TOWER HAMLETS

D0410081

THE EXPLORER

Also by James Smythe

The Testimony

JAMES SMYTHE

THE EXPLORER

HARPER
Voyager

HarperCollins*Publishers*
77–85 Fulham Palace Road,
Hammersmith, London W6 8JB

www.harpercollins.co.uk

First Published by Harper*Voyager* 2012
This edition 2013
1

Copyright © James Smythe 2012

James Smythe asserts the moral right to
be identified as the author of this work

A catalogue record for this book
is available from the British Library

ISBN 978 0 00 745675 8

This novel is entirely a work of fiction.
The names, characters and incidents portrayed in it are
the work of the author's imagination. Any resemblance to
actual persons, living or dead, events or localities is
entirely coincidental.

Set in Sabon LT Std by Palimpsest Book Production Limited,
Falkirk, Stirlingshire

Printed and bound in Great Britain by
Clays Ltd, St Ives plc

All rights reserved. No part of this publication may be
reproduced, stored in a retrieval system, or transmitted,
in any form or by any means, electronic, mechanical,
photocopying, recording or otherwise, without the prior
permission of the publishers.

MIX
Paper from
responsible sources
FSC™ C007454

FSC™ is a non-profit international organisation established to promote
the responsible management of the world's forests. Products carrying the
FSC label are independently certified to assure consumers that they come
from forests that are managed to meet the social, economic and
ecological needs of present and future generations,
and other controlled sources.

Find out more about HarperCollins and the environment at
www.harpercollins.co.uk/green

PART ONE

I had the ambition to not only go farther than man had
gone before, but to go as far as it was possible to go.
— Captain Cook

TOWER HAMLETS LIBRARIES	
91000001850080	
Bertrams	14/01/2013
SCI	£12.99
THISWH	TH12002373

1

One of the first things I did when I realized that I was never going to make it home – when I was the only crewmember left, all the others stuffed into their sleeping chambers like rigid, vacuum-packed action figures – was to write up a list of everybody I would never see again; let me wallow in it, swim around in missing them as much as I could. My name is Cormac Easton. I am a journalist and, I suppose, an astronaut. Part of my job on the ship was to be in charge of the communications with home, taking video and writing updates, sending them back to Earth directly. There wasn't a guarantee of how long any of the broadcasts would take to get there – if they got there at all, as far out as we were, what with the chance of interference – but it was something. It was how I had been sending all my reports, but I assumed that they'd know what to do with something more personal, that they would pass it along. The list was deep. Elena was at the top. I had missed her before we'd even left. On the days leading up to the launch I had been trying to get hold of her, leaving messages, telling her how I felt, because what screwed us up was *this*, my job, this trip; and I wanted to see if, when it was all over, we could try again. There's always hope, that's what they say. As soon as I worked out that there wasn't ever going to be that chance for reconciliation? It became something else. I wasn't missing her any more: it was despair, maybe, or another word for when you fall apart, when you can't cope, when it all crumbles. I hid my feelings from my crewmates because I didn't want to ruin their trip, didn't want to bring them down. That went into my messages. I told Elena that I missed her, and that I would always miss her, and that, if there was a God, we would see each other again someday, even though I didn't believe that. It just felt right to write it, in case.

Some other people that I'll never see again: My parents, my mother and father. My parents are – were – teachers. My mother left my father in the late stages of their lives, post-retirement, and he decided to cut himself off from me completely. In books, they say that familial rejection is often a direct result of one's coping mechanisms, but I think he had been looking for an excuse. We barely ever got along, and when he disappeared, he really disappeared. No phone call on my birthday, no letters, nothing. It's been over five years since I've seen him. He might be dead for all I know. Sometimes that's what I assume. It's easier than explaining what really happened. My mother died six months ago, something to do with her heart, and my father didn't come to the funeral, or call, or anything. I had a cat as well, though he was missing when I left, which was typical – a packed suitcase on the bed usually meant a holiday, and he went off and hid somewhere, unforgiving of us for abandoning him. It was bad enough with Elena gone, frankly. My friends, though they all lived elsewhere, kids and jobs and the breakup with Elena dividing us. And then my crew: the crew that I came out here with, that I started this journey with. My crew died in bits and bobs, dribs and drabs, up here, with me. My crew: I was never really a part of them, even after all the training, because they knew more than me, technical things. This trip relied on them to happen. I was chaff. Civilians never fit in completely; those people had been training their whole lives. I was here for PR purposes; they were here for the science. I would argue that I was here for the adventure, as well, for the sense of exploration: they would understand that, I think, but I can't tell them that now. They died one by one, falling off like there was a checklist. First to go was Arlen.

Arlen was First Pilot, from somewhere in the American Midwest – Ohio, I think, but he spoke about the country as if he'd lived all over, throwing names of cities and towns into conversation, always with a tale to tell about them. He was a storyteller, one of those types, and older than the rest of us by a few years. When we all met he was clean-shaven, but he grew a beard for the trip, because he wanted to see what happened to it when we were in stasis.

'When we get out,' he said, 'this sucker might have grown. I want to know just how frozen we actually are in those things.' We were only in them for a fortnight, but he said that if it grew fast enough he'd be able to tell the difference. He thought that it would be hilarious if it grew so fast he would go from tidy to unkempt over the course of a single sleep. He was all about the joke, Arlen. He died in stasis, or just didn't wake up, however you want to think of it. We all came out of the pods one by one, as we had in training: his was meant to be first, so that he could switch on everything, run diagnostics before the rest of us turned out; but, for some reason, his bed didn't open. By the time we prised it open he was gone. Something must have happened to it during the launch period, because everything was fine when we got into them; we had run stress tests to make sure, and those things were meant to be idiot-proof. In a worst-case scenario, they were even meant to be our escape pods: the thought of one malfunctioning didn't exactly fill us with confidence. We all came out of our pods soaking wet, because something about the sleep made you sweat, made your entire body lose its water. Arlen wasn't wet: his skin was a filthy grey-blue, hard and crusty and starting to flake off in fingernail-sized chunks of dust. We tried using the defibrillator on him but nothing happened. The skin cracked, and his eyes were so dry they looked like marshmallows, and we realized that we were going to have to put him back and seal him off. We said some words, told Earth, a few of us cried; but that wasn't a *mission ending critical*, as Ground Control called it. That was why we had more than one pilot.

'Things can go wrong,' Ground Control told us. 'You have to be prepared.'

Second to die was Wanda. We jokingly called her Dogsbody, because she got all the awful jobs, and pretty much did whatever her superiors told her to do. That included me, for some reason; even though I had no official rank, she acted as if I did. Respect, maybe, or honour. Something. She had been recruited straight out of some Ivy League university, and she acted it. When she did what we asked, it was always grudgingly, and she was surly, sad. We speculated that she really missed home. She was American as well – she and Arlen, the American contingent, first into action, first to leave, like some old joke about one of the wars – and her accent was Southern, but she always said that she was from DC. We had something in common: headaches. I get bad headaches in low gravity, which I didn't realize, of course, until we were up here. I think most people have the potential to get them, over long periods of time. It's the pressure. I never had headaches before we came up here, and neither did Wanda. We were the worst to get them – or, maybe just the worst to feel them, at first, before we got used to them. Wanda died outside, in space. Her suit had a tear, or a crack, and we ran so many checks, over and over on all the suits, that when she died we couldn't believe it. There was a routine maintenance scan on the hull every few days; we cut thrusters, made sure that the outside was holding up, that the hull's integrity was normal. We were pushing ourselves into new parts of space; the first time that we had been here, manned, this far out. The hull could have developed issues, so we sent Dogsbody – Wanda – out to check it, on her wire, and we ate breakfast. She reached the apex of the craft and her line went taut, and she drifted off, her helmet filled with blood, thick enough that we couldn't see her face. When we dragged her in her eyes had burst behind her eyelids. Her head had drowned, really, flooded the helmet like a bathy-sphere, like a goldfish bowl. She'd kept her mouth shut, squeezed her eyes shut like we were told in cases of depres-surization, but her nostrils . . . We hadn't even thought about the nostrils. Guy suggested that we all wear earplugs in our noses after that, when we went on walks, but we didn't, because we knew that if the helmets failed us, no amount of plugging cavities was going to keep us alive.

Guy was third. He was German, and that wasn't his real name. His real name was Gerhardt, but we had to prise that out of him, really bully him to tell us. He hadn't used that name since he was a child, he said. To hear it made him angry. Guy suited him better. Gerhardt suggests a fat man, a chef, huge and mustachioed and swirling. That wasn't Guy, who was thin and tall and bald, almost hairless. He was chief scientist and engineer. We debated turning around after Wanda died, head back to Earth whether Ground Control gave us permission to or not – could we even do that? The systems weren't meant to put us in reverse until half the fuel had been depleted, but Guy helped develop the tech that made the ship run: he would almost definitely know the safe codes to reprogram the systems, to manipulate our journey, change the coordinates, change where we were heading. Everything was safe codes and protected routes that we weren't able to change. We went silent as we put Wanda's body back in her stasis pod, stopped – although, we never actually stopped, of course; we were always drifting, because that was the nature of space, no stopping, nothing ever ceasing – and we sent a message home, and waited for the reply. There was an eight-minute wait for messages to reach home at that point – four minutes to send it, four to get the reply, but we had to give them extra time for any anomalies. We sent the message a few times, to make sure, and waited and waited. Eventually, they told us we were carrying on; that we couldn't afford to stay still, that we should turn the engines back on a.s.a.p. The life support in the ship is piezoelectric, charging itself from the vibrations that the hull makes as the engines rattle it, so as not to deplete the fuel supply; the longer the ship stays static, the less time life support has. The ship was built to keep us moving. We were told that we had to progress, that Wanda's death wasn't crucial, so we did, for a while. Quinn and

Emmy didn't like it: they argued, wanted to turn around. I supported them, and when they told Guy that they were turning the ship, it turned into a full-blown argument. Quinn was screaming at him, using nothing other than a sense of morality as his argument (people had died, we owed them something) and self-preservation (people had died, and there might be more), and Guy grabbed the walls suddenly and he had a heart attack, scrabbling at his chest with his hands, beating at it like he was fighting off another man, an actual physical attack. In zero gravity it was scarier than seeing it normally; normally you imagine people crumpling to the floor, but Guy was a cartoon version, a terrified and confused wolf plummeting down a ravine, clutching at his chest as he fell. As Emmy kept saying that night, consoling us, or trying to: it would have happened anyway. And Guy had been losing it: he accused me of things, started getting paranoid, seeing things. There's no telling what this amount of pressure can do to the human body, let alone to the mind. We were past any point where anybody had been before, and we had to accept that, and move on. We were as fit as we could be; we would either cope or we wouldn't.

Quinn was next to die; and with him, it became almost funny, or like a setup for some awful TV show, where you expect the presenter to reveal that it had all been an overly elaborate joke. He was the second pilot, though he always referred to himself as a caretaker.

'I only push the occasional button,' he told me in his first interview. I am a journalist. That's why I'm here, that's my motivation, to document this, to take film clips, to write about this. We live in a time of interest, of being able to remember this stuff forever: it's not like when it was paper, which faded and peeled and tore. Data lives forever, and we're in a new age of journalism: the age of permanence. I could win a Pulitzer for this, everybody said before we left. I was writing up the adventures of those who go further than anybody ever has before. This is the stuff of sci-fi movies and books, of dreams: it's humanity exploring again, crossing the deserts, reaching the poles, scouring the depths. *We're doing it because we can*, is the first line in my article. In the film of this, I am the fourth actor's name to appear on the screen. I'm the everyman. The stars are Arlen – it's a shock twist when he dies so early, so his part is almost a cameo – and Quinn, but Quinn's face is biggest on the poster. Quinn was handsome, charming, roguish. All those things. He looked like a prince, or some sort of Arabian herald; dark hair, sharp jaw, blurry blue eyes that were at odds with his heritage. Quinn was British-Sri Lankan, but had spent most of his youth in California. He had a curious English drawl, slipping into it when he asked for stereotypes, for tea, for a sandwich, to wear some trousers, but the rest of the time it was pure West Coast, smooth and swift. Quinn died when I was outside the ship, working on some wiring to try and get control of the computers. We shouldn't have been out alone, but we were down in our numbers. We had lost all contact with Ground Control, so we panicked; he was trying to turn the ship around, which meant overriding the systems, which meant working on something outside the ship as well as the computer system inside the ship at the same time. When I came back Emmy was crying, absolutely hysterical. Irreconcilable. I couldn't make out what she was saying, but she was gone, inconsolable, and Quinn was on the floor, his eyes rolled right back, blood around his head because he'd fallen down – the engines were off, and we were still, and gravity, being what it is, had taken its toll – and he had hit his head on the wall at the wrong angle, a cruel accident, the sort of thing that could have happened to any of us, and I couldn't even get Emmy to try to save him because she wouldn't stop screaming. I looked in her eyes, and she was just petrified. It was terrifying, really. There was blood on her hands, and it looked like – or, it *could* have looked like – she was responsible, but she didn't say anything about it when I asked her, and I had to have faith. I had to. When I had cleaned up the mess and turned the engines back on, I bundled his body into the stasis beds – have you ever tried to move a body in microgravity? It floats and wobbles and hits you, inadvertently, and you almost forget that it's a body, because it's suddenly all physical mass and form, but with no weight behind it – and sealed it up, all the bodies there, peering out until we got home. They all looked like they were asleep, apart from Wanda, with the blood around her eyes. I don't know why we didn't wipe it before we put her to sleep. And then there were two. Last – apart from me, if I'm going to die – was Emmy.

Emmy died – I use that word, but, really, maybe it's not that bad, maybe there's something can be done, I don't know – only hours after Quinn, really. We were barely speaking, because something had gone wrong with her, I think, in her mind. That was the other thing they warned us about: snapping. She seemed to blame me for the deaths of the others, and she wouldn't look at me, not properly. She screamed at me that it was my fault, that I was somehow responsible for everything. She called me a murderer. We didn't speak, and she refused to sleep. Eventually I worried about what would happen to me when *I* slept – because she seemed, suddenly, like she could do *something* – so I had to keep her sedated most of the time, strapped into her bed. They had warned us, when we did all the training, that this would be psychologically tough. I seemed to be fine, but Emmy bore the brunt of their warning. They bandied around words in training, in a joking way, but you never knew if they were actually joking. And then after our journey, and all the deaths! How could you stay sane? Even I don't know how I've held up; *if* I've held up. We powered down and I sent another message back, not knowing if it would reach home, but praying, and praying that, somehow, they could reply, and we let the time tick as the life support system whirred. With only the two of us we knew we had enough life support to stay there for a day or so – a full complement of 6 had 6 hours, so we did shaky maths based on the sizes of our lungs, and the backup tanks that we could wrench from the now-spare suits and fit to the system. So we sat, and she was silent until she finally decided to speak to me. She sounded so threatening, like some villain from a movie, telling me that she was fine, trying to psychoanalyse me, getting nowhere. When I was scared enough – for my life, for what she might try and do when I slept or when my guard was down – I was forced to put her to sleep. I had to. I had to sedate her, and then I put her in stasis until we could get home, when they would wake her up and fix her. I had to.

That was a couple of days ago. She missed the best part of the trip, when we – I – hit our fuel limit, the 51% mark, when the ship was meant to turn itself back, send us all home. It didn't. I watched it creep to 52%, and then tick over, and I waited for something to happen. I assumed *deus ex machina*: there would be clanking, something mechanical, and the ship's engines would kick in, boosters taking us into that beautiful curve, and then I'd suddenly see Earth in the distance, a pinprick of light. I would get to watch this all on the monitors, trying to remember the star formations that we had passed, laughing as a formation that was on our left was now on the right, as I tripped past it and gaily waved. I watched it creep to 50 from 51, and then I stopped the ship. That much I knew how to do: there is a pause button, big and green, like you would find in a cartoon. All systems are frozen before they shut down automatically. They are kept on a hyper low-energy standby to preserve them, like a TV set or a computer. They Ding! when you bring them back online. When there's a problem, a red light flashes and there's a beep, a long, solid, irritating beep from the system speakers. The designers must have loved sci-fi films. I froze the systems so that, when they came back on, they would kick-start. I imagined the computer's AI as being like a late student, realizing that the alarm hasn't gone off, and then running to compensate. It wasn't, and when I rebooted all I got was more forward movement. I spent 2% percent of the fuel wondering if we had already turned, and were heading in the right direction, heading home, but we hadn't and we weren't. That was that: I travel forward until I run out of fuel, and then I use the life support – a week, maybe, given that it's just me, if I breathe in shallow breaths and then rely on the spare O_2 tanks in the external suits – until I run out of air, and then I die. In many ways, it's calming, knowing that it will probably happen: I remember reading something in the papers years ago, an article about a journalist who knew that he had cancer, knew that he was going to die, and said that it eased him. He moved on, and he had his family move on as well.

There were rumours that his wife started dating before he was even dead, because that's what he wanted. Not everybody reacts that way, but he did: he found a tranquillity in it.

All that I've got up here is tranquillity now, I suppose.

2

I eat meals by myself; or, rather, I eat them in the room with all the sleep pods and my dead colleagues, because it's either that or the cockpit, or one of the other parts of the ship. We've got expansive engine rooms; massive chambers full of tech that I don't understand, all to process the air and the water, keep us going; and storerooms, spaces that would be empty if they weren't filled with crates of supplies we'll never use. The power supply is cutting edge; until a year ago, it was touch and go as to whether they'd get it down small enough to actually even launch. They did. I don't know how we ever doubted them.

It's amazing how fast you can get bored. Emmy's been dead for two days – I keep using that word, because in an ordinary situation we would get home and she would be brought out of sleep and somebody would be able to help her, with drugs or surgery, something to balance her. But here, she's dead. I know that we're not going backwards, and no pods have returned to the ship to tell me their rescue plan. I mean, not that they could have one in the first place.

It would take them so long to reach me that I'd be dead by the time that they did. There is no Plan B.

I've become like a vampire, sitting here in the dark on my own, lusting for something – anything – other than this, other than here. I've turned the lights off – I flicked the switch when the computer shouted that we were crossing paths with an asteroid (Nereus, the on-screen prompt told me), just to look at it, really. Couldn't see it though, the real version. There's technology on the screens that shows you images, composites of what's really out there with CG stuff, to give you information. It painted in the path of the asteroid for me; I see its tail in the distance, as it runs towards Earth, where it'll swing around, passing close enough for bedroom-astronomers to get excited. From here, Earth is a speck, a twinkle, a flash of light. We were in space for two reasons. Guy was running tests on anomalies, things that probes and satellites and telescopes couldn't even begin to fathom, all to further our knowledge of space. That was only the secondary reason, though: science taking a back seat to something less tangible. Our primary remit was to inspire people, to be explorers. To show the people of Earth that we – as a race – were able to take ourselves further, to push our limits, our scope. Nobody explored any more, so we were the new vanguard. It was so exciting, so important. We were going to be heroes.

The lights are off now all over the ship, and I have decided to not switch them back on again. I don't need to, not yet. There's very little to see here, and the lights inside the sleep pods and from the panels keep me going. Nobody's been here before, and it'll be years, maybe more, before people come here again. Why would they risk it? I like that nobody will know what happened. An assumption: the contact-capsules never made it back to the Moon, never made it back

16

to Ground Control and DARPA, and they will think something happened to us. There are so many possibilities, each of them worthy of a movie. We made first contact, and now are in another galaxy, being tortured, or prepping an invasion force. We exploded, and now orbit the Earth as chunks of what we were. Somebody in the crew got Space Madness and killed everyone else. We had a hull breach. We crashed into a moon, an asteroid field, a spatial anomaly that nobody had factored in, or seen before – we made a discovery! We popped a fuel cell, ran out, we're adrift. We never left Earth, and it was all a cover-up, our launch filmed on a sound-stage. There are different scenarios that they'll run because they just want to know what happened to us, and this will set them back fifteen years of research. Next time, it'll be safety first; minimize the risks. They'll take years deliberating about whether it's worth it; they'll only go out with a real purpose, a reason to do it (colonization, or fuel, maybe). It'll be decades before they think it's safe, and the ship won't be a prototype: it'll be tested to near-death before it's sent up. They'll try to save energy by launching from the Moon, maybe, and the ship will be bigger, and it will have more fuel, and a crew of pilots and engineers. No useless straggler of a journalist. It'll be packed to the gills with the fail-safes we went without, like an AI pilot. Whatever happens, that ship will go up and then come back down, having done what it was meant to do, even if the crew all suffer a fate that couldn't ever be predicted. It might not even have a crew to begin with: keep it less fallible.

The ship is clean, absolutely clinical. It's like an operating theatre, not a doctor's surgery: there isn't much around to tinker with. There are no lines on the floor to give us directions, no screens and beeps. There are panels that run computers, and there's a table with a transparent lid that shows what we keep inside it – food bars, books, medical equipment. On one wall of the main cabin run plastic chairs that fold down from the wall like a cinema, all with clips on the sides that click onto the pins on the sides of our trousers to keep us sitting down if we don't want to float. On the other wall is a table, a booth, built in, enough seating for all of us, same principle with the clips. We were meant to sit together once a day for meals. There was a list of rules that some psychologists thought up, to help us deal with being out here for so long on our own.

'It brings about a sense of camaraderie,' they said, 'to remind you of the comfort and security of being together: not alone, but part of a unit, working together towards a single goal. Subconsciously, it will remind you of eating home-cooked meals with your family.'

'That's a great idea,' I remember Quinn saying, 'but my mother never cooked shitty meal bars from cellophane packets.' There are no knives and forks, clearly, just hundreds of sachets of meal bars. They're all sponsored by fast-food companies, and they taste just like the real burgers and chips and puddings, only in these reformed bars, hard and crispy when they've been heated, soft and damp when not. We have exercise machines, all designed to provide physical stress, resistance, and we're meant to use them for half an hour a day to prevent bone loss. Then there are the beds, designed for comfort and stasis, used every night. They sit at a 45-degree angle, and we sleep with buffers around us to stop us slipping in any direction. There are padded straps to hold us in. We all, at one point or another, floated whilst sleeping. It seemed silly not to. They all have doors. Their glass is frosted, but you can still see the bodies through it. We have everything we could ever need up here, in the front, in what passes as a cockpit, a lounge, a bedroom, a cabin. It's almost upper-class.

I've thought of killing myself, but something stops me. Just think, it says, you'll go further than anyone else has ever been. You'll see deeper into space than anybody else has ever seen. You'll make history.

'But nobody will ever know,' I reply, and the something doesn't say anything back to me, just sits there in the dark. I take my place in the chair at the front of the ship and decide to ride it out.

I take sleeping pills. I don't know what I'm trying to achieve by this. Sleeping pills are a cry for help, right? I take a handful, because I don't know how many I'm meant to take. They're not even kept in the medicine cabinet: we were given our own supply, because we were told we might have trouble with sleeping. I vomit them up into a white paper bag, then dispose of it in the refuse. It makes me feel awful. I don't know why I did it. I've never been that sort of person. I've never had that sort of strength.

When things beep on technology you don't know how to operate it's the worst thing in the world. There's a flat panel covered in switches, next to the big Go/Pause button, and there's a screen covered in jargon that means nothing. It's fine knowing about the placements of stars: why they build this thing for only engineers to understand I cannot fathom. I understand the fuel readings, and I understand the energy cell readings – we are running at 42% fuel, 93% piezoelectric-efficiency, six hours of reserve energy in the cells – and I understand how to tell that Life Support is working. On the screen, a tiny number flashes: 250480. I don't recognize it, or know what it means. It's in a small box, the kind that pops up when the computer crashes or when you open a program or when you've got a meeting scheduled. It starts to beep as well, and there's a tiny red light, the size of a pinhead, that starts flashing, a solitary LED that I wouldn't even notice if I wasn't floating directly over it. There's a Help system on the computer so I boot another screen and type it in, to search through the thousands of documents about how this shuttle works, but nothing comes up. 250480. Nothing at all. It doesn't seem to reference anything; it doesn't seem to have any meaning.

'I have to ignore it,' I say to myself.

Something that might be of interest: we could have travelled faster than we have been. The engines that we're fitted with are two-year-old tech, and the advancements that have been made since then are incredible. We could have been doing this almost three times as fast, but the rate of fuel consumption meant that we would have been lucky to reach the Moon. Signals through space, though, they're different; they're waves. They travel faster than we can, because they don't weigh anything. We give them a distance and a direction and fire them off, and Bang! We hope that they hit their targets. We haven't had a long-distance message since we left our orbit – or, technically, the magnetosphere, so the scientists told me. Maybe this is what happens when a message arrives. Maybe there's some sort of subspace signal, and this is the information. 250480. This is their way of telling me I'm going to be getting home.

The light stops shining just as I am getting excited, and the beeping stops a second, maybe two, after it. The 250480 is still there on the screen after the prompt, but it rapidly gets shunted down the list as the fuel readings – 41% fuel, 93% energy, six hours' life support – tick by and replace it.

Outside, the sky is beautiful. We – that is, those of us in space, travelling here where nobody has been before – we don't think of it in terms of sky, or even as space. We think in terms of an actual space, of blackness, of The Dark, that which we don't understand. We over-word it, write about it in terms that we think people will find attractive, beautiful, moving, meaningful. We mystify it: It's what we don't know, something else entirely, something abnormal and terrifying and still and completely other-worldly, in the most literal sense of the phrase. Here, where you're close enough to touch it, it is just space; there's nothing to touch even if you want to. And there's no definition of a horizon, no way to tell where we actually are, not really. We can say, 'Well, we've travelled this far' – *I* can say, 'Well, I've travelled this far, I know how much fuel the ship has used, there's no resistance, the readings must be right' – but the relationship I have to what's out here is nothing. It's a number. This deep into space, there's nothing. It's dark, like oil or tar. I can't see stars. If this wasn't already fucked up enough, I'd worry there was something wrong. As it is, I revel in the nothing. I drink it in.

The ship has this thing that we call the Bubble, built into the ceiling of the main room, a raised dome of impenetrable plastic where we can get a 360-degree view of everything around us – and when they were all still alive I could see it, and they told me what it was we were seeing, what was Earth, when the light was right. From that distance it looked white, almost. Shiny, like a tiny coin.

When we first woke up it was all I wanted to stare at, even

21

when we were dealing with Arlen's body. Using the telescope computers' highest zoom. We left in August, and the clouds were thin. Those first couple of days I would just catch myself watching Earth behind us, marvelling when the planet was half in darkness, a nearly perfect line jutting across the land, scraping along as the planet turned, a duvet being slowly pulled back, waking people as it went. At any given moment you could see how much of any country was still asleep, their cities lit up like embers, and how much was awake, lights off, going about their business. Through the digital telescopes we could see ships in the sea, the path they were cutting, tiny dots with white trails like slugs. We could see planes hitting the atmosphere, commercial flights. We could see the shape of cities, and make faces out of them; we could see faces in the clouds, only from the other side of them.

Being in space gives you a sense of philosophy, a sense of something other than yourself. You look out at the sky – because we're used to that thing above us being sky – but when you're part of it, what is it then? It's nothing, or it's everything. It's just where you are. Here, in the middle of space, or at the end, or the start, I have no idea – here is just where I currently am.

The beeping starts again. It's been hours, days maybe, and I've barely thought about it. I've been sleeping. Being in constant total darkness makes you far more tired than you realize. I wonder how they do it in the Arctic, in Iceland. And we have clocks here, but they're hidden, on computers, so you forget when day starts and night ends, or vice versa. It's easy to sleep when you ought not. I might be on a ten-hour cycle of days now, for all I know.

The beeping cuts through the hum of engines, and the light, even as tiny as it is, can be seen all the way across the main room. The screen has that same message, that same chain of numbers, and, again, the search box on the Help software doesn't offer anything. 39% fuel now; it seems to be going down faster than I predicted, and faster than I would like. Faster than it should, actually, and by some way. I try typing the numbers into the computer back at itself, like it's a line of code, an instruction – maybe this is its way of giving me help, offering me a sort of sentient way to turn this thing around? – but nothing happens. I'm sure that the pilots would have known what to do with it. Arlen would have flicked a switch, one of the hundreds labelled with numbers and abbreviated codes, and that would have stopped it. Quinn would have tapped the screen, smiled at the number.

'They've found us!' he would have said. 'All the way out here! And they've brought our favourite food and drink with them!' And we'd have had a meal at our table with the gravity switched on, not worried about how much of the energy it would waste, and not worried about whether we'd make it home because we would already be there.

A few hours later the beeping finally stops. The ship is now on 38%.

It drops around a percentage point every few hours. I've taken to watching it properly. There's a diagnostic control you can input that I read about in the Help files – I've read them all now, digital-cover to digital-cover – that shows you exact values, so you can watch the fuel tick down in milli-litres, but that takes the fun away from it. This has become a game, seeing if I can predict when it will next click over. I can get it down to an art: the engines have a remarkably constant rate of consumption, and there's no resistance out here to bog us down, slow us, change the maths. My first guess is three hours off; my third just twenty minutes. By 33% I nearly have it at a countdown.

This is the moment in the film where that word repeats – countdown, countdown, countdown – and we fade to the beginning of the mission, as we're all being strapped into our stasis beds. We were only allowed to stay in them for two days – a number that didn't rely so much on science as the few tests that had gone before (which we assumed were on monkeys, but didn't ask) – because they were depriving us of oxygen, to keep us under, to keep us stable. We asked what could happen if something went wrong and we had too much or too little oxygen, and the doctors told us that we could get cramps, that sort of thing. As a journalist, you notice tells. It's like gamblers: there's a fine art to seeing when people are lying, when they're holding aces. What you develop in my line is something else, though, a stage past that. It tells you when the giveaway signs are something you shouldn't push. Leave it alone, it'll be better that way. The doctors knew something, or suspected something, and we signed documents that agreed that they had no legal control over us; that we chose this trip, and the inherent risks therein. You don't want to know. The launch itself was automated, and we were all asleep before we even heard the countdown voice over the loudspeaker (which I assume that they did, though I have no proof). Stasis is odd: it's not cold, but you're frozen. Really, you're just asleep, but whatever drugs they give you shut down as much of your body as they can without causing any damage, and, as you sleep, they lower the temperature. When you come out you are soaking – the sci-fi films of the 1970s got that much right – but from your own sweat. But there's no shivering, no hang-over, no feeling of sickness. You come out, you shower. (We have a pod in the back, in the changing room next to the airlock, that you climb into. You press on the ceiling – which stops you floating upwards – and the pod fills with soapy water, which is sucked out, and then fills with recycled water, which gets sucked out again. I haven't used it in days. I keep forgetting.) We did the stasis because of the G-forces – the acceleration, Quinn explained to me as we were strapped in, was so great that we could all be damaged from the initial launch to break from the Earth's atmosphere, and we were going to pass so close to the Moon that we would maintain the speed until we were clear of it, and we were going to be going so fast that there would be an atmospheric change, a drop in temperature that we couldn't even hope to survive. Stasis kept us whole and kept us alive. We only needed to be there for a few days, but then, why not miss as much of the trip as possible? We woke up when we were well past the Moon, and we found Arlen, dealt with that, then we took turns in the shower, and then opened the vents for a few seconds to suck out all the water that was floating around. We were awake then, and we went about our business: checking the systems, checking we were all healthy, making notes, recording interviews, watching the Earth become a dot through the Bubble.

I'm halfway through a percentage-cycle. Dinner tonight is McRib pulled pork flavour bar, dessert a Cadbury's chocolate cake bar. Later today I will open the cap on a bottle of water and watch it hang like a balloon in the air, and use a straw to try and suck it up as I float around in the chase.

I look at my beard in the mirror of one of the reflective silver wraps of a meal bar; it reflects me distortedly, like it isn't really me. I haven't yet questioned my sanity, though I probably should; but I can see this beard that has started growing, because I haven't shaved, because I haven't taken the care of myself that I probably should. I'm still exactly the same. I look at the crew, one by one, to see how they're different. Arlen's beard hasn't grown; they say that it happens after you die, but I've frozen him. I've frozen them all. We never change, even out here.

27%, and an all-stop, hitting the big button in time with the tick of the fuel calculator. There's six hours of backup life support charged in the batteries – but, again that's based on a full complement of crew, so for me that's well over a day, maybe even closer to two, two days of just being able to sit here, ebbing about on nothingness. I wonder if I'll drift over that time? I log onto the computer, open my drive. This is where all my recordings of interviews are. There's hours and hours of them, all broken down into categories: pre-launch nerves, childhood histories, moments of greatness, thoughts on the crew, thoughts on space, thoughts on each other, the interview process, how they want to be remembered, the problems with space, the problems with the craft, the concept of what it means to be a hero, the concept of what it means to be an explorer. I sort them chronologically and click on the first one. Emmy's face fills the screen, fills the screens on the bulkheads further down the room, and her voice comes through the speaker in the ceiling, clear, perfect.

'I started off working in a hospital – I did my training in Brisbane and Sydney, then I moved to UCL – and I worked in St Barnabas' Hospital for the first three years, and then was recruited, I suppose.' She laughs. 'Recruited! That's what they called it. And then there was three years of training before I was even asked if I wanted to go on a mission. We did Zero G triage tests. They have this shuttle that we went up in, hit the atmosphere, and we had to operate on it. Nothing real, only these dummies, but blood bags, so we could watch that stuff floating around. What happens if somebody, I don't know, needs an amputation of something and we can't get gravity stabilized? We might have to operate in Zero G, and we needed to know the intricacies of it, how to deal with it. There's a lot more clamping involved.'

Just hearing her speak is the best feeling I've had in days. On the screens she looks young, pretty, blonde, Australian; like you'd expect her to. Through the stasis bed her blue eyes are pinned open – I forgot to close them, I don't know why, probably subconscious; I wanted her to keep looking at me, a shrink would say – and staring out in the light of the screens. It's a trade-off: I decided to take seeing them open and dead in the stasis and alive and on the screen over not seeing them at all.

'I used to work in the Sudan, doing health-check runs – there were a few people who needed surgery, torn ligaments, that sort of thing, but nothing out of the ordinary. For most people it was starvation, hunger. I saw some awful things. And then they asked me if I wanted something bigger, more challenging, more inspirational.'

I watch the videos until I pass out. She reminds me so much of Elena, and I don't really know why.

Elena was of Greek lineage. She was a stereotype: passionate, annoyingly so sometimes, with this huge laugh, like a roar; all bust and arse for the first few minutes, until you get past that – usually with the laugh, the passion; a magnificent cook, which she got from her mother. We met when I was on holiday one year with some friends, and I was the only single one. I had decided that I'd spend the time there taking pictures, trying to make that part of my skill set stronger – that was my excuse, as the rest of my friends all smooshed up against each other and fed each other bits from their plates – and I met her the first day, holidaying by herself, because she really wanted a break from her old life. She ended up tagging along with our group. There's no great whirlwind romance there: we met, we liked each other, we fell in love, we got married. Sometimes the simple stories are the best ones; the ones that don't need explanation, that just happen, and that you accept as being The Truth, as being fate. In the movie of this, she would be played by a classic actress, beautiful but believable, dark and mysterious and loving. But, the film is about me here, now, and how I survived as long as I did on my own, in a capsule, just myself for company. Nobody has gone this far before, and people will want to know about this. They'll queue to see it. They won't mind who plays Elena, I don't think.

I've finished my videos of Emmy, and moved on to videos of Quinn. We – the rest of the crew – wondered if they were having a relationship. They probably were; they're both so good-looking, like models. I still have hours and hours left of backup power, by my reckoning.

Starting up again by pressing a button is anticlimactic, but it's a necessity: the air is getting thin, and my headaches have gotten worse. I have stopped complaining about them – they are just there now, just something I can't really do anything about. I never even asked Emmy if I could take a tablet for them before she died. There's a cupboard full of medicines if I need them: I'm sure an aspirin won't do me any harm. The cupboard carries everything, every sort of pill, like a tiny pharmacy, prepared for any eventuality. They didn't save any of the crew. I press the button and the engines whir into place and we chug off, a steam train. There's no concept of the speed we're actually going right now. You can't look out of the window and see the stars whizzing by. There are no markers or reference points; there's just the darkness of space.

3

I slept heavily last night, and I ache when I wake up. I think that my sleeping patterns are fucked up, that I'm not sleeping at night, or what should be night. The not-day. I don't actually know if it was night-time, not really. The clocks say something different to what I feel it is anyway. They're all on Earth time, to acclimatize us, to help for when we made contact. Up here, it's totally different. Twelve hours can feel like a lifetime. I wake up to the beeping again, 250480, little red light, and it takes me a few minutes (that I spend typing the number into the computer again, hoping that it might suddenly work out what I was asking, searching around it, yawning) to notice the fuel gauge. 25%, a full 2% lower than when I went to bed. I sit and watch the screen again, bringing up the detailed analysis. This can't be right. Each percentage of fuel has its own smaller percentage, a mini-countdown, and it is ticking swiftly, a percentage point every couple of minutes. Something's wrong, or more wrong, worse than it was before. We seem to be losing fuel at an accelerated rate. I don't know why, and it hurts to be this clueless.

In one of Emmy's videos she spoke about the worst moment of her career: treating a patient with internal bleeding, trying to save her, but watching the blood failing to congeal even after they had done everything that they could do, closed her wounds, healed her.

'Being a doctor who can't do their job,' she said, and then trailed off. I drag myself to the Bubble and try to see as much of the ship as I can, but there's nothing outside that might be causing this. There's nothing on the computer, aside from the beeping, but I can't even tell if that's related. Sense says that there must be something outside. An engineer would know, a pilot would know. Even Emmy would probably know. I pull myself back to the main cabin and hit the full-stop button. Two hours of life support with the engines off, it says.

It takes me forty minutes to get out of my clothes and into one of the External Suits, check that the seals are tight, that there's nothing wrong (because of Wanda's mishap, and because there's nobody here to even try to save me). They are incredibly warm, running off some sort of chemical reaction designed to help you out in deep space. I've had a couple of microgravity tests in these things, in the hangars on Earth that they set up for us to practise, to log hours; and two actual runs (if you count the one when Quinn died, and I hovered outside, uselessly).

'Make sure you alert the rest of the crew when you do one of these, check that somebody is on the end of your Safe Cable at all times, ready to pull you back in if you need it.' That was one of the major rules of the suits. They taught us how to work on the outside of the ship, in case we needed to. 'You won't need to,' they said, 'the ship is perfectly capable of taking good care of itself. But if panelling comes loose, something like that, you may need to assist one of the pilots in repairs.' I'd give anything to be assisting right now. I float myself down to the back of the ship and step into the Exit booth – there's a one-man exit, like a revolving door, with depressurized seals, and a door that slides back when you hit a button. It pulls wide to reveal the nothingness. The suit I'm in is fitted with loose magnets over all the limbs, designed to help you stay in an orbit of the craft itself – the scientists were thrilled with how difficult it would be to lose yourself, to float off into space. I cling to the ship like those baby monkeys you see on nature documentaries, and pull myself along on all fours. It's silent and cold and I haven't got a clue what I'm doing out here. I don't even know what I'm looking for: damage, maybe, or an open petrol cap. It's going to be that simple, I tell myself; you'll see it, and fix it, and that'll be that. All the stuff under panels, the broken and bruised parts of the ship's guts, they'll be fine. I circle the main body of the ship, never having any sense of which way is up as I cling to the cylinder and I look up and down the panelling, at the clean lines, at the lack of scratches and scuffs, at the perfect cleanliness of the body. There's nothing. I get back into the ship and change again, and there's ten minutes on the clock before life support would have run out. I start us up again, and watch the numbers. They have to be wrong.

Wherever you are, when you're alone, you feel eyes on you. I sit at the desk and write my entries for Earth – because they could still be listening, maybe these would get there eventually – and as I type, I feel eyes on me. No matter where you are, no matter how alone you are – in the dead of space, in the middle of nowhere – it always feels like you're being watched.

22%. Something's definitely awry, something mechanical. I hoped for a while that it would be the computer maybe, just fucking up. It isn't. There's a pattern again, but it isn't constant: each percentage point seems to be taking less time than the one before it. That means I have three or four days left at most. A few days of flying, moving, whatever, and then, assuming that the piezoelectric batteries charge to full, another day or so of sitting around, waiting for the air to run out, or to be rescued, whatever happens first. Less than a week of my life left. People achieve a lot in a week: in a week you can cure a disease, write a song, create a child.

Elena and I had spoken about having children. A recurring theme, running around a track passing a baton to each other wherein we make excuses. We tried, two years ago, and she lost it. The worst moments in life come when you are happiest, like the cruellest anvil of irony. We were happy and laughing and in a taxi going to a party to celebrate an award I was getting – to celebrate me! – and she cramped up. Dinner had been asparagus and steamed salmon and dauphinoise, rich and stodgy and hearty, and we were going to the party afterwards – like a real celebrity, an after-party with invites – when she grabbed the headrest of the front passenger seat and wrenched at it.

'Are you okay?' I asked her, because she was never one for indigestion or heartburn. (I used to say that she had a stomach made of iron. She would poke her belly – her normal, not-fat belly – and I would clarify that I meant inside, and she would mock-take it as an insult.)

'I'm fine,' she said, 'must have eaten too much.' She sounded so convinced that I didn't worry her while she checked herself; as she puffed to control her breathing, like they would have eventually taught her to do in antenatal classes. I didn't notice as she reached down to grab at the cramp, to claw it out of her; I only saw what was wrong when her hand came up covered in blood, the front of her dress sodden, the still-cold cream leather of the car – an expensive one, that had its own business card, that we argued was worth it on this Special Occasion – smeared red, and she started crying. I got the driver to pull over and she lost the baby right there at the side of the Uxbridge Road, halfway between a pub and a police station. I took my jumper off and she clutched it to herself to soak up the blood, and we threw it away in the bin when we got to the hospital, an expensive jumper, just like that. I don't even know if it was big enough that you could call it a baby. I don't know what you'd call it. We weren't even sure she was pregnant: we'd been trying for a couple of months, and this was the first period she had missed. It happens, we were told, sometimes; sometimes, it's best not to get your hopes up at that early stage.

'I said we shouldn't assume it would be fine,' I offered during the conversation, and I'm still not sure if that was me consoling or accusing. It took another year before we spoke about it again, and then we agreed to try, but another month. There were bills, or too much work, or the time that it would be born was wrong – we planned everything nine months ahead, verbally positive that nothing would go wrong. And then I got my trip, or the promise of it.

Here are other things about Elena: she had a temper, but never shouted; she once threw a cup at me across the kitchen, and she hit me square in the forehead and caused this scar, and I mercilessly teased her about having the best throwing arm in the world, saying she should join the London Meteors, help them win some games; and only once more did she throw something at me, a book this time; and she begged me not to go, saying that the time we would be away from each other would be too much. She was right. This is too much, now. I am left with the sterility of space and so much else of nothing.

19%, and I don't want to go to sleep. I have been awake now for what feels like hours and hours, and my eyelids are tugging themselves shut, but I don't want to sleep. I want to watch this tick, in case. I look outside. There's no sun to keep me awake. I've switched all the lights back on: there's nothing to see but they keep me irritated every time I start to drift off. My headache is here, a comforting neighbour come to borrow a cup of sugar, who stays to have a drink and will Never Fucking Leave. There's a library of books, films, music, all in the computer, and none of them even slightly fascinate me: I'm in space, and I'm slowly dying.

17%, and something hits me. What if the message – the numbers, the beep, the light – is coming from aliens? What if something is out there, watching me, hailing me, and this is how it comes through in our system, like an error message in an operating system? We don't know what's here. We've been here by video, never in person; they might have been waiting for us to get this far.

'Congratulations,' they would say, 'you are the first species to get to us. Here are our secrets.' I spend the next few hours looking at the blackness out of the Bubble, and there's nothing. No ship, no aliens, no stars. Nothing.

15%. Another day. No sun rises. I eat a coffee-flavoured protein bar for breakfast – it's actually coffee ice-cream, but that feels more like a dessert, and I like to act socially acceptable, even when by myself, so tell myself that it's just coffee – and run the recycling units, get some fresh water. I've been drinking stale for days. I should start living like a king. I have food supplies enough to feed a full contingent, including special occasions. We had the resources for a party, for when we reached the halfway point, when the ship turned itself. We were to celebrate and film it, and that would be what they showed on the news. There are a couple of bottles of champagne, hidden here for celebrations – the halfway point of the trip, probably. That was the good intention of them. They're a good way to celebrate, I suppose. I decide to drink them, to eat the Roast Beef meal bars – the best meal bars, sponsored by some celebrity chef – for as many meals as I can, then work my way down the list. The Fried Chicken and Pepperoni Pizza bars get to stay in the box, where they can forever taste like the stale crisps that they are. I am no longer rationed. The champagne is loose and crisp, the bubbles almost larger here. If there was anyone else here I would ask them if they actually were larger, if the pressure or the gravity or the speed, whatever, if it made the champagne different. I can feel my headache wilting under the alcohol. I drift up to the Bubble and stare, and feel something rising inside me, a swell. It's like music: when you hear an orchestra warming up, tapping at their instruments, rolling their snares, cleaning their reeds, checking their tuning. I am swigging from the bottle and trying to remain totally still, pressing my hands against the side of the frame to steady myself, to focus the stars in the distance and see if I can actually watch us move. I drink as I stay there.

Oh god I am so sick

I spend a full day passed out, I think. Maybe only hours, flitting between being conscious and being not, and I see things; I see myself, how I could be, up and about, instead of strapped into my bed and trying to not throw up. Vomit in zero gravity is the worst you've ever seen. I can't even remember how I got myself into bed. I am so close to death, and I'm not even being histrionic.

I wake up and look at the gauge. It's like an alarm: you've been lying down, happily asleep, and you think you hear something, so you sit bolt upright, startled. Have you missed your wake-up call? Your eyes focus immediately – far quicker than they usually do upon waking – on the numbers on the little screen next to you, and they read whatever number you want to hear, the exact time that you wanted to wake up. You didn't oversleep, and your alarm is about to ring, or play the radio, or start your morning coffee being made. I didn't oversleep. I am still alive, still ticking down, still with miles and miles and percentages to go until I am gone. 11%.

I will, if my training is right, sleep through my own death. Assuming that I push this to the very limits of the fuel and then ride out the battery backup I will pass out as the life support systems start to fail, as the oxygen dribbles out. What I'm breathing out will be more potent than what I'm breathing in, and I'll start to feel tired, and I'll nod off. My death itself, my actual moment of passing – an inevitability now, surely, as much as breathing itself – will come as I dream of something, and I'll be oblivious. It's a gentle way to go, the way that my mother always said that she wanted.

'I want to be asleep, and it to just happen,' she would say, and my father would quote something from when he was younger, from a suicide note of this rock star who killed himself.

'It's better to burn out than to fade away,' he said. 'I want to burn out.'

'You'd be lucky to do any burning at all,' my mother said, 'and if you set yourself on fire I'll kill you myself.' I miss them. Not as much as I miss Elena. My mother died long enough ago that I've done my mourning, and my father . . . I mourned, and he might yet be alive. There would never be a chance of reconciliation. Maybe he might step forward to get money for an interview, a spewing of what I was really like – siding with his enemy, the one he beat and emotionally destroyed for so many years – but then he would disappear again. I still miss him: he's my father, for better or worse. Elena was everything, though. She was my all, my entire, my absolute. When we got married, our vows promised to love and honour and obey, and I broke those last two, a majority number destroyed, because I had plans and dreams and aspirations that I failed to take her into account with. She didn't want me to leave, couldn't believe that I would actually go ahead with it. I was always saying things: that I would go to Africa, to do refugee reporting; that I would climb a mountain and write about that; that I would someday like to go to space, or to the depths of the ocean, or to those still uncharted parts of the rainforest where there are those few civilizations that we've left alone, to develop naturally, technology free, staring up at the helicopters as they take pictures, wondering what those things in the sky are. I said all those things and she used to cradle my head and stroke along my hairline and listen to my dreams about that, but she didn't actually believe I would do it, because those things, they're not the sort of things that people accomplish. Her dreams were of rising to the top of her field, of the family we could have, of realism. Even I didn't believe in mine, not until I saw that they were looking for people for the space mission. Even then, as I filled out the forms, I questioned every single answer, and wondered if I shouldn't just sabotage myself. Back then it would have been so easy to invent a heart murmur and keep my dream intact.

'I would have gone, but the doctors wouldn't let me,' I could say, and then, when the trip actually happened, that would be my story. 'I was up for that job, but health reasons stopped me,' I could say; and if I said it enough, maybe I'd start to believe it.

My head aches, a combination of the old-faithful pressure and the alcohol from last night. I am sure – there's an old joke, in comedy shows, cartoons, about the stages of mourning, where characters run through them as they describe what they should be feeling. I should be suffering them. I look them up on the computer, in the encyclopedia. Stage 1: Denial and Isolation. Ha ha! There is nothing to deny, and I can't help the isolation part of it. I would if I could, but I can't. Stage 2: Anger. There is nothing worth getting angry for. Stage 3: Bargaining. Please, God, if you do exist, save me. Turn me around, turn this ship around. Flick it with your mighty fingers; spin me back to Earth, to the Moon, even. I'll take whatever I can get. Stage 4: Depression.

This is often accompanied by addictive problems to help deal with the pain, such as the use of alcohol or drugs. Stage 5: Acceptance. I'm going to die.

I start watching Arlen's video. I barely recognize him. It's been so long – and it seems even longer – since I last spent any time with him, and the only video isn't much like him, because he's working in it, running diagnostics before we even left Earth. All work and no play. I laugh when I see his beard. We were an attractive crew, for the most part. It seemed like it was part of the overall package: find relatively charismatic crewmembers, make sure that we're photogenic; you get people to care about the project. Guy comes into frame, over Arlen's shoulder, and they shake hands. Guy clasps Arlen's hand in both of his, pumps it up and down.

'When you going to get around to me?' he asks, and I tell him that it won't be until we're up in space. He smiles at that, like he's remembering where we're going. 'Oh shit, well, I guess you'll know where to find me, yeah? Fuck!'

'They're really good people,' Arlen says, when I ask how he likes the rest of the crew. 'It helps, you have a good crew, this whole thing will go a lot quicker.' Now, here, that makes me wince to watch him say that. Nothing can possibly make this go quickly. 'But all of them – you included – you all seem like good people.'

'What are you doing now?' the me on the video asks him.

'Now, right now, I'm testing the propulsion systems, checking that they're working.' He flicks a switch, a light goes green.

'What do you say to those people who argue that you aren't a pilot if a computer is doing all the flying for you?'

'To those people I say, well, you come up here and fix

that computer if it all goes wrong, or you land this thing upon re-entry. The *Ishiguro*'s a costly girl, I can tell you that much.' He smiles, and the video clicks at a stop. There are no manual controls, and I don't know how to fix the computer. I pull myself to the back of the main room and unseal another champagne, and drink. Stage 5: Acceptance.

The *Ishiguro* was one of the last things named or revealed about the expedition. There was a board of name suggestions, with DARPA wanting to move away from their traditions.

'We've had enough of the grandiose,' they said, 'and there's only so many *Voyagers* that people can stomach.' They ran a competition through the website to get suggestions, and the one that ran the highest, that tested the best, was *Destiny*. 'The *Destiny*,' people walked around saying, trying it on. 'The *Destiny* is boarding. The *Destiny* is ready for take-off.' When we signed up we didn't know about a name; it was kept under wraps, for a huge media reveal. The day that they selected us they told us the name, showed us the banner that they were preparing to slather all over the ship itself. Our faces told them all that they needed to know. (Afterwards, Guy made a joke: 'We're fucking astronauts,' he said, 'not fucking My Little Pony jockeys!') The next day there was a meeting that we weren't party to, and after that they took us back for another reveal.

'We're thinking about using the name *Ishiguro*,' they said. Hidenori Ishiguro was the man behind the initial design of the ship's engines, the engines that were going to let us make this journey, before the team of scientists – including Guy – tore the project away from him and made it something globally funded, huge in scope, and definitely going to happen. He was enigmatic and brilliant, and we all respected him.

'It's a fine name,' we all agreed, and they announced it at a reveal a week later, where the man himself whipped a cloth off the name-plate and the audience clapped. The press weren't taken with it.

'It's too subdued,' they said. 'It doesn't mean anything. Where's the sense of magic, of reaching for the stars?'

'Can't please everyone,' Arlen said when we read the articles. 'Especially when they want fireworks and you're giving them dust.'

After Arlen, and the tick over from 11 to 10%, comes Guy. His videos are shades of light and dark, veering wildly from him being happy, singing for me, laughing about a joke, playing up to national stereotypes – he was a good sport, most of the time – and then suddenly being serious.

'We've signed up for this; we accept our fates, if they occur.'

'What fates?' I ask.

'Well, what if we reach the turnaround point and we don't turn around?' He's prescient: I didn't even realize that we had this conversation. Oh God.

'They've run the trials three times now, unmanned, and it's always turned around on those occasions.'

'There's always a first time,' Guy says. 'Those were much shorter runs, as well.'

'Could you fix it, turn us?'

'Perhaps. The computer is intricate, temperamental. I would give it a go, but I wouldn't need to.' He flashes a smile – he's missing a tooth, three or four across from the front centre, and I only now really notice it, and find it fascinating: why didn't he have it grown back? Why did he

42

leave that gap there, a gap that could be gotten rid of so easily, just one injection?

'Why did they not put manual controls in, Guy, in case something goes wrong?'

'In case? Nothing goes wrong. The computers are perfect, and it keeps us from making any fuck-ups. We are only human, you know? You see us, we hit a switch, we play with a joystick, we fuck it all up. The computer has a course, we stick to it, we get home. Simple.' In the film I would pause the tape at this moment, freeze him on the screen. Famous last words. I think that's how the film might start, with that chunk of premonitory exposition, that interview, and then the freeze, then a draw back to reveal me alone in the craft, the others dead, in their beds, and then pull back further, the ship in space, puttering along as the fuel gauge flicks numbers over like an antique railway station clock. Cut to: The opening credits.

There is a way to fix this. Guy knew it, he could have done it. He died too soon. If he was me, the last one, last of the Mohicans, he could have gotten home, told them what happened.

'I spent so long alone!' he could have cried. 'Alone!' And, 'I had these messages, and they didn't mean anything, so I ignored them!'

As if by magic, another beep, another flash of the red light. 250480. The message never changes, telling me that there's something wrong, but not what that something is. I just can't fathom it. I write it over and over as I write my blog entries (which I've maintained, even now, alone, with no idea if they're reaching home or not). I contemplate writing it on the walls, all over the crisp whiteness, so that if I'm ever found they'll think I have succumbed to Space Madness, but decide that it's a pointless joke. It's not a systems warning, not a fault, and, as best I can tell, not a message. The AI in the computer hasn't become sentient. I don't believe it's an alien trying to reach me – there's nothing out here, that much is clear when you get here into the stillness, the darkness – so it's just a beep. Perhaps it's a way of telling me that there's a problem with the fuel. Perhaps it's just nothing. It stops, the light, the beep, just as the computer drops to 9%. There's stillness again.

4

I write my blog entries into the computer every day, and I send them, telling Ground Control what's been happening, just so that there's no confusion. I want them to know that it's just me up here now – or, me and Emmy, really, if they wanted to save us, two bodies, not one – and I tell them about the warning, the numbers, because they might find a way to send me a message back. They probably could. Or: they always told us that they could travel faster, just not for as long. Maybe they've fixed that? Maybe they've had a breakthrough in the last few weeks, and there's a ship roaring towards us right now, and it will pull alongside us and lower its doors and I'll get to drift over, and I'll be saved. I write that in the blog, and everything else, even down to my dreams and what I've seen outside the ship, to give them a better idea of where I am. I write them and then I click Send, and then I don't look at them again, because I really can't stand the thought. It's one thing to watch videos of the others, seeing stuff through their eyes for a second. I couldn't stand to relive this trip through my own eyes, I don't think.

I miss gravity. So many days into nothing, into my floating inside the ship that is floating in space, like a Russian doll, and I have decided that I want to feel the floor beneath my feet again. We were never going to put the gravity field online when we started off: all I know is that it burns through the piezoelectric batteries like nothing else on the ship.

'The sheer energy required to sustain it is monumental.' I can't remember which one of the crew told me that. I flick the switch, and there's a humming coming from all around the walls, making us shake, a subtle vibration, like a washing machine, and I push myself towards a standing position for when it kicks in. I am suddenly pushed to the floor, and there's a sound like jumping on twigs. Something in my leg snaps. The pain is monumental. It roars up my side, and I collapse to the floor, my other leg buckling under my weight, twisting behind me. The sting from that one is negligible: the injury in the other has caused blood to start spilling out of the root of my trouser leg, puddling out around me into a pool. Amongst all of this, the beeping starts again, and I am heaped on the floor, unable to see the screen. Deal with the leg first. There are bandages in the medical cupboard, I've seen them, and painkillers, and probably whatever else I'm going to need. I try to roll the trouser leg up but something stops it, something hard and sharp and like being stabbed, and I assume that it must be a bone. Scissors. I need to cut it free.

I drag myself across the floor to the table, trying not to look at my leg, trying not to let it drag – or worse, snag on anything, the jutting bone facing outwards like a little hook looking for a catch – and hoist myself to the seats. The cupboard is above that table, and I manage to get it open without having to push myself up any higher than the seats themselves. From there, the scissors. My shaky hands don't do justice to the fabric, tearing and ripping as best they can, until I can finally see the damage itself. With the pink of the blood, the yellow of my skin, it looks like coral. It looks – as with coral – almost aerated, fine holes, bubbles running throughout. This is my shin, pushed out and upwards and through the skin, a one-inch punch, as neat and delicate as my own surgery on the trouser leg.

In the kit there is a huge roll of bandages, some elastic strips, some plasters, a self-cleaning syringe with multiple doses of morphine in it, another with some sort of anaesthetic, another with antiseptic. There should be tens of bottles of painkillers, as well, but the tray is nearly empty, their slots sad and vacant, only one bottle left. I wonder which of the crew was using them; we were warned that they could be addictive, that the headaches, the sickness we might feel would pass, that the painkillers were strictly for emergency use. There's a metal splint. I take the syringes and the splint and the bandages and shuffle backwards on the bench, pulling my leg by the thigh until it is flat – or as flat as I can get it – on the bench with me. The beeping persists from the computer. Fuck.

I use the base of my hand to hold my leg at the knee, pressing down to stem the blood, tying a bandage off around it, pulling my hand free. The blood is already darker, already congealing. I wonder if blood finds it harder to do its job in space? I wonder if bones heal the same? Technically, I suppose, it's a surface wound. Two injections of antiseptic, two of anaesthetic, the morphine on the side for when I need it. I clean the area around the rupture, wipe it down, and then put one hand on my calf, the other on the nape of the bone, using the base of my palm. I brace myself, count to three, breathe, and then push down. The bone – seemingly my whole shin – shifts, sliding down, and there's an almost satisfying click as it meets whatever it is that it slots into, like the clunk of a car door sliding shut. It doesn't really feel like anything. I inject another antiseptic, wipe the area down, bandage it, and then extend the splint, rest it on the front of my leg and wrap the arms around my calf. Activating it makes it tug itself tighter, and I can feel the pressure on my bone, and then the pain starts to come back, just as the splint thinks it's found the right level of tautness for my muscles, and it hisses as it shuts itself off. The pain crescendoes, and I take the morphine, inject it into my neck. Pain, or morphine, or something, makes me pass out.

I dream of space. At least, I think it's a dream: otherwise, it's just nothing.

I wake up to the beeping, still. My leg is swollen, but the pain has subsided slightly. I inject more anaesthetic into the puffed skin around the bandages and give myself a far smaller dose of morphine than I took last night and shuffle to the edge of the seat. It's five metres to the control panels, maybe slightly more. In zero gravity, that's two pushes, maybe. Here? I put my good leg onto the floor. It winces, but only slightly: the second injury was just a mild twist, I think, nothing fatal. (Ha! That I should worry about fatality! Here!) From there I push myself to standing, and from there grab part of the bulkhead and shuffle myself towards it. I grab the inside wall and pull myself along until I reach the chairs in the cockpit section, and sit down in the pilot's chair. I have avoided this one until now: I've always used Quinn's. I don't know why.

The computer tells me that there's an ALERT, and that the battery is down to 10%. It must be the gravity field. I had no idea it took that much power. I've just managed to lose a week of my life, all so that I could shatter my leg apart. Fuck it. I switch the engines back on. I start drifting upwards as the battery power percentage disappears to a corner where it displays a recharging symbol, and the 9% moves back to the centre of the screen. 9% of fuel, and the life support ticks down on cue, matching that number. 9%. My life, in single digits.

I sleep, but I don't remember actually dropping off. I remember lying against the bed, the straps tugging slightly at my side, my leg hanging limp. The lack of gravity makes this wonderful, my leg floating free and easy behind me, swinging like a cat's tail. I remember wondering why I couldn't sleep, getting annoyed at the hum of the engines, the light from the monitors. I remember thinking about Elena, and then the computer beeped to 8%, and I decided to wake up. I'm not even tired any more.

I put on Wanda's videos, and in them she is cleaning the front console. 'This is the fun part of the job,' she says, 'this is where the action is.' She seems so sad, like she doesn't want to be here.

'Do you have to be careful when cleaning this stuff?' Video-me asks. She shakes her head and leans in towards the camera conspiratorially.

'No,' she says. 'None of this actually does anything; it's all smoke and mirrors.'

As the computer ticks down to the 7% mark I am sitting at the backup terminal, reading about the propulsion systems. There is a schematic showing me the sequence and code to enter into the computer to accelerate the engines, to take us to maximum power. We are using most of the power of the ship, apparently. The piezoelectric batteries have barely charged, certainly not enough to make it worth my while to use them. I don't want to wait, not any more. I'm going to end this. There's a self-destruct, like how all the best old films and stories had one, built in to stop American technology falling into the hands of our enemies. I don't know why it's here; all I know is that it is. It's called something else; it's labelled as a 'Crash Assist', in case we were headed back to Earth too quickly, and we needed to shed the craft and let the stasis pods float back to Earth on their own, with their own in-built parachutes. It makes the hull break up into pieces, like Lego, and leaves everything else to fall of its own accord. Everything shatters. It feels appropriate. It makes the engines accelerate briefly, just for a few seconds, far beyond their natural ability, to short them out; and then the ship opens itself, and here's all the people. I have just enough energy to do it, according to the computer. Just enough.

The guidelines tell me that, in case of emergency, I am to jettison all unnecessary cargo. I seal the main hull off from the back of the ship and open the external rear doors and the food stockpiles, the external suits, the oxygen tanks, everything gets sucked out. It's much faster than I imagined, a real 'blink and you'll miss it' moment. I shut the doors and read the next guideline. *First, ensure the rest of the crew are safely in stasis.* (Ha! Emmy looks at me through the glass, safe and sound, tucked in.) *Next, prepare your stasis bed for yourself, and enter these instructions.*

I type the complicated string of numbers into the computer. Ensure that everything is secure – hatches, doors, the stasis beds – and then press the Enter key. *Caution! Upon pressing the key a countdown will initiate, and when finished, the engines will reach Maximum Efficiency. The countdown will last 30 seconds.* I take one last look around the ship. There's nothing here for me. I pull myself to Arlen's chair again, stare out of the view screen: It's so peaceful. There's nothing but blackness for as far as I can see. I strap myself in, and lean over to switch the gravity on again. If I'm going to do this, I want to feel it: I don't want to be floating, airlessly. I want the stress. I want to know what it feels like. I want to see it, and I don't want to have battery backup left to keep me here, all broken bones and torn limbs, lying in pain, waiting to die, before finally choking to death, suffocating without air. I think I am saying all of this aloud, to nobody. I think.

Gravity kicks in immediately, and the pain clambers back up my broken leg with the weight I'm suddenly putting on it. I hit Enter, and the countdown starts. 30, 29, 28. My life, the last few weeks, has been dictated by numbers. 27, 26. I go years without thinking about them, thinking instead about words. 25, 24, 23. Suddenly I find them the most important things in the world. 22, 21. Countdowns, percentages, time: they all matter. 20, 19. And the message, the numbers on the screen. 18, 17, 16. I'll die, never knowing what they mean. 15, 14. They'll be a MacGuffin, always eluding me. 13, 12, 11. Like everything else, they'll just fade, I suppose, 10, as I move on, wherever it is that I'm going, 9, and nobody will ever know that I didn't know what it was, 8, just another batch of trophies and 7 commiserations on somebody's 6 shelf, and I hope she 5 misses me as much as I 4 want her to, because oh, God, Elen3a, I miss you so 2 much, so much 1 it hurts.

I can't move. I can barely see. There's water everywhere, it feels like, and I try to gulp in breaths through my mouth, but I can feel it twist and move, and never actually get the air that I want from it. I can make out the shapes of the numbers on the screen, but they aren't important, not any more. This is it. I stare at the window in front of me, at the cracks that are starting to form in the plastic (another me would have asked why they don't test this!) and at the space; there's suddenly something in the distance, blacker than the rest of it, somehow. It's more tranquil than everything else I can see, with no stars, just an expanse of pure, absolute night, so black that it almost looks solid, like I could just reach out and touch it. I'm focused on it when the crack directly in front of me splits like my leg, and it pulls the window out almost wholly. All the sound dulls away, and I feel the clasps attaching me to the chair being pulled at, tugged, yanked. As we reach the blackness of space I come free and I can suddenly hear that blackness, that somehow, here in the vacuum, it has noise, a roar, a filthy, gasping roar, like a whirlpool, a maelstrom, but I'm spinning out of the ship, and out of myself, and out here, in the deepest part of space that man has ever been, it feels like somebody is holding me, telling me that it will all be all right as I take one last breath of air, of actual air, the last one left on the ship, and I swallow it down and let it wash all over me, knowing that it will be the one that I take as I die, and then I regret this, because maybe I gave up too soon, and Elena wouldn't be proud of me, giving up like this, because she always told me that I was the strong one, and I see the blackness, worse than space, worse than anything, utterly black, and it swallows me whole.

PART TWO

We live, as we dream –
Alone.

> – Joseph Conrad, *Heart of Darkness*

1

Elena's voice; soft, eager. She asks me to wake up, so I do. I lean over to her, tell her that I've heard her say this before. She laughs.

'Cormac,' she says, 'you have to save yourself. You have to wake up.'

I open my eyes, and it's the same blackness for a second, so dark I can't think, even, and I can feel it in my eyes, in every part of me; and then the roar of the ship's engines, but with that noise behind them, like an echo, like a microphone that distorts your voice into the timbre of some horror-movie villain. Then the noise stops, but it's still so cold I can barely see anything, and it suddenly hits me; the temperature, the noise. The ship tore itself apart; or I thought that it did. I try to pull myself to my feet, but then I realize that I'm not on the floor at all; the gravity is gone still. These are the rules of space travel. I can barely see anything, because the cold is making my eyes hurt, and I can't hear anything, even myself when I try to shout, because the sound from the engines – it must still be the engines, although they should be gone, destroyed, sucked into the void – is like a howl, totally decimating the air, filling it with itself and nothing else, like white noise. I feel my way around, hitting every surface I brush against in slow motion, trying to work out where I am. It's freezing cold, so cold that it hurts, that when I gulp for breath it almost burns my lungs to take it in. I am back on the *Ishiguro*, or I never left. Either way, this is my ship. I feel the rounded screen-door of one of the beds, find the handle, wrench it open. They're all dead, and I'm not, but if I don't get inside I will be. All of a sudden, here and now, I want to save myself. I wonder how much of what I felt before – what I saw, my drift into the darkness, the ship exploding – how much of it was real. Did I even do the self-destruct? Did I somehow imagine it all? The door hisses open, and I see his face, suddenly clear: Arlen. His already-dead body is worth far less than my survival; even though my bed is only feet away, I can feel the pull inside the ship's atmosphere, threatening to tear me apart.

I unclip him, push him to one side and slide in in his place. I remember sleeping in these things from the first time I did it. It's hazy, distant, but still there. You don't forget something this important. There's thirty seconds before you sleep, thirty defined seconds and then there's nothing. I stare out of the glass of the pod and then I remember my leg, which now is healed, the blood only a tired stain on the clothes, faded almost completely, and I can move it, flex it, and I know that something – either the end, before, or this now – cannot be real.

The door to the bed opens and spits me out. This is how it was the first time, still totally familiar; the weirdest sensation, leaving you soaking wet, gasping for air, as if, almost, you've forgotten how to breathe. For that first second it's so alien, so complicated, and there's so much water dripping off you that it feels like you're drowning, maybe. The water drips off me, and the ship sucks it into its vents, ready for reprocessing, for turning into drinking water, shower water. I'm dry in seconds.

My eyesight is still screwed up, so I rub at my eyes, blink wildly. I jam my foot against the corner of the room, steady myself. The whir of the ship – engines on, moving quickly, but nothing like the noise I heard before, when I woke – is nearly distracting, because it's so quiet again, that same hum as it always was, engines working fine, ticking along. Then I see Arlen. I had forgotten. I'd forgotten what he looked like when we opened the bed, found him there. He looks the same; almost blue, flaking like an old wall.

'I'm so sorry,' I say to him, 'I had to get into the bed.' I pick him up – he weighs nothing, like an over-full sack of dust – and put him back, strapping him down, tying him in. I hate to touch him, but I have to, so I'm careful. The ship is so dark still, and I'm suddenly not used to it. 'Lights,' I say, and they flick on one by one. Everything here is like it was. I look to the cockpit: I remember it being pulled off, cracks spreading across the view screen, then being torn out. It's all so clean. I look around to see if Emmy is okay in her bed: she's still strapped in, as if nothing ever happened. She looks utterly tranquil, peaceful. Her eyes are shut. I look at the rest of them: Arlen, so blue and chalky; Quinn, handsome and sharp-jawed, stony-faced; Guy, his face in a smirk, almost; Wanda, Dogsbody, but her eyes aren't red any more, and her face is clean, which is odd. Then I get to the last bed, my bed, which should be empty; but there's a body in there already, like all the others, and I take a second before I focus on the face, recounting, wondering if I've fucked up, and then I really look at him. It's me, my face. He's clean-shaven and pure and his cheeks are glossy and his hair parted and neat. He looks as I did weeks ago, when we left on this mission. He is in my bed, and he is breathing softly, the gentle rise of his chest, the puff of his cheeks, sleeping as I sleep, the exact same way.

'Fuck,' I say. I hit the glass front with my hand, wanting to stay where I am, let me focus on the face; I try to breathe, but it clogs in my throat, so I cough it out, force it out. I pull myself up, until we're face to face, look through the glass. 'This is a trick,' I shout, 'who's fucking with me?' but I know that it isn't a trick, that I'm not being fucked with. I feel my guts roar, faster than I can control, and I taste it in my mouth, vomit, awful and bitter. I swallow it down on instinct, because I don't want it floating around. Every part of me wants to open the bed, but I don't. I can't explain it. I don't.

Shaking – quivering – I hurl myself across the room towards the computers in the cockpit, look at the date on the computers, at the updates from Ground Control. The screen is emblazoned with the message that we had waiting for us when we woke up – *Dear crew*, it reads, *Welcome to your new home for the foreseeable future!* – and it's time-stamped, marked as unread. I check the monitors, the gauges and dials and numbers that I know how to read. We're on 93% fuel, which means we're only hours out of warp, and that's what it was when we woke up, one by one, popping out of the beds ready to be the explorers we were destined to be. Arlen was meant to be first up, first out of bed. When we got out of the sleeping pods, Arlen didn't. He was meant to have been up hours before us, preparing the ship, turning the lights and heat on, checking that the life support systems were working. He died, and we assumed that the system malfunctioned. It was unexplainable, no matter how hard we tried: the diagnostic tests showed everything working perfectly. It hits me again: the system didn't malfunction; *I* did. I opened his bed during warp, and I dragged him out and I squirrelled myself away in his place. I pull myself across to him and examine his body through the glass. This is what the scientists warned us could happen if we weren't in stasis: rapid dehydration, massive decomposition of the flesh, incredible bone loss. I wish I had closed his eyes before I put him back in, because they look like they're fake, like they're made of paper, the pupils drawn on in dusty black pen.

I killed Arlen. It's all I can think, and all I can see, and I'm so confused that I start crying, and I have no idea how I can stop.

Arlen had an hour before the rest of the crew were woken up, and now I have that hour, somehow. I swear into the space around me, and I cry so much and watch as the tears peel away from my face before they drip off, and I stare at Arlen, who watches me, letting me know how guilty I am. This is my fault.

I have to hide, I think. They can't see me like this. The ship is just a huge fucking coffin, rigged to explode, dragging its crew into the furnace as it goes, and we exploded because *I was there*, and this – all of this, seeing myself, like a mirror, like a trick of the light, like a magician's finest hour – all of this is wrong and unreal, because it has to be.

Only: it feels real. I gasp and feel the floor, and it feels real enough, and everything is how it was. I don't know how, but I'm back on the *Ishiguro*, and it's the start of the trip, and I'm not the me that I was.

I panic, because I don't understand what's happening, how I can be here, and pull myself through the rest of the ship, turning the lights on all the way down to the engine room, past the airlock and the changing room. There are rooms back here. We barely ever had cause to go into them, because they didn't have anything that we needed. Two rooms near the back – the base – of the ship were exclusively for fuel cells and engine access panels, another exclusively for the battery; they had routine checks, mostly by Guy or Wanda, but the rest of us didn't touch them. We weren't trained to, and we didn't want to. One of the storerooms was where most of the food supplies were kept, but that was too frequently used; and then the storage room for walk supplies, emergency power tools, that sort of thing. This is the one: I don't remember ever going in here, because we so rarely needed anything from here. If you needed to hide some-where, this would be the place. From where I'm floating, the ship is actually enormous, cavernous, far bigger than six people needed; so much space filled with nothing but fuel cells or enormous batteries or storage crates. This is where I'll hide. I find a crate, full of spare parts for the ship, piping hose and sheet metal. It's fastened to the grated floor with clips and carabiners, to keep it rigid in no-gravity. I loosen the straps, only slightly, just enough to leave a gap about a foot deep underneath it, and I slide under it. This will be fine as a hiding place, unless they put on the gravity and the box falls down to crush me. That won't happen. Assuming that what I think has happened has actually happened – I am back here, at the start, and everything is going to happen the way that it originally did – the gravity won't be put on for a short while yet.

I think about what I'll do when the crew wake up. I'll go to them, and tell them what's happened, surprising them as they do their routine checks on the systems, as they run their diagnostics. When they find Arlen's body, I'll explain: they all died, and I was alone, and then I died as well, blowing up the ship because I didn't want to die slowly and ingloriously, and now I'm here, and I killed Arlen, dragged his body out of sleep before I should have, left him in the coldness of the ship to choke to death, to freeze. Hello, I'll say, take pity on me; even though I know that they won't. They'll hear my words as the ranting and raving of a madman, of an identikit stowaway. They'll brandish their pitchforks and storm the castle, and demand that I'm killed for what I've done: or, at the very least, held accountable. They won't listen. I know that the me that'll be out there won't listen, that's for sure. He'll stare at his hitherto-unknown twin as if he's insane. He'll want to know what's happening, and he'll be overly aggressive, to prove he's not a part of the conspiracy, and they'll want answers, proof that I'm me, that he's me, or that one of us isn't me.

'Cormac,' I'll say, 'here's something that only you know,' but he'll deny knowing it, or accuse me of reading his old diaries. He'll lead the charge against me. He'll put me in the airlock and flush me into space, and they'll watch as I scream and die, an alien, a clone, a gutless, brutal anomaly, and the guilt he'll feel will be negligible. He'll be desperately confused, sure, but he won't feel guilt, because he's the real me, and that's how I would feel. I don't know how I know this, but I can almost see it playing out in my mind, or like a gut feeling, like intuition. I have to stay here, or they'll think I'm insane, or he is.

Is he? Am I?

I listen as the crew wake up, pulling themselves from their beds. I am crouched, hiding under the box, terrified, sobbing, biting my lip to keep from making noise. I can hear my own voice: it carries down the corridors more than any of the others, it seems. That's probably just my mind playing tricks on me; I never thought that I spoke so loudly. Quinn was first up, and he found Arlen, woke Emmy, and they got his body out, tried to bring him back. As they were strapping him to the table – the medical table, the same place we ate our meals, everything with multiple purposes, wiped down after single tasks to prepare for the next emergency/meal – the rest of us woke up. I listen as Wanda cries, as Guy offers to examine his bed, as Emmy closes his eyes for him.

'What a way to wake up,' Quinn says, talking about Arlen but meaning himself.

'Something must have happened to the air supply,' I hear myself say, my voice like when you hear it on a recording: more nasal, not quite right, but definitely mine. 'Or maybe there's a crack?'

'No cracks,' Guy replies. 'If they've got a crack, the door won't lock. It's a closed system: needs to make a circuit to shut properly.'

'Maybe the seal itself?'

'If the seal is torn, the door won't lock either. It'll be something else. These things can happen, fucking errors in the code or the wiring or the chips shorted out. Extremes of temperature, you know. These things can happen.' We used to joke about his stereotype, about how he was German and so fucking efficient. It started before, when we were in training, but this was the first time we really noticed it. I remember it all. If I tried, I think I could exactly predict what I'm about to say: I mouth the words as they leave the other me's mouth.

'They can, but they shouldn't.' I can't see it, but I remember what happened then: I hugged Wanda, told her that it would all be all right, even though I barely knew her. It was consoling. When Guy couldn't hear us, we spoke about how he was too cold, too clinical. Quinn told us that he had to be, said that, if he wasn't, who would be? And Wanda wouldn't stop crying: I totally forgot that she had to be sedated that day, that Emmy had to take her to her bed, put her back. When we slept in them we just used the straps, closed the doors, but they weren't locked or anything. I forgot that, for a while, it was like Wanda was dead as well.

I listen to the crew arguing as they try to revive Arlen, but they give up so quickly, because Emmy says that there's no coming back when the body is in the state his is. She's the one who tells them to stop, finally, and she calls the time of death as if this is a hospital. When she does it they all sigh, and Quinn shouts something in anger, and Guy doesn't even pay attention, it seems, because there are things that need doing. This ship, he would have said if he had been asked, won't run itself.

'We should tell Ground Control,' Quinn says. Nobody disagrees with him. The wait time at that point was only a few minutes, because of how close we still were to home, but I remember that it felt like forever, having to deliver that news. 'This is the crew of the *Ishiguro*,' Quinn says into the computer microphone, 'and we've just come out of the pods, just checking in. Ship is stable, fuel reserves at 93%, which is in line with expectations. Captain Arlen Bester didn't wake up after stasis, however; attempts to resuscitate him have been unsuccessful. Time of death was called at oh-seven-forty hours.' He left out all of the details – about his blue skin, his chalky eyes – because there was no need to pass them on. We were warned, when we signed all of our disclaimers and NDAs, hundreds of pages of the things, that the beds could malfunction. It was one of the multitudinous ways that we could die, and DARPA couldn't – wouldn't – be held responsible. When Quinn's finished, he suggests that we say something. We're already standing around Arlen's body as if it's a proper funeral; all that's missing are the clods of dirt to throw onto the coffin, the priest, the black suits. He turns to the other me, the original me, tells me that I should do it. 'You're good with words,' he says. I remember my speech; I remember how it fell out of my mouth, like I was being sick in fits and bursts.

As the other me talks about Arlen's beard, about what a cool guy he was, tells stories about stuff that happened in training, I hang onto the wall and wonder once again if I'm completely insane, and if any of this is real at all. I notice my leg, where I hurt it – where I remember the blood, the bone sticking through, so painful – and realize that, even though it still hurts, the wound isn't sensitive. I wind up my trouser leg, expecting blood, a scab, a gash, but it's healed. Along the line of my knee is a scar, like a sideways grimace, but it's healed. I ball my hand to a fist and hit it, trying to see if it flinches with pain, and it does, but it's only dull, like an echo, a memory of how sharp the pain used to be. As I keep listening to the crew it hurts more and more, until it's aching again, creasing along the line where it feels slightly healed, where the scar is; until the pain starts creeping up my whole body.

I must have remembered it wrong. I must have. Despite how it looks, after a while it hurts so badly that I'm shaking slightly. The pain gets worse with each passing second. I have no idea how I'll make it go away, and I shake and moan, because none of this makes any sense.

The crew are running diagnostics, sweeping the ship for anything that might not have been spotted. At the time – and again, now, as I listen to it for the second time in my life, word for word the same – Guy told us it was to make sure that we were safe.

'Think of this thing as a rubber boat,' he says. 'You go for hours along a river that's calm; it's great, nothing wrong. You hit some rapids all of a sudden, and it gets a puncture, something tiny, barely even visible; you might not realize. But, you know, you made it through the rapids safe, and you're alive, so you relax. When you're then in the huge river, or the sea, in this instance, it doesn't matter how still it is, how calm and relaxing: if you don't find that puncture, that could be the thing that kills you.' We had to search for the puncture, in case it existed. 'This is nothing to do with Arlen's death: it's standard protocol. There's nothing to worry about, it's just something we have to do. Back to work, you know? Better to be safe than sorry,' Guy said. Each member of the crew was assigned a room; each member scoured that room to check its integrity. I put myself behind the boxes, in between them; they're curved, like a U in the room, a perfect human-sized space for me, and there's space under them where they've been strapped down, where I can hide, like a criminal clinging to the undercarriage of a vehicle, praying he isn't caught. I hide in there and wait as the door opens and somebody walks around the room. I don't know who it is, because I don't look, in case they hear me move. I know that it wasn't me, because I was checking the main room: it was all I could be trusted with, because what else did I know? I wasn't like the rest of them.

I first met Emmy months and months before the flight, along with the rest of the crew. There was a bank of seventeen astronauts and pilots that they were going to draw from, all of whom had been training, and all of whom were at various stages of that training; six doctors; four scientists. There were three of us journalists, and we had all done the physical checks, all the psychological profiling: days worth of questions about our lives, our hopes, our fears, our families. We had a week-long camp where we did physical exercises, pushed our bodies and our minds to the absolute limits; and then, at night, we socialized, but not too much. They let us out of our rooms every day for a few hours, kept us moving around the groups to see who we worked best with. There were no phone calls home, and they – a subdivision of DARPA, a government-sponsored conglomeration of companies that was privately funding the space trip – watched everything. It was like a television show, a reality one, where we waited for the viewers to vote us off. They had to make sure that we got along, or that we could work together. I told Elena afterwards that I think they wanted to check that there wasn't any sexual tension amongst us all, or anything that might breed into aggression. Any emotion that wasn't just friendly camaraderie was discouraged. They put us in training rooms in our underwear and made us work out; no secrets, no hiding our superficial scars or those slightly saggy love handles.

We would all watch Emmy from across the room, all of us men. I remember meeting Quinn early on – we bonded in that superficial way that men can when they're slightly embarrassed, in social situations that they don't know how to deal with. He was less nervous than I, less self-conscious – his body, his manner, they afforded him that privilege, because he was chiselled – and he bolstered me, gave me an extra shot of confidence. He was better looking than I was, but he was one of the cool kids, and my association alone lifted me up. He had the looks, the charm; and I could talk for myself. I was the perfect wingman. I pulled myself together so that, when I stood next to him, I didn't feel quite as inadequate. We spoke about Arlen's moustache – it was just that back then, a handlebar, like a stereotypical brigadier in a World War I film – and we spoke about Emmy, about the way that she carried herself.

'Oh, she's out of my league,' I remember Quinn saying, which was a lie, and we both knew it. But he maintained it, I think, for the sake of staying amiable with me. Nobody likes a show-off. I didn't speak to Emmy that entire week, apart from when we were put in exercises together. It wasn't until the second week, when they whittled some of the group down, that we got to have a proper conversation.

Most of the crew sit down in the main room and eat. Wanda is showering, because she's so upset after the death of Arlen that Emmy recommended she try to relax, try to calm down; and the rest are cooking, warming meal bars. I listen as they drink wine – we left with a few bottles, only enough to commemorate a few different occasions, and the champagne for the halfway point, of course – and then they make a film for back home, all crowded around. Ground Control, when they replied, asked us not to mention Arlen; they told us to look happy, to smile, to say cheers, to wish the world the best. We fought about it for a few minutes, but then Guy spoke up, trying to be a voice of reason.

'It's no good starting this off with tragedy,' he said. 'Think about what we're meant to represent, okay? Fuck's sake, think about something other than ourselves.'

'This is a new age of discovery,' Quinn said to everybody watching at home, to the millions – billions, if we were lucky – that would be crowded around their TV sets just to see how far we could get, what we could find out here. It was so cheesy, but that helped us believe it, I think. When the recording had stopped and been sent, we spent the evening talking about what we thought everybody at home would think about. I listen as they all talk about their families. We had all lost loved ones, near and dear to us.

'Wonder if that's what made us all want to be space cadets,' Quinn jokes. I remember Emmy laughing especially fake-hard at the joke: she doesn't let my memory down, and I hear her voice carry down the corridors, through the lining of the ship's walls, a big laugh, as if barely a care in the world at that point. They talk more about Arlen. I don't remember it being this miserable; but mourning always looks worse from the outside. Me? I barely remember Arlen now. The other me tells the story of Elena, leaving out key details – why she actually left me, what we said to each other, what happened before I left for the trip – because I don't want anything to change the way that I'm painted. Guy laughs at me.

'Everybody says that they're innocent after a divorce,' he snorts. 'Nobody ever says, Sure, it was my fault we broke up. The other party is always to blame, and we try to tell it any way we can that isn't true.' The others don't agree with him; they defend me, and I sit quietly, letting them. Quinn tells him to be more considerate, that it's not fair. Emmy nearly shouts her defence of me.

'We've all been hurt,' she says to Guy, 'stop being such an ass.' He laughs it off, slaps my arm, tells me that he's only joking.

'You know that, right?' He turns to the rest. 'He knows that.' I listen as they move on, tiptoeing around topics, avoiding anything that might spill secrets. Within the hour, it's like we've forgotten that Arlen was with us at all. It isn't until we're getting into bed that Emmy brings him up again – a casual mention, that she's sad he didn't get to see this with us, that he would have been so proud, that she hopes he's honoured when we get home – and Wanda starts to cry.

'We have to sleep with him there, looking out like that?'

'I'll shut them,' Quinn says. He tells the crew to look away, and he opens Arlen's bed and does it. Such a heroic gesture. 'It's done,' he says, as if that's enough.

Wanda doesn't stop crying; the rest of us – Quinn, Guy, the real Emmy, the other – real? – me – go to sleep. Eventually Wanda falls silent as well. I don't remember that first night, whether I actually slept or not. Now, I listen, but I can't hear anything that suggests either way.

2

In the main body of the ship – the cockpit, the living areas – the noise of the ship is almost comforting, or was. It became a constant thrum, a neat humming that you knew had purpose behind it. As long as that slight vibration existed, so too did our life support, and when it bugged you, that thought reassured. After a while it became something you were used to, as well; we stopped talking about it completely after a couple of days. Here, however, in the storeroom, the walls seem to shake. I take straps and fasten them to the floor behind crates, hooking them to the standard fixtures using their carabiner hooks, strapping myself down. I lie down and strap myself in, holding myself in place; the vibrations through the thick straps rattle every part of me, my teeth, my bones. My leg aches, and my back aches, and I shiver, and I'm in pain.

'I can't do this,' I say aloud. It feels like I've been doing this for so long; before this, on my own, as they died, one by one; and here, now, a second time, to watch them, or claim responsibility.

* * *

I can't sleep. I lie on the floor – or, slightly above, most of me touching the hard metal panelling, the rest of my body seemingly floating underneath the crates, like an upside-down bed but with none of the rest that a traditional mattress might bring with it. When I don't move for extended periods, it feels like those parts of me that pressed against the crate above me have become loose, detached. It was never like this before, the first time. In the main cabin, they are in their beds, strapped in. They don't have gravity for them, but they have bumpers, holding their bodies in. Part of our training was – can you believe this? – practising sleeping when in confined and constrained spaces. We slept in normal beds with rubber frames around our bodies at first, then they tilted the beds, like we were patients in a hospital, the bed-frames controlled by the specialists. They explained that they had to save space: the beds on the ship were to be at an angle, not unlike that found when sitting up in bed.

'It'll help blood flow as well,' they said, though Emmy always said that they were lying about that.

'A lot of what they tell us about the medical stuff they're doing is a lie,' she told me one day. 'They just want to cover themselves, and if you don't ask questions it's a lot easier.' I asked her about the bone loss, because that was another warning. 'It's an issue, sure, but not for us,' she said. 'You'd have to be out in space for years for it to really cause you issues. That's space station health worries, for the guys who are up there on six-month or year rotations. We're not up here for long enough. You eat your meals, drink lots of water, exercise, you'll be fine.' She was so sure, and that reassured me. I trusted her, because that's what we do. It's who we are, as people: we're intrinsically built to trust.

As I lie there, shaking with something, I don't know what,

like I'm ill, actually sick, I wonder what's happening. I'm so scared, because I don't know what's going on, and I don't know what it means, and all I can do is pray that I have actually gone insane, because the alternative – I can't even say it – is far, far more terrifying.

I unstrap myself, no concept of what time it is. The rest of the ship is completely dead, however (that word, like a prediction, a crystal ball); one of the benefits of the crew sleeping in their pods is that they're pretty much prevented from hearing noise from the rest of the ship, by design, blocking out voices. We were meant to sleep in shifts but never did: there was always to be somebody watching the ship, making sure that everything was fine, but with no need. Everything was so automated we might as well have been at home, were it not for the *purpose*, for our being the eyes and ears of the people who might want to be in our position. Guy said it best as we waited for the lift to take us up to the ship, the day we launched.

'We're the new explorers,' he said. 'This is like Columbus, or those guys who first went across the Antarctic. We're adventurers, right? We're inspiring people.' That was the only thing that he ever seemed passionate about: what we were doing, that it was important. To me, specifically, he spoke about how important my role was. 'You have to tell it like it is: tell the world that we're *not* heroes, we're just people seeing what can be done. That's crucial, right?'

I open the door to the storeroom, sliding it back. The lights in the rest of the ship are still on, and they make me blink, blinding me slightly again. I drift down the quiet hallway towards the main room, the cockpit.

'This doesn't make any sense,' I say, aloud, quietly, into

the nothing. I cross the threshold, and there's the other me: looking so much younger, clean-shaven, peaceful. I stare at the sleeping crew for a while, taking them in. My eyes keep flitting to myself, to the scowl that I sleep with. Elena always told me that, that I looked angry when I slept. ('Like you're planning vengeance,' she would joke.) I wonder what it is that I'm so angry about at that moment; what my dreams are of.

In the changing room I look at myself in the mirror for the first time since I woke up. I am a wreck; it takes me seconds to come to terms with what I'm seeing, because it's wrong. I don't recognize this face; it's so thin and drawn, weak and loose and grey in the skin. My face has pockmarks, shaving scars, scars from what looks like acne and scratches, as thin as blades of grass. I examine my chest: marks, more slight scars, faded but still prominent, and every single rib there outlined, jutting, trying to punch their way out of my white, almost translucent skin. My arms are a picture of self-harm, scratched-in scars from my wrist to my elbow on my right arm, nearly as many on the left. I'm covered in them. In my mouth, my gums have drawn themselves back, exposing yellow and brown teeth that cling desperately to the inside of my jaw. At the back, two or three teeth are missing; my breath reeks, even to me. I shake, again, poking at myself. This is scarier than any film I've ever seen, any nightmare I've ever had, because it feels real; that sheen of it being fake – false – is gone, and I'm left with myself: a fragile, broken shell.

'Was this the crash? The explosion? Did that do all of this? What the fuck has happened to me?' I ask aloud, my voice – harsh, like I'm not used to speaking – cracking into tears, but there's no reply. I didn't expect there to be.

* * *

Day two was spent outlining exactly how the trip was to work: what everybody's individual roles were. I conducted interviews with the crew as they worked, or as they sat for me, like this was a TV show. Every day I beamed a broadcast back; there was a slot reserved on the BBC, sold to hundreds of other channels the world over, where they would watch the mini-documentary each day. It was basically edits of the interviews (and after a while I would start interviewing for single sentences or sound bites only, because they were all that ever made it into our miniature documentaries) and some shots of the crew working, or of the space around us – from the Bubble, or, on rare occasion, taken out on a walk. It was the first time that they had the tech to receive these broadcasts, at least during the early part of our trip, so that was part of the job. (To some extent, the money from the sales of the broadcasts funded part of the trip: DARPA sold the rights, and they pocketed the profits. It probably paid for some of the fuel, or the hull, or us.) I wrote everything down, because after this, it would become the article. I wrote at the computer – though it was harder than it ought to have been, because of the microgravity, because being strapped to a stool wasn't comfortable, because the keys seemed to be harder to press than at home, not having their usual give as I tapped at them. Day two was when I established those things. Now, here, I listen to the me that's out there asking the questions I barely remember asking, that now, in hindsight, sound so banal.

'What made you want to become an astronaut?' I ask Guy.

'No, never wanted that. I wanted to be an explorer,' he corrects.

'Okay,' I say. 'What made you want to become an explorer?'

'Really? That's your first question?' He laughs at the camera, at me, because he sees something intrinsically funny in all of this. That was Guy. 'I mean, Jesus, who wouldn't?' That was the clip from him that went into the first broadcast back; he looked so happy when he said it. I knew it was a self-satisfied pleasure, but it played as excitement.

I listen as the other me delivers a fake eulogy for Arlen, a second speech especially for the camera, standing in front of the cockpit so as to keep his bed – his body – out of shot. I remember that Wanda held the camera, because she was still crying whenever we said his name, and Ground Control said that they didn't want it in shot. We were to report that he died a hero's death: that he died for the betterment of humanity, in trying to further the reach of our species, to further the concept of what it means to be human.

'It's something we all feel passionately about,' the me says, 'that he died a noble death.' We don't say what happened to him; just that there had been a malfunction, and we would be bringing his body back for a state burial upon our return. 'May he rest in peace,' I say, and then we go to a picture of him that we've got on file, superimposed with the dates of his birth and death.

After that, it was back to work; I remember, because we had to. No rest for the wicked.

Our journey was incessant, unless we had to cut the engines to do a mandatory stop, fix something, check something out; or if we simply chose to. There were no issues with it wasting energy or fuel for the most part, so it wasn't a huge deal. If we wanted to stop, however, we needed permission from Guy. What I did, when I was on my own – what I will do? – stopping the engines as much as I did, that was rare.

The noise of the engines covers up for me now, hiding any accidental noise I make. My beard itches, and I scratch at it, worrying that the noise will somehow carry. One of the rules was that we were presentable for the videos. That went out of the window after a while, but for those first few broadcasts we shaved and cut our hair, and Emmy put make-up on, because she said that it was important. For the day-to-day, we didn't bother. Now, all I want to do is shave, clean myself – I stink of the sweat after the stasis, of whatever I've been through – and I want to reset everything. I'm starving, and I rifle through the crates and find a few spare food bars, and I eat one, but that doesn't stop the shaking, and there's a water bottle, pure stuff, filtered, which I drink, but it barely soothes my throat, and doesn't do anything for the fever I'm sure I've got, or that I'm developing, or the desire to put myself back how I was. And through all of it, I concentrate on that beard, which doesn't suit my face at all, would be far more suited to a harder face (like Arlen's), and which I constantly want to itch at, tear at. I need to cut my fingernails: they scratch my face when I itch it. I can't bite them, because I'm worried about the stability of my teeth. The beard needs to go, I decide. I need to cut it off. Before this, I'd say it was pride, or care, or a desire to feel better about myself. I never got frustrated with my personal hygiene before.

Our third day of training had been one of the hardest. We were evaluated by psychologists, taken into small rooms one by one and shown pictures, asked questions.

'How do you feel when you see a long, unlit road?'

'The sound of running water: soothing or terrifying?'

'What would it feel like to dream and never wake up?'

'What is more important: purpose or reason?' We had hours of the questions, one by one, alone with nameless doctors in little grey rooms. When we ate lunch, it was on our own, sandwiches handed to us in sealed plastic packets. The sandwiches didn't say what was in them, and visually, there was nothing given away; it was a colourful paste, like sandwich spread. Before I'd even taken a bite I knew that it was a test, that I was still being watched. 'What does it mean to trust? What does it mean to take?'

When we were finished I sat in the annex, waiting to see what was next; if we were allowed to leave, or if there was more. Emmy was the next to finish; she sat next to me on the strict white bench and asked me about my day. We compared questions, answers.

'You reckon they're still watching us?' she asked.

'I'll be a monkey's uncle if they're not,' I said. She laughed at that.

'I've not heard that before,' she said. 'What is that?'

'Something . . . it's an old phrase. Something my parents used to say.'

'Monkey's uncle.' She smiled, and we stayed there, chatting, until Quinn arrived. He sat on the other side of her, took over; that was his role as the leading man.

I rummage through the storage boxes for paper, so that I can write down everything I can remember that happened from my first time here. I can't remember exact days: after Guy died, when we stopped sending broadcasts back to Ground Control – because they were markers in the days, stop signs that told us what time it was, almost – I completely lost sense of what was day and what was night. Quinn tried to stick to rigid sleeping patterns for the few days that he survived, but I gave up on it altogether, sleeping when I was tired. Emmy . . . I don't remember what Emmy did. I scribble down rough estimates of the days on which everything occurred, starting with Arlen's death. Wanda's was a week after Arlen. Guy was five days after Wanda. Quinn, a day, maybe, after Guy. And Emmy I sedated a day later. I try to remember how many days I was here afterwards; how long it took for everything to degrade. It seems so long ago, like another lifetime, or hundreds of them.

'It was only two days ago,' I realize, 'that the ship . . .' I try to count backwards – to calm myself, to run through the days, simultaneously practical and controlling – but can't. I scrawl a seven next to my name – though it could have been as little as a three, as much as a fifteen, I really can't say. I read over it a few times, saying the name aloud, counting down the days on my fingers as I go, as if I'm remembering exactly what happened, as if that counting will make a difference. And then there's the hole: that gap between what happened and now, when my body became ruined, and I became ill (I shake, I shiver, I sweat) and I woke up again.

In the main cabin, they have seats with belts across them, to hold them down. They have beds with buffers, with rubber panels to stop them slipping, to keep them safe, to frame them and ensure that they get the maximum amount of optimum rest; and blankets, attached by Velcro, to keep them warm and simulate the sense of being in bed, of sleeping; and the ability to warm the meal bars, to heat them in the branded microwave ovens, to eat them and feel some semblance of normality in mealtimes, and being able to choose flavours, to alternate meals, to drink something other than re-cleaned water; and the ability to exercise, to strap themselves to the rower or the weights, to press against something and feel actual stress, pressure, feel their muscles working against something other than just the lack of gravity, pressing against each other, working their bones, stopping those tiny slivers from wearing away in their joints; and computers, where they can send messages back to Earth, and receive them, write to their families, their friends, and to hear that they are all safe and sound; and to speak to Ground Control, reassure them that the trip is going smoothly, get orders, hear back that everything is running fine at their end; and they have other people to talk to, even if they don't actually get along with them, even if they wouldn't choose them as friends in any normal social circumstance, but find themselves able to converse, to argue, to fight, to discuss; and other people to look at, to just be aware that they're not alone; and they've got the Bubble, and the cockpit, and they can see where they are, see the astonishing feat that they're accomplishing in real time, first hand, see what nobody else has ever seen outside of a recorded video, grainy and somehow unreal, because it needs to be seen by the naked eye to ever actually become totally tangible; and they have other people to share this with, to assure them that they're still sane. I have nothing. I have myself, and the dark of the storeroom, and no control over anything that's happening to me, because it's all been controlled once before.

That night, the ship creaks. I notice it quietly at first; like a stomach ache in the person lying next to you in bed, something you hear but can't place the origin of, can't pinpoint. I press my ear against the wall and listen as hard as I can, but it's only there as that tiny creak, that murmur; and then it's gone.

'If I haven't gone insane, I'm somehow back on the ship,' I say out loud, to make it real.

I think about changing everything, and every time I do I halt myself. Every time I do my stomach knots and I feel more sick than I did, and I stop and tell myself it's better this way. I remember something from a film I watched when I was a kid, a sci-fi thing where somebody time travelled – ha! That's what I am! A time traveller! – and they were told that they can't change the past or it will break everything. *It's impossible to change, they were told*. I wonder if they're right, but my stomach, my every instinct seems to agree with them.

I hear Guy saying that he's coming to the storeroom before he does, which is a relief, a mercy; I've been nearly asleep, or halfway there, trying to think of something other than how sick I feel. He shouts something in the hallway, speaking to Quinn, saying that they need something – a plug to close the filters on Arlen's bed, designed to allow air in, something that the corpse of Arlen no longer needs – and Quinn shouts that they should be in the storage crates.

'Along with all the other crap,' he says. We hated the crates when the ship was being loaded, because everything in the boxes was contingency stuff. When the scientists told us what was in them, it was always prefaced by them telling us that we wouldn't need what they were giving us. Nothing was necessary.

'Just remember,' the scientists said, 'the most important thing is the mission. Get as far as you can, and use whatever you have to in order to get there.' Those boxes were the *whatever*. (I remember why Guy wanted to plug the filters; Wanda was worried that Arlen would start to smell. Emmy reassured her that he wouldn't, but she wouldn't listen. That was Wanda.)

The hardest part of staying in the room is the worry that somebody will just appear; with microgravity, there's no footfalls, no early warning system. Guy's shout let me know to keep my head down – the boxes I'm under are full of nothing, spare parts for the external panels, in case we hit an asteroid or something, I don't know – but they're not what Guy's going to be looking for, but that doesn't matter. I quickly loosen the straps on another crate, behind where I am, and I slide under that, watching the shadows made by the light outside the room as Guy approaches. I stay totally silent as I hear the door slide across, Guy heaving it, locking it open. He grabs the box he's looking for, drags it towards the light from the hallway, peels back the lid and rummages.

'*Verdammt du Hurensohn,*' he says, then shouts the rest down the corridor. 'These boxes are such a fucking mess.' I listen as he roots around, takes things out and puts them on the floor. 'Are these labelled?' He puts them back, walks around the front part of the room. 'It says that they're in here, in this box. Where's Wanda?' He shouts her name, and she shouts back. 'Have you got the inventory?' She tells him that she'll bring it down, so he leans against the box, waits for her to bring it to him. I worry that he'll hear my breathing, so I try to calm down.

Wanda finally arrives with the inventory; she and Guy read what's in the boxes (which are all numbered, one to eleven), and then they find the plug in a box on the far side of the room. They leave after a few minutes of putting the boxes back together, of barely speaking – they never got on especially well, always frosty with each other, never really talking much – and then shut the door after them. I listen as it slides across, realizing that I've kept my eyes shut the whole time, like a kid playing hide-and-seek. I can't stay here, I realize. I need somewhere better to hide.

The first time we were allowed to walk around the ship was a VR simulation. This was before construction was finished, when it was still just a fantasy, when the promise of our trip was still eighteen months away from being realized. We – most of the people who were being offered the jobs, deep into our training and analysis – were led through, given a guided tour by one of the scientists. They showed us every nook and cranny, clearing the rooms, spinning all the features, stripping the walls of their panelling and showing us what was inside them: the wires, the pipes, the tubes. They showed us how the piezoelectric energy worked; the little sensors rubbing across the metals, the gap between the outer shell and inner walls that carried the sensors. It had to be wide: the hull of the ship picked up the vibrations, and the inner wall of the hull carried the sensors that converted those vibrations into energy, which then ran off into the battery. I remember standing in that room with Arlen and a doctor who didn't make the final team.

'It's like a closet,' Arlen said.

'Wouldn't even hold half of my wife's clothes,' the doctor said.

'Good job she's not going to be coming on the trip, then.' We were shown around every part of the ship, then the outside, the hardcore electrics, the mechanics, the stuff I would never understand. The panels were all designed to be removable, in case we needed to reach the electrics, to do vital repair work. Remove them, fix the ship, we were told. If the battery fails, open the walls and get inside, and fix the piezoelectric stuff from the inside. Everything is repairable. These things were vital to the continued journey of the *Ishiguro* and her crew of explorers.

I wait until the crew have gone to bed, then grab a tool from one of the boxes, a thin sliver of metal that's not dissimilar to a crowbar. It slides between two of the panels at the back of the room, and I heave the panel off. There, I see it: the ship's insides. Her guts. They run like veins and intestines and arteries and bones and nerves and synapses and *blood*, and they line almost every inch of the panelling. It should be dirty grey metal, like they showed us in the VR mock-up; instead it's technicolour, wires of every type, bound together in lines. There's insulation, as well, white and foamy and unlike anything you can buy to do your roof with; future insulation. The space between the walls is wide enough for a man, even for a man turned sideways, lying flat, stretched out. I pull the panel out and slide in. It's colder than the rest of the ship, but not by much, and the noise from the panels is so loud that it makes my head throb as soon as I'm in there. But after I've pulled the panel shut behind me, tugging it into place, listening to the clack of the plugs sealing me in the pitch-blackness, I feel totally safe. None of the crew will be able to find me here. It's perfect.

I'm crammed in when I feel something in the cargo pocket of my trousers, pressing against me. It's under a zip, and I open it, and there's a bottle of pills, a quarter full. They're labelled as painkillers. I don't know where they've come from, but it doesn't matter, because they're all I've got, and as I'm looking at them I feel the over-whelming need to take one, the sheer blunt desire, like a hunger, a craving. I take one, and ten minutes later I can barely feel my leg, and the shaking and shivering has gone, and I start to actually, genuinely relax.

I breathe for the first time, and take stock. I have no idea how I'm here, or why. I feel my chest as I inhale, and I know that this is real.

I shut my eyes and try to sleep, but every time I'm nearly there – my eyes so heavy I can't open them to see if the darkness has cleared, the filthy noise of the ship so black in my ears that I feel almost physically sick, even through the blunt ache afforded to me by the painkiller – every time I'm nearly there I start thinking of something, one solid thought that breaks me from sleep.

This is impossible, I think. This is utterly, utterly impossible.

3

When I signed up – at the behest of my agent and my editor, both desperate for me to take my career (such as it was) to the next level – there hadn't been a manned mission in ten years. In 2010 – I think – NASA (as it was then) announced that they were going to start work on Mars missions. Everybody expected colonization (or something) on the Moon, but that never came. Instead they worked on optimizing launches, ways to break gravity better. It would, they thought, save thousands of dollars in fuel costs. Then, in 2015, there was the Indian launch, and the mistakes that they made – not making it to the Moon, even, and losing their crew. They replayed that footage over and over, of the craft exploding like a firework, and we all watched it in grim fascination. After that, all the governments went back into their shells where space was concerned. We weren't getting anywhere; it was a waste of taxpayers' money. Everything suddenly became about the private companies, those heads of industry who established small research teams to send probes into space, to look into ways of making fuel more efficient, to develop new propulsion systems. In the 1960s, the race had been to land a man on the Moon, with all the world's governments desperate to stake their claim. After that, the companies were racing to get a man onto Mars. They put money into places that the governments didn't: marketing, publicity, the entertainment business side of space flight.

And then an unmanned mission to the red planet came back with news, about the landing, the atmosphere, the temperature; about how it would be impossible to put us – I say Us, but I mean humans, our race – down there with the technology that we had. We developed everything in the wrong way. So they shifted tack. We're launching anyway, they said. We're just going, a test case to see how far we can get with maximum power, and how much we would need to make it to Mars when we finally did. I had just left school, was just writing, working freelance for newspapers for no money but bags worth of experience, and nobody understood it. I wrote an article about the launch during a week dedicated to it, about how it was important that we knew more. We send probes and cameras, the article said, but we never send our eyes; this way, we'll be looking back at ourselves from further away than anybody has had the chance to before, and we'll – hopefully – be able to understand ourselves a bit better because of it. The craft – unmanned, robotic, piloted from a crew planted on the international space station – ended up alongside Mars. They took samples and pictures and watched everything, and then they came home. A flag – featuring every flag of the world, like a blurry collage – was planted in the soil using a mechanical arm from a remote-controlled UAV, and the footage was played for weeks, the triumphant moment that we took our first planet. Then it came out – via leaked video, up on YouTube, never officially released – that the flag fell over seconds after being planted, blew away in some wind, and people started speaking out about it, talking about the lack of achievement in what happened. It wasn't even comparable to the Moon landings, they said. In the 1960s we conquered something; here, we barely visited. Make it manned next time, or don't make it at all: that was the resounding message.

Only, there wasn't the money to do anything more. The governments of the world were standing as far back as possible, refusing to offer any of their cash. Everything went completely private, and the private companies found that they didn't have a clue how to raise the funds they actually needed to make it a fully crewed mission. So, they adapted. They hired other companies who knew how to put prices on things, and they branded. Nothing crass, was the rule: only the tasteful and practical. The food on the ship was all going to be branded; the tech we used would all be stamped with the names of the companies, and everybody would know the companies that were providing the jets, the fuel. And, more than that, the private companies funding the mission – under the umbrella of DARPA, now an independent part of the US government – only had the cash for one trip. It was the be-all and end-all. They knew that, if we weren't going to land somewhere, we had to do something extraordinary, something that inspired. We had to do a feat that nobody had ever done before. Probes had gone millions of miles away from the Earth before, but never a person, and that was where our flight came in. They built our ship to deal with extreme temperatures, made the fuel as compressed as possible, in as great quantities as possible, and they decked us out with recording facilities, cameras, a crew that translated well to screen; likeable, attractive, for the most part. The extraordinary feat would be to hit the realms of classic science fiction films, of pulp novels and comic books, and to stretch ourselves, to travel further than anybody had ever done before. That was how it was sold: a voyage to rival Columbus, to rival the stories of Jules Verne. It would be, DARPA (in association with McDonald's, Coca-Cola, BP, British Airways and News Corporation) announced, epic.

It was all done cloak and dagger, more so than most things to do with space, where they were subtly announced years in advance to little fanfare. This was planned and organized and then announced on TV, and everybody watched. Smaller companies from forty-eight different countries were utilized by DARPA, which meant that the whole thing was totally international, no boundaries. It was a big deal. We would run science tests as well: to explore anomalies that we were picking up with the telescopes, stuff that we couldn't pin down from the ground. I remember that being announced. We were only going to take readings, send reports of stuff, nothing that really required work, but stuff that we could do, as we were out there. The work couldn't be done with probes: the things that needed to be done had to be done manually, which is where Guy came in. The research was his life and work. The DARPA people told us that they had one shot, because if they could prove that space flight was important – to humanity, to the people of the world as a race, that it inspired, brought people together, united them – the governments might be inclined to reinject funding. That's what they wanted: a proper space programme again. They wanted the glory days back. The flight was sold and commissioned and divided between corporate partners, and every part of it was to be broadcast and tracked. They ran trailers for the announcement of the first part, where they told the world that they were building a ship, technology, a crew.

When news went out to the various agencies that they wanted a journalist on the flight, everybody leapt at the chance. We had to audition, first – print and video media were both up for it, so they had to make sure we were all on an even footing – and then they whittled us down. When I told everybody that I was shortlisted – totally breaking the NDA, but it was my closest friends, my family – they threw a party for me, and all night people kept telling me how proud they were of me, that I was going to do something so incredible. I kept saying to Elena that it was amazing, that I was so happy.

'I'm glad for you,' was all she said.

In the morning I hear the crew through the walls as they wake up, shout to each other, go about their business. For a second I pretend that I've forgotten, and I listen to them as if this is one of those old-style radio plays. The actor playing me is so good in the part, just like the real thing. If you didn't know, you'd never guess.

It's their third day. On the third day we did more interviews, and sent more broadcasts home, and tried to pretend that we weren't irritating each other. All alone, and still reeling from Arlen's death, we were bumping heads. We all awoke irritable. I listen to myself snapping at Wanda when she says that she doesn't want to do another interview – when I remind her that it's part of her job description, that it's part of what she agreed to – and I listen as she reels off information for me, curt and blunt. I'd forgotten that she spoke that way because she hated the imposition, not because that's how she was. I mean, the two were related, but she gets colder on video, with the camera pointed at her face. I ask her to do something, to enact some action for the video, so that the people at home can see what it was like. She picks up a cleaning cloth, floats to the table, scrubs at it.

'None of this is real,' she says. She's on the verge of tears, about to break. She clings to the table as I interview her, and I listen as her voice cracks when she speaks. The me that's talking to her snorts. We don't get on. I don't think that Wanda liked any of us. It was so easy, after she died, to rewrite all this. In my reality, she was an unpleasant person. Why did we call her Dogsbody? Because she was slightly irritating, because we were older, better trained, more respected, more knowledge-able. That's why you give a person a nickname.

This is exactly the way it happened the first time, and yet, isn't anything like I actually remember it.

The lining. That's what it feels like, being inside the walls: like I'm inside the lining of something far more important. I'm pressed against the electricity, the heat, the water, the source of everything that makes the ship run. It's dark, apart from cracks of light through the vents: I can navigate with them, though, with the sounds of the voices that come through the air conditioning channels. I can shuffle through almost the entire length of one side of the ship, room to room, until it branches for the engines, where the lining gets too thin for me to slip through. I also can't get further than the main living quarters; the cockpit is too thin again, and not tall enough. At points – behind the beds, above the table, in the changing area next to the airlock – I can see through the vents and grates in the walls, if I press myself up against the wall and peer downwards. I can see everything, a futuristic version of the peeping Tom, the voyeur. I creep around all day, listening to every conversation, playing them through in my head, trying to remember what happened next in them – if I led, or allowed myself to be led.

I'm watching through a vent. I can see the table as the crew eat dinner, fastened into their seats. We've just sent a broadcast back, led by Quinn – his jaw was made for television, Guy jokes, such a pretty little fucker – and we're eating branded meals, burgers in the form of compacted bars, drinking from cartons with semi-permeable seals, and we're talking about home. Wanda starts, because Guy prompts her to.

'My dad died, and my mom went home, back to Korea. She might see this on TV, and then . . . I don't know, she'll see it and realize that I made something of myself.'

'You're doing this to prove a point?' Quinn asks her. She nods; from my grate I can see her jawline moving, creased up and tense. 'Because she'll, what, see this – see you, up here – and think, Oh, she was worth something?' He sounds almost incredulous when he says it. 'This is a hell of a long way to go to say *Fuck you* to your parents.' He sounds so angry. Emmy coughs, to break the mood, but all I can see is Wanda's jaw, still gritted. 'I'm not here to prove a fucking point,' Quinn says, 'I'm here to do something good, something worthwhile.'

'So am I,' Wanda says.

'Right, right, okay.' I hear him slurp from his drink.

'So how did you get involved with this?' That's Guy, diverting, turning his attention to Quinn. He was so hard to pin down; furious and antagonistic one second, single-minded and driven; then a calmer, a leveller, desperate to bring everything back to zero the next. 'You always been such a pretty-boy pilot?' He treated every inquisition like it was a joke, like it meant nothing. Answer, don't answer: Guy's had his fun either way.

'Started in the Indian air force, then the RAF. Dual citizenship. Then some much smaller, privately funded projects until the big boys grabbed me.' We told these stories so many times, over and over. 'My mother wanted me to be a pilot in wartime. She thought that there was a glory in it, because that's how my father died. He was honoured, and I never was. When she passed away I joined a little project looking at stealth fighters, funded by the US, and got out of the military. I always hated the military.' We didn't say anything after that, because Arlen had loved it, and Wanda. They both lived for it, and any conversation that followed that chain would only end in tears.

'So, we're stopping tomorrow?' I hear myself ask.

'Yeah; it's hull-check time.' It was our first scheduled stop, and we were so excited when it happened we could barely contain ourselves.

In training, gravity – or, the shift from not having it to it suddenly being there, solid and concrete under our feet – was spoken about only briefly.

'It'll feel odd,' we were told, 'that you didn't have any weight, even when sleeping, and then suddenly you do.' They showed us how to brace ourselves before the gravity was switched on, how to plant our feet and anticipate the drift downwards. 'It's not like in cartoons,' they said. 'There's not a sudden plummet, you're not going to hurt yourselves unless you fall badly. Listen to these rules, and you'll be fine.' We listened, or pretended that we did, and then disregarded them. They were health and safety rules, like the video you get shown on your first day of work, the warnings that never came to fruition. We would be fine.

I sleep for the first time in days, but it's fitful, transient. I manage to wedge myself in between two pipes, rubber-lined hoses the circumference of my arms, the bracket of one against my shoulder to stop me hitting the ceiling. It hurts like hell, but I take more of the painkillers that I found and it's fine. They help me sleep, in fact, for those fits and bursts, twenty minutes at a time. Every part of me aches. I tell myself to stop moaning about it, because I'm annoying myself, even; but I can't. Once an ache sets in – once it's there, niggling away, coursing through with every movement – you can't shake it.

The excitement is amazing. The me that's with the crew is giddy, filming everything, talking so quickly. I listen as I type something, my fingers thickly beating the keyboard into submission – it's a report, part of my article, the diary that's going up on *Time Magazine*'s website to chronicle what we're doing, all first draft, no editor, my writing at its most raw – and as Emmy and Quinn laugh about something, and as Wanda and Guy prepare the airlock for the walk. When they're done, Guy speaks to us all.

'We want to be still for as short a time as possible,' he says. He's all business at times like this. 'We stop, do the stuff we've got to do, get started again, right?'

Emmy laughs. 'Why can't we stop for longer? It's not like we're using fuel or anything.'

'There's a schedule,' Guy says. 'What else do you want? I let you do that, you'll stop every time you wish you were sitting on a fucking toilet, or have a funny tummy and want to eat food sitting down.' He's at that curious halfway point between anger and laughter. 'There's a schedule.' The crew brace. I push myself against the wall, jamming myself as tightly as I can, my feet resting on the floor in an approximation of the pose that we were told to take. Guy asks Quinn to hit the button to bring us to full stop, which he does.

'Feet don't fail me now,' he says, and then everything seems to slow. From the cabin I hear the gentle clatter of shoes touching the metal flooring, settling in; inside the lining I slump down. The pressure of my weight on my leg makes me wince, even through the painkillers; I keep it under control. If they heard me, they would tear the walls apart.

'Shit,' I say, forgetting about my voice. They don't hear, but my whisper echoes across the pipes, through the lining and into the electrics. I listen as Guy and Wanda head towards the airlock and their suits, as the me that's part of the crew goes with them, filming them as they go on their first walk. I remember standing outside the airlock, looking through the glass at them; watching as the door was heaved open by Guy, and as Wanda took her first drift, totally unlike those that we did inside the ship; perfectly smooth and effortless. She went out of the door and disappeared, and the safety ropes went tight, and then she pulled herself back on them, towards the door. I remember filming it all, because it would be brilliant footage for the broadcast home, the footage of her freely drifting. Only four days later she died – will die – and the footage becomes eerily prescient, predictive. Part of me wants to tell her, to stop it happening. Something in my gut tells me that I shouldn't.

My leg hurts, so I reach down to my pocket, take another painkiller out, swallow it dry. I realize that my provisions are running low – my water bottle is nearly empty, and I have no food bars left – which means that I'll have to make a move into the ship again, back to the storage crates and their bounty. In the cabin, Emmy and Quinn talk about Wanda, saying that she's too high maintenance. It was something that we always moaned about.

'Can't believe that Dogsbody gets all the fun of the walks,' Emmy says. 'She whines all day and then gets to go out there?'

'She's with Guy,' Quinn says, 'it's not like it'll be anything resembling actual fun.' I hear him walking around, coming closer to where I am, to where Emmy is seated at the table – actually sitting down for the first time in what felt like forever, we all said. 'Besides, you'd rather be in here with me, right?'

'Don't,' Emmy says. 'Just, don't.'

Elena and I rowed about my taking part in the testing. This was well before they even came close to announcing that I was part of the crew. We rowed from the day that I applied, but I said that it was important to me, that it might be the most important thing that I ever did. When there were four journalists left – when we were all told that they had to be sure we were made of the right stuff, ready for the hard work that space would take on us – they took us to Florida for a week, a solid week above and beyond the day-to-day that we were doing in New York. We joked and called it space camp, but when I told Elena, she flipped. We had been living in a hotel near to JFK airport, because that's where the hangar where we underwent most of our training was, and she had been writing reviews from there, going to restaurants in the city and eating alone, then telling the American branch of her magazine what she thought of their bread rolls, their creamy desserts. When I got back to the hotel room and told her that I was leaving for space camp, she broke down.

'How could you?' she asked, because I was suggesting that she stay where she was and I would go. There were others on the trip with wives and husbands and partners, and they were all staying in the same hotel; I casually suggested that she might get to know more of them while I was away. 'You're really going to go?' she asked.

'I haven't come this far to stop now,' I said. 'It's only a week.' Elena was depressed, or had had depression. I don't know if it ever leaves. She took a pill and went to sleep, and when we both woke up the next morning told me that she was going back to London.

'I'll be there when you get back, and we can talk,' she said.

'I want this,' I told her, 'and I want you. I want both things.'

'I know you do,' she replied. We kissed goodbye at the airport, and I paid a grotesque amount of money for her last-minute ticket, and she left. I waited there until the end of the day, when the rest of the cadets – we called ourselves that, buying into the fiction we were so in love with – turned up, and we got on our plane. I sat next to Emmy, completely by chance. We hadn't seen each other in a week or so, not since the psychiatric evaluations.

'Hey, Monkey's Uncle,' she said. 'I wondered what happened to you.' We were all in different groups, being trialled for compatibility as a crew. We were to be together in space for a long time, and they wanted to make sure that we could all work together. Emmy was with all the other medical staff. Doctors in one group; pilots in another group; researchers and scientists in another; journalists in the last. They wanted to break us down to our core components before they spread us around and let us form bonds. 'Did you ever work out what it means to trust?' There was another journalist sitting on the other side of Emmy; she craned over, looked quizzical. Emmy explained. 'We had the same questions in our psych tests. Didn't you get stuff like that?'

The journalist sighed. 'I missed those; stomach bug. They're doing them when I get back.'

'Ah, we won't spoil them for you, then.' Emmy laughed. 'Seriously, it's not that bad, but this guy here, he looked so sick when he came out of them.'

'*I* looked sick?' I asked.

'Oh God, yes. That's why I spoke to you; thought I could calm you down or something, stop you from climbing the walls.' I realized that she was joking, to wind up the journalist. 'Had you been sick?'

'Loads,' I said. 'One of the worst days of my life.' When the flight had taken off and the journalist next to her had fallen asleep, Emmy leant over to me, half-whispered at me.

'It's a competition, right? Like that *Charlie and the Chocolate Factory*. There's only a few golden tickets, and I'd rather you got one than she did.' She put her hand on my arm, squeezed.

For a second, a brief second, I forgot about Elena.

Guy and Wanda come back in from the outside, and Emmy begs Guy to let her try it.

'We're stopped,' she says, 'doesn't matter. Just ten minutes.' He lets her do it, because he's still on the high from being out there. We all go down to the airlock to watch her suit up – she goes with Wanda, who somehow has the most time spent training for this, the most hours logged on the simulators – and they dance around outside for a few minutes.

Now, here, I stay in the lining and try not to be heard, as

the pain ebbs back into my leg, and I contemplate when I can take the next pill. I don't have a watch.

Fifteen minutes later the engines are switched back on, and I slowly drift off the ground again, my little space suddenly feeling even smaller. In the cabin, Emmy sighs.

'That was amazing,' she says. She leans over to the me and Quinn. 'You guys have to try it.'

'Next time,' we both say.

When they're all asleep I sidle along the lining, taking my time, and then ease open the panelling in the storage room, taking care to make sure that it doesn't fall. I swim to the food crates, stuff my pockets with meal bars – a handful of breakfasts, lunches and dinners – and a few bottles of water. We never even used the emergency water the first time around, because the recycled stuff was fine; they won't miss it. The pills are different. With the space, the light, I roll back my trouser leg and look at the muscles, the bruising. The swelling seems to have gone down, but there's something else in there, something bad. I press my fingers to the bone and the pain snaps at me, telling me to stop. It's only one patch, but it hurts more than anything I've ever done to myself before. It must be a break, I think, a fracture. They say that: you can have a fracture, and it can be thin – hairline – and it'll just sit there until it gets infected if you let it. I can't risk an infection, not here, not now. It can't have healed fully: there must still be problems, under the skin.

I drift through the room, slide back the door as quietly as possible, and move towards the cabin. The crew are all asleep still, in their beds, the doors sealed. I keep forgetting about Arlen, and yet, there he is. I open the medicine cabinet, pull out a carton of the pain pills, exactly the same as the one I found in my pocket – we left with thirty cartons, which was more than enough; or should have been, at least – and some of the generic antibiotics, the stuff that any doctor would prescribe for a small infection. It's all labelled – I suppose, in case anything should have happened to Emmy. (Which it did, and will.) I take another bandage as well, a support for my leg. Tight, constricting elastic to keep it still and in place. It's a frantic scramble through a slow-motion filter, as I struggle to make sure that nothing drifts away from me, that everything stays in the sealable plastic Tupperware-esque boxes it was given to us in. I go to the computer and sit down, load up my folder and look at the pictures of my loved ones that I brought with me. I miss them all: I zoom in on their faces, force myself to remember exactly what it is that they look like. After that I read through my blog entries, what I wrote about that day, what I sent back to Earth. It's kind and excited and in my voice, and I can't even imagine being that person, now: being the person who would write those things. I remember writing them, though. I remember the turns of phrase I used, florid and overwrought, filled with metaphor and implied meaning. If I could only have seen me now.

I log out after looking at the picture of Elena again, and when I turn around I see myself staring at me, from my bed: eyes open, watching. I haven't put the lights on in the cabin, so it's dark out here, darker still from behind the tinted glass, but his – my – eyes follow me around the room, a creepy old painting on the walls of a pitch-black mansion. I don't know if he's awake: I don't remember this happening, don't remember catching a version of me skulking around the corridors while we all slept. I move towards the doorway and leave, and quietly retreat back to the storeroom, listening for the hiss of his door opening, but it never comes. I fasten the wall behind me, slip back inside the lining, and swallow antibiotics, painkillers, water.

I spend the rest of the night unable to sleep, even with the dullness given by the pills. I think about why I'm here, and what happens: I know how this ends, and I know that it can only end with my death – both the me in the cabin, and the me here. I picture myself trapped here, in the lining, struggling to breathe, kicking against the walls as the air – the oxygen, the only thing I really need – is replaced with *nothing*, taken away and not given back, and I choke here. I beat the walls, and the only person who could hear is me, and I'm already dead, out there.

When they wake up, the me doesn't say anything about what he saw, if he saw anything. He didn't, I'm sure: everything else is exactly the same. The ship moves quietly, a slow, long day of tests and write-ups. Everything has to be detailed and noted, every single change, every measurement. The ship is mounted with cameras, and stills and video have to be taken at various milestones, markers for future generations. The fourth day is a day for this, for record-taking. I hide, and stay awake, and then, when they all go to bed, so do I. It's a routine. I listen to their conversations and still remember them, their ebb and flow. It's all so natural.

Every noise wakes me up from my sleep. I'm getting so much less than I need. Every time I wake up I wonder how much I'll need to function the following day, and that thought keeps me awake. I sleep for no more than an hour at a time, and I worry that it all means nothing.

The crew gather around the table for another live broadcast, something to be beamed home, something inspiring. I watch through the grate as they pull themselves around the table unnaturally, so close that they're all touching. The connection is established, and the crew smiles and cheers. On the screen are the smiling faces of the DARPA Ground Control; their mouths move first, and then their voices fill the cabin from the computer's tiny speakers.

'Hello to the crew of the *Ishiguro*! Greetings from Ground Control!'

'Hey there!' Quinn says, then the rest of us follow.

'How are things up there?' they ask, an absolute, unequivocal formality, because we submit three reports a day when nothing is happening, hourly reports if anomalies occur – when Arlen died, for example – but this is for the press. The world likes to imagine us in solitude: it's part of the great deceit. Astronauts were almost conceived by fiction, by books and television and movies, and then they became real; but those conceits created with the first image of a man travelling beyond the bounds of Earth, and heading towards the stars, those have stayed. The astronaut is alone. He drifts through space. He explores. He discovers. Since it all changed – since the India tragedy, the dearth of funding for governmental space agencies, the down-sizing of NASA – that was lost. Our purpose was to give that back. The people back home read my diary, a one-way transmission. We were like a television reality show, unaware of what was going on outside the TV studios; and then we made contact every few days, our faces beamed down to let them know that we were okay, that we were happy and doing our job, and *exploring*. 'We're going to cut to some of the extraordinary exterior footage, now; why don't you talk us through what we're seeing here?' Ground Control are in charge of what we do. This stuff is pre-edited, taken by us, but chosen to show points of interest, grabbed by the cameras attached to the Bubble, a full 360 degrees-worth of footage. In the distance, that's Saturn. Mars. That cluster, that's the Eagle Nebula, which seen through a high-powered telescope looks like this. As they show it, the crew stop grinning, but not completely.

'I'll say the next bit, about the full stop, introduce the clip from the walk,' Guy says. Quinn looks surprised, but lets him, because he actually doesn't mind sharing the spotlight; that sort of thing has never been important to him. I watch as Emmy squeezes his hand behind their backs.

I called Elena from Florida, to check that she got home safely. She told me about her flight, about how her seat was at the back, with all the children. We had first spoken about children before, only months before, when I was debating whether to even go through to the second stage of the application for the project – when it was still just words on a page, imagined concepts of what might be involved, before I got my award, before it even seemed like something that could manifest. We both wanted them, and neither of us were getting any younger. We had always said that I would stay at home with the kid, raise it and work freelance, and Elena could stay on full-time, editing and writing for whatever magazine she worked for at the time. She was always on salary, I was on contract, so it made sense. She mentioned it when I was filling out the forms.

'What if I get pregnant?' she had asked, speculatively, but in that way that made me wonder if she knew something I didn't – if she knew that she had stopped taking her pill, that we were already trying without my consent. 'Will you still go?'

'It's space,' I said. 'If we've got a baby by then, I'll stay.

If we haven't, and if, by some miracle, I get selected to do this, I'll go. Deal?'

'Deal,' she said. Then we lost the baby we had been brewing, growing inside her before being rejected, and the doctors told us to wait for months and months before trying again, and that was that. When I spoke to her from Florida, she sounded almost grateful. The kids next to her had howled the whole way, and the family – foreign, she said, but without the qualifier of a country of origin – didn't clean up after them. They changed nappies and stuffed the filthy ones in the pockets of the seats in front of her. 'It was so unhygienic,' she said. 'Just ridiculous.'

'But you're home now.'

'Yes.' She left it at that, and didn't ask how my flight was. 'Who else is there?'

'Everybody. It's everybody.'

'Oh,' she said, 'I assumed that they would be doing it in groups.'

'They are, I think; but we're divided day to day. It's less strict than I was expecting. There are a few social events, that sort of thing.' I told her that I would call her the following night, let her know what had happened. What happened was: we spent the day getting measured for suits, and then we got into the suits, white latex things that showed off every single part of your body, good and bad, and then we stood in a hall that was a giant wind tunnel, a turbine built into the floor like nothing I've ever seen, and on top of that a grate, and then, in groups of three they blasted us upwards over the fans and we were flying, for the first time. Then they kept us in those same groups – I was with Guy and a female pilot who didn't make the cut, a gruff, businesslike woman from France – and they put us into a chamber that was completely sealed. We stepped inside, were told to brace ourselves, and then the room began to growl, and the pressure fell, and we struggled to stay on our feet. I was first to fall: Guy and the woman braced for a good ten seconds after I lay on the floor, spread-eagled and slightly in pain. When we were let out of the room, I told Guy that I was sure that I just signed my own dismissal.

'You both survived, and I gave up,' I said.

'It isn't always about surviving,' Guy said. 'Sometimes, that's the least important thing.' That evening, I sat with him for dinner, ate deep-fried chicken with him, and we spoke about the others. He had his own thoughts about their chances, evaluating them all from a distance. Quinn, he guessed, was in. 'He's pretty, which makes for good TV, and he knows what the fuck he's doing.' He didn't guess Arlen, who he dismissed as being too 'corn-fed', and he wasn't sure about Wanda. 'But Emmy,' he said, because we all knew her name, by that point, 'she'll definitely make it. I mean, who wouldn't want her on a ship with them?' Guy was gay, and didn't mean that in a sexual way: he just meant her energy, her presence. 'You're stuck nowhere for what could be a couple of months, you're going to want people with a bit of something to them, you know?'

'Do you think I'll make it?'

He snorted when I asked that. 'Probably, maybe, sure,' he said. 'All the other journalists have such a stick up their asses. You're the only one with a bit of life to you.' After that meal, we drank, all of us. Some went to bed, because those days of testing were hard; but the rules weren't against us. We were told to unwind, so we did. I called Elena from outside the hotel bar, told her about the day.

'You sound like you're having a lot of fun,' she said, angry at me, that bite in her voice. She was so funny: sometimes, when she was stressed, she almost had an accent, the same hint of Greek that ran through her mother's voice. She'd never lived there or anything; just the accent.

'I am,' I told her. 'How are you?'

'It's the same here,' she said, 'same old London.'

'I'll be back soon. Will you come back to New York to meet me?'

'How long do you think you'll be in New York for?' It was a loaded question, with no right answer. At least, no truthful right answer.

'A few weeks.'

'I'll think about it,' she said. Back in the bar, Emmy had bought a bottle of Black Sambuca, which most of the Americans had never drunk, and was pouring shots, thick and dark brown and reeking.

'You've drunk this shit before,' she said, 'I know you have.' She beckoned me over, gave me a glass, counted to three, and we drank, first myself and Emmy, and then most of the people in training. At the end of the night, when the bar closed and we were forced to go to bed, because the hotel was in the middle of nowhere, purpose built for the convention centre rather than a town, Emmy asked if I wanted to go to her room and carry on drinking. 'I've got a mini-bar, and I know how to use it,' she said.

'I can't,' I told her. I meant to say, Because of Elena, but I didn't. I left that part out.

'Sure,' she said, 'big day and all that. Maybe another time.' She reached over and took my hand and squeezed it. 'I'm not even nervous about getting onto the ship, now, because this has all been such a trip.'

All I could think about, as I lay in bed and tried to sleep, was how little she seemed like a doctor: she was more like a friend, or a lover, or a dream.

I watch as the me with the video camera, with no facial hair or scars or pain, who has been sleeping and is totally unaware of me watching him, as he takes his place at the table, fastens his belt, listens as the crew eat and talk about themselves more. I've always been a good listener. They ask questions about me, about my past.

'So, you don't say much,' Guy says. 'You get to ask all the questions, but we don't know much about you.' He knows about Elena, about what I do, where I come from. That should be enough, I think. The me out there jokes with him.

'You know how I feel about you,' the me flirtatiously says, and the table laughs.

'Fine, but we should interview you, shouldn't we?' He picks off parts of his bar, throws them into his mouth, chews with his mouth open, talks as he chews. 'I mean, you're part of the crew, you're going to want to be documented just as much, right?' I don't say anything. 'So, after dinner, we'll film you.' He grins. He's got one of those smiles, smiling as he chews the food, as I see it flopping around in his mouth. When we've finished, true to his word, he picks up my camera. 'Does this just work?'

'You press this button, for a new file,' I say, showing him. 'This is the focus.'

'It doesn't do it automatically?'

'It does, but in case you need it.' He doesn't even put his finger on the focus button, or the zoom. He points and shoots. This isn't about the film.

'Tell us a little about yourself,' he says. The others sit at the table, strapped in, and watch. They don't say anything, or even react. They just let Guy get on with it. 'Where did you grow up.'

'London,' I say, 'West Ealing.'

'Parents?'

'Gareth and Erika. Teachers. Dead.'

'Wife?' He says it deadpan, but there's a question in his voice, a probing. I remember this. I remember being furious with him, because he knew something, and this was his way of letting me know. Emmy hits him on the arm.

'You've asked enough questions, Guy.'

'I don't want to do this any more,' I say. 'I write a fucking diary every day for the website, they'll know more than enough about me.' Guy laughs, puts the camera down.

'Fine,' he says. He walks off, back towards the engine rooms. Wanda gets up from the table.

'I'll talk to him,' she says. 'He's just frustrated, being up here. They said that it would get to us all, didn't they?'

I remember this bit: I remember putting the camera away, and wondering why Emmy wouldn't look at me. I bent over, trying to get eye contact, but she stared at her hands, at the buckle of her strap, at the table, and tried to not see me doing it.

I've adapted the straps on my suit to work with fixtures inside the lining, fixtures that weren't meant to take the straps, but can be shoehorned into their new use. It meant letting the length out a bit, so that it stretches, but now I can sit down, at least, still wedged in, but not drifting as much. I take a pill, because I realize that I haven't in a few hours, and push my back against the wall and try to sleep, even though the crew haven't gone to bed yet; I can still see the bleed of light through the grate I could be looking through, if I were less tired, and I can hear Quinn singing some song from twenty years ago, something that I barely remember but that he knows every word to. I roll back my trouser again, look at my leg, but there are no marks, nothing distinguishing. I poke it, scratch it with my nail, but the pills have made me numb, and I feel nothing.

I need to sleep, but I can't. I close my eyes and see that light-bleed, hear Quinn's voice, even long after I'm sure they've all gone to bed; that same song, a solitary line of lyrics rolling around my head, over and over; not so much a refrain, more a rolling eddy of words, washing over everything I can possibly think. I try to count down from a hundred, measuring my breathing – something that Elena taught me when I used to have trouble sleeping, to breathe in synchronicity with the counting – but it only makes me think of her. And when I'm thinking of her, there's no chance of me getting to sleep. I close my eyes and struggle, trying to move on, to forget and go blank and sleep, because I need it so much.

'Why don't I tell them that I'm here?' I ask into the darkness. 'Why don't I say something?' I take another painkiller, and I shut my eyes, but all I can see is myself, struggling. 'Why am I back here?' I ask. There's nobody to listen: it's just me, the darkness, the lining, and on the other side of the wall, the crew, all asleep, even the me that doesn't need it. And then I sleep, but it's only for a few minutes, and I know that it'll only be for that long before I'm awake again, and wondering.

4

Emmy is screaming. It wakes me up . . . I'm not sure if the Emmy that screams is real or not: if she's screaming because they've found me and I'm not meant to be here; or if she's just part of a dream. The reactions of the crew tell me that it's neither. They panic and bluster.

'No, god, I just had a nightmare.' She gasps, laughs, asks for somebody to fetch her water. The psychiatrists told us that nightmares were common for people in our situation: that being confined, nowhere to go, in such a volatile and extreme set of circumstances could only lead to confusion and possible night-terrors. Emmy had it once, a few days in, and this is that time. I remember this. I unlatch myself from the floor and shuffle towards the cabin wall, where I watch myself and Quinn helping her up, both soothing her. I'm surprised at myself, at how forward I am. I didn't realize. Guy passes her a water flask, Quinn bends down, tells her to Aaah for him, jokingly, and I stand behind them all and watch. Another thing that I didn't realize: I'm quieter than I remember.

Emmy tells us all about the nightmare.

'I was trapped in the bed. Like, I opened my eyes, woke up, and wanted to get out, but I couldn't, so I thought I'd bang on the door, but then I realized that I wasn't able to move or anything, so I started to panic, because I thought, Holy shit, what if I can't breathe properly, even though that's insane, right? Because I could breathe, but whatever. So I thought, I'll try to scream, see what happens, and then I screamed and you guys opened the bed and got me out.' She smiles; I can hear it in her voice. 'I mean, for whatever reason, I really thought I was a goner, there.' Wanda comes over, puts her hand on Emmy's shoulder.

'You're safe,' she says, 'it's all right.'

Wanda's only got two days left, I realize.

As we went through space camp, Wanda was aloof and distant. She didn't spend much time with anybody else, because she was focused, totally single-minded. She was the youngest person there, I think, by a good few years, just out of university, and she seemed to act like she didn't know why she was there herself. We – that is, every person that I sat next to at dinner, or had a training session with – managed to get bits and bobs out of her about who she was. Her parents hadn't lived in the US for long, only since the year that she was born. Her mother worked in a restaurant, her father an electronics shop, until he died, and her mother decided that she wanted to go back to Korea. Her mother, we guessed, didn't ask her to go with her, and she signed up for something to take her mind off it. She did a degree in aeronautics, and didn't expect to be chosen for the training, let alone the mission itself.

'This part,' she told me when we were waiting to be examined by medical officers one day, after a session in the pressure tank, 'is all just amazing experience for me. Even if, on my CV, I just put that I was here, that I was selected for this, that might open doors to something great.' Others – I forget who, but they didn't make the final cut – didn't think she even wanted to get on the final crew, that the thought of achieving it was so far from her mind that it wasn't even a factor. This was an experiment that could end with her holding her head high. She went in to see the medical examiners before I did, and I watched them talk to her through the window into their office. She sat on the chair opposite them, smiled and laughed when they made jokes, looked coy and embarrassed when they asked her questions (that I later found out concerned bladder and bowel movements), and then she stood and let them examine her – which they drew the curtains for, but I knew was happening. The room was soundproof, but she looked happy, perfectly happy. When she left, I asked her how it went.

'Oh, you know,' she said. 'If it's possible to fail a test where there's no wrong answers, I'm sure that I just did.' She didn't smile for me when she said it, slipping away from that veneer. I never questioned whether she wanted to be on the trip itself: seeing her acting (either for me, or for the doctors who ticked their boxes and said that she was fine to carry on with the process) made me realize that she wanted it as much as anybody else.

I follow Wanda through the ship. We all called her Dogsbody behind her back, never to her face. We thought – I thought – that it was a gentle nickname, harmless, that she was in on the joke, but she isn't. I watch her cleaning, running the basic diagnostic tests, the stuff that Quinn can't be bothered to do. I watch her helping Guy in the Bubble, and ensuring that measurements from the telescopes and cameras are recorded and logged properly, all to be sent home. I watch her do everything that we don't want to do, and nobody thanks her. She goes into the changing room, alone, and cries, gently sobbing into her hands like some 1950s movie star, floating in the room, scrunched up and foetal. That was one of the best feelings, about being weightless: being able to do gymnastics in the air. She revolves slowly, involuntarily, as she sobs. Nobody hears her.

She goes back to her routine, and I follow her through the ship. In the main cabin, she prepares the meal as Emmy laughs about something with Quinn, as I sit at the computer and type. Quinn leans over the cockpit instruments and taps a screen.

'What does this message mean?' he asks, and Guy heads over and looks at it.

'It's nothing,' Guy says. I wonder if they're talking about the number that I saw before I died. Maybe it's the same. Maybe I'll solve that puzzle. 'It's just an alert about some of my research.' He disappears back towards the Bubble. I can't see the screen: if it is the number, I'll never know now.

Wanda warms the food in the heaters, bars that taste of fast-food fried chicken, and serves it with flat Coca-Cola in crisp white sachets.

'Dinner's ready,' she says. We strap ourselves in and eat. I join them, peeling open one of my own packets – this one some homogeneous freezer-meal branded bar that tastes vaguely of sausages and potato – and nobody really speaks, but then Quinn reminds Emmy of the dream that she had.

'Hope you don't wake us all up again tonight,' he says. She hits him on the arm.

'I couldn't help it.' I'm filming them all – part of my remit, get the stuff that looks friendly, that shows how well we all get on, how much fun exploring is – but I'm not paying attention to Wanda, who is quiet, and still. I watch her now, and see it all.

Wanda's walk will take place in twenty-four hours' time. Full-stop is scheduled for first thing in the morning, as that's when the broadcast home will happen – our first with gravity – and, after that, Wanda will get into her suit and head out into the darkness as we eat our breakfast, and she will die. I watch her wake up, not knowing. I watch her record interviews, talking about nothing, bullshit, her day-to-day, what she does. The me that's interviewing her ignores everything, ignores all the questions that might actually tell us something about her, or help her through whatever the hell it is that she's going through. Instead, he finds out about how statistics help the ship be efficient, about how much oxygen gets used and how it's measured. I remember watching these when they were all dead and thinking how dull she was, how she had nothing to offer. Hindsight.

This is how she spends her last day. I struggle with my eyelids, which want to close, even though I know I won't sleep; and I take more painkillers, because the pain is absent, or only niggling, like a memory of the pain, and I want it to stay that way, even though they make me even more tired. I watch everything she does, because somebody has to. Somebody has to see how she lived her final day, what she did. But she does nothing. She cleans and records things and sits in the background, even further back than I do, somehow.

113

At the end of the day, she talks to Guy, corners him in the corridor, leads him to the storeroom.

'I need to talk to you,' she says.

'Fine,' he says. 'What's up?' He tries to sound casual, but never can. Everything is brusque and bitter when he's preoccupied.

'I'm having trouble,' she says. She seems like she needs a shoulder to cry on, but Guy shrugs her off.

'Look,' he says, 'fucking deal with it. You knew what you were getting into. You wanted to be an explorer, wanted your name to go down in history, or you wouldn't have signed up. Man up and get on with your job, okay?' He leaves her in the storeroom, in the dark. I think about getting out and telling her that I'm there, holding her, because that's what I think she needs. Instead I wait in the lining for her to stop crying again, and move back to the cabin, and to pretend that everything is normal.

Wanda was the last into the room when we were being told who was on the crew. I had been third, after Arlen and Guy, and I knew them both fairly well, so was happy. I was happy to see Emmy, and Quinn, and then Wanda came in, and none of us really knew her. I reintroduced myself, because I didn't know if she would remember my name.

'I'm terrible with names,' she said when I did it, apologizing for me, pre-empting anything that I could say.

'Yeah, we didn't really get a chance to talk to you much,' Arlen said. He introduced himself then, and the rest of the crew. She knew Guy; they shook hands, smiled.

'So you're going to be my dogsbody,' Guy said, which is when the name began. 'Tell you what, that ship won't clean itself.' He was joking, but he wasn't. Everybody else had experience, reason to be there. Wanda was the anomaly, of sorts. There were others who could have had her job who were far more qualified; when Guy led Wanda off to tell her how the day-to-day would work for them, the rest of us crewmates questioned the choice.

'It's not even like we know her socially,' Emmy said. 'You can't even argue we get on really well with her or anything.'

'She must be the best person for the job,' Arlen said. 'No two ways about it.'

I listen as the crew get into their beds, as they say goodnight like they do every night, like they will until there aren't enough of them left to bother; when it's just me and Emmy, Emmy and I, alone. They say goodnight, and they seal their beds, and they go to sleep. I hear Wanda saying goodnight last, and think about how sad I am for her – that she's got so little time left.

'I don't want to watch it happen,' I say to myself as I lie in the lining and try to sleep. 'I have to try and save her.' If there's a reason for me to be here – if it isn't just chance, or some accident, if the universe (ha!) has put me back here for a reason, maybe it's to save Wanda?

I listen to the air for hours, until it's totally still. There's no noise, apart from the engines, and the moans of Emmy dreaming, murmuring in her sleep. I slip back to the storeroom, prise open the panel and drift into the ship again. Wanda dies in space, her suit torn, compromised; there must be a tear. This won't be like Arlen, I tell myself, where I caused it. In Wanda's case, I'll save her. I'll change what happened, for the good.

I get to the changing room and look at the suits, trying

to find the one imprinted with her name. I don't know how the tear was caused but I'm careful, cautious. The suits have diagnostic panels; I switch hers on to see what it says, see if it picks up any tears, but there aren't any. I check the helmets then, all of them, because they're generic, one size fits all. None of them have cracks or bleeds. I run my fingers across their seals, gently, trying to find anything, but there's nothing there. Not a thing. Everything is perfect, totally perfect, and I haven't caused anything, and she shouldn't die. Maybe they just needed the diagnostics to be run to make them okay; maybe I've already changed it.

I pull myself back to the corridor and towards the store-room when I hear her crying. I can see her, floating in the corner, hands on her face again, these tiny little sobs. She's right in front of the panel that I came out of, that I've only loosely re-fixed to the wall. I decide to do the unthinkable.

'Wanda,' I say. She's the first person that I've spoken to in what feels like forever, the first time I've used my voice properly in days and days. She doesn't look up at me: she wipes her face with the palms of her hands. I stay back, so she can't see me, hidden slightly by the darkness. If she sees how thin I am, sees the scars, my hairline, my beard, bushier and fuller than the me in the cabin, the manic look I'm sure that I have in my eyes almost constantly . . . If she saw those things, she'd know that there was something wrong straight away. She's upset, not stupid.

'Cormac,' she says. It's so strange to hear my name, and to hear it addressed to me, not the other version. 'I thought you were asleep.' She doesn't look at me, because she doesn't want me to see her eyes, to see that she's been crying. 'I didn't mean to wake you; I just wanted to look at the ship like this, when it's quiet.'

116

'It's okay,' I say. 'You've been crying.'

'Homesick,' she says, which is a lie, because I know that something more is wrong, something deeper.

'You want to talk?' I ask her.

'No,' she says, 'I'm fine. Honestly.'

'You can talk to me,' I say.

'No,' she tells me. 'I can't.'

'You'll be all right,' I say, meaning it; wanting to reassure her, and myself.

'You should go back to bed,' she tells me, wanting me to leave her alone. 'Big day tomorrow. Aren't you going to get to walk?' I had forgotten that: I was going to get a chance to go out there, after she was finished with the diagnostic checks. I'd forgotten that, when she died, one of the things I felt was disappointment, selfish disappointment.

'Goodnight,' I say, and I push backwards, away from her, down towards the cabin. When she's not looking I duck into one of the fuel rooms and wait until she gets up and leaves, sliding the door shut behind her, going back to her bed. The me she thought I was is already there; the me that she actually spoke to rushes back to the hole in the wall, opens it up, gets inside. My eyes have adjusted to the darkness now, and there's no chance of me sleeping. I take another pain pill and move to the changing room, and watch the suits to make sure that nothing can possibly happen to them.

The crew wake up at the same time, because there's an alarm been set. Guy tells everybody to brace, which they do, and then he presses the button, and the ship stops moving as fast as it was, begins to rely solely on momentum – which, we were told in training, could take us a long way in space. When there's nothing pushing you backwards, nothing to force you to stop, you can keep going forward, a car with no brakes barrelling down a hill. Gravity falls, and I find myself steady. I'm doing less exercise than I was first time around, and this is harder, much harder, because my legs aren't feeling nearly as strong, and whatever I did to my leg before, it's not what it was, even with the painkillers, and even though it's not as bad as I remember it being. The crew gather around and greet home, and everybody grins and smiles and updates them, lets them know that we're happy and fine, that everything is going to plan. When they're gone it's back to business, and Wanda shakes slightly at the side, testing her legs, almost, as she leans against the table.

'Wanda, you're up,' Guy says after a few minutes. She doesn't say anything, but leaves the cabin. I scurry along inside the walls to follow her: she goes to the bathroom first, washes her hands and face, splashes water onto her cheeks, rubs them. (That was something that Guy recommended to us during training. 'It's a survival mechanism,' he told us, when we asked him why he did it – this was in the final stages of training, when we were taken up in a modified jet to the stratosphere. 'Humans have got this thing built into them, where water, on their faces, wakes them up, kicks adrenalin in. It's to stop us from drowning, something that we've evolved to do.' He always splashed the water, he said, because it helped him to think clearly.) From there she strips to her underwear, a vest and pants, and then walks to the changing room and pulls her suit on. It's the same suit that I checked last night, checked and found to be fine. She takes her time, following all the protocols, and then, when it's pulled up and fastened, takes a helmet down, puts it on, locks it in place. Guy comes in, checks it for her. 'You ready?' he asks, and she nods. He tests her oxygen, that the seal is okay, and then puts his hand on her shoulder. 'You're feeling better?' he asks, and she nods.

'Much,' she says, but I can barely hear it through the helmet. He takes the safety cable, clips it to her back, and the proxy cable, in case of failure.

'Good girl. See you in a few.' Guy backs out of the room, heaves the door closed and instigates the airlock process. He waves to her through the windows, like a little salute. She doesn't return the salute: she suddenly flashes a glint of something sharp and metal, and jabs it into the seal between her suit and her helmet, which is only a thin rubber thing, and the door behind her opens, and she plunges backwards, like she's falling from a diving board. She doesn't squirm or wriggle; it's graceful, peaceful, almost. Guy doesn't scream – the rest of the crew don't hear anything – but his face falls, and he realizes what she's done. His decision flashes over his face, and he decides to keep what happened a secret. He watches what I can't, because I can't see out of the ship, but I remember what she looked like when she came back; burst, swollen. None of us knew that Guy saw it when it happened; he didn't say a word.

I wait and listen as everything plays out like it did before: Guy tells the crew that something's wrong, that he's bringing Wanda back – and he calls her Wanda, not Dogsbody, even though she can't possibly hear him use the name that he first birthed for her – and Emmy rushes down to her, tearing off her helmet as soon as the airlock finishes its cycle and we could get past the door. She feels for a pulse but there's nothing, so she pumps at her chest as Quinn rushes to get the bumpers, but then she calls to him, tells him to stop, that Wanda's gone, that there's no chance. We all stop and bow our heads, because she's the second to go, and because it's a tragedy, and because we're all wondering what this means for us, as a trip, as individuals. Guy steps onto whatever it was that Wanda was holding, and as soon as he gets the chance, he grabs it from the floor and slips it into his pocket.

'We need to move her,' Emmy says, so we do, myself and Quinn and Guy, like pallbearers, shuffling down the corridor with her, trying to not drop her or spill any of the blood that's pooled around in the folds of her suit. We put her body on the table and Emmy stands at her feet and sighs. 'I don't know what to do,' she says. 'She should maybe have an autopsy, to check what happened.'

'It was a seal,' Guy says. 'Something must have gone wrong, or not been checked properly. This is what happens when there's a leak in the suit; this is how you die.'

'Put her in her bed,' Quinn says. 'I'll get a connection to Ground Control, see what they say.' He looks at all of us, in turn. 'This is too much now, right?' Myself and Guy move Wanda's body again, after Emmy has used tissue to soak up the blood from the suit, wiped it from her neck and face. It's still around her eyes, and we put her in the bed and seal it as fast as we can, put her in stasis.

'This uses energy,' Guy says, meekly. He's not complaining; just stating a fact. We listen as Quinn establishes his link, and then wipe down the table as he leaps through the security protocols. When he's finished we're all seated and waiting to be told to come home, but Guy knows what they'll say.

'The mission is too important,' Guy says. Emmy fights, Quinn fights, I stay out of it. 'We've come so far,' he says. 'And this is important.' From the lining, now, I don't believe him. 'Wanda shouldn't have died like this,' he says, 'but the mission prevails.'

'Fuck you,' Quinn says, then tells Ground Control we'll stay where we are and wait for an official response. He severs the connection and nobody says anything.

Emmy says that she needs some air – which isn't literal – so she goes to the back of the ship, towards the storerooms. Quinn follows her, and Guy snorts.

'They're fucking,' he says to the me that's in the cabin with him, 'I'm sure of it.' I watch as I ignore him, because I'm not sure that I want to know. 'Can I have two minutes with her? I want to say goodbye.' I nod, pick up the camera from the fixtures on the desk and leave. I remember: I went to the airlock and filmed it, silently, suddenly some sort of auteur, thinking that a poignant shot of the room – cold, empty, sparse in every single way apart from the hoses and safety cords lying bundled on the floor – might make a good part of the story of this trip. Now, here, I watch Guy. He stands in front of Wanda's bed, making a fist, gritting his teeth. I worry that he's going to punch the glass, but he doesn't. He shakes it, and he stares at her. He tries to breathe but finds it hard; instead, he makes these small gasps, quick draws of breath. He swears quietly, under his breath, and he shakes, and he holds the door of Wanda's bed. His hand creeps down towards the catch, but he doesn't open it. He isn't crying. He isn't furious. He just stares at her shut eyes and scowls.

The signal that we're being hailed crackles to life and we assemble in the cabin.

'You're moving onwards,' Ground Control say. 'Miss Khan – Wanda – will be honoured with a full state funeral upon your return. For now, please continue with your mission.' It's not a conversation; it's an order. Guy moves over, presses the button, and none of the rest of the crew look at him as we drift upwards, and the ship starts moving again.

I got the telephone call telling me that I had been selected for the final stage of the selection process – selected to be selected – one night at home, just after Christmas. We had the family with us, because Elena's parents were back in Greece and we couldn't afford to go and see them, so her sister stayed at ours and we invited my mother along (and it would be her last, but we didn't know that then), along with a few of the cousins I had who lived in London but never saw. I cooked a goose, because none of us actually liked turkey, and my mum and Elena split the vegetables between them, each on a half of the hob, each with their own knives and chopping boards.

'My girls,' I called them as I rushed around doing the meat, mixing the stuffing, ladling spoons of gravy juice over the skin to make it crackle and crisp and pop itself open. Neither of them laughed, because they didn't get on that well – my mother was a classic case of the matriarch, and Elena liked attention far more than my mother was willing to pour upon her, so – but we tried, and Christmas was happy. We had eaten, and then we watched television, and then we slept. It was the next morning, sometime that it was still dark outside, that the phone rang. We didn't have one in the bedroom so I had to run downstairs, because Elena's sister was sleeping in the office, and I took the call from the DARPA people there in the hallway, standing in my underpants.

'Merry Christmas, Mr Easton,' they said. 'We're thrilled to be able to tell you . . .' It didn't kick in immediately; I went back to bed, lay next to Elena, draped my arm across her and rocked her gently, hoping that she'd wake up and not realize that I had done it; and then I drifted off again, only a bit, but it was her getting out of bed hours later that dragged me back.

'Did you sleep okay?' she asked, because she could see something in my face, I suppose.

'I got in,' I said.

'In?' She thought that I was making a joke, a vulgar joke, because that's what I did with her; that's what she expected of me.

'To the space thing. I've got a shot at being on the team.' She acted happy for me, hugged me, told me that she was proud of me, and we went downstairs, where my mother had already made breakfast. ('So that I couldn't get around to it,' Elena told me later, 'because that's her proving a point, that's she's still in charge. Oh my gosh, I hate it when she does that.')

We didn't say anything until we were all sitting around, and then I said, 'You're all going to have to wish me luck, I think.'

'What's going on?' my mother asked, immediately suspicious.

'He's going into space,' Elena said, jumping the gun. She put her hand on my arm, squeezed it as if she was proud, and everybody around the table cooed. None of them knew anything about the training, about the process – it had been ten months in the making, ten months of me getting fewer bylines, doing less small stories because of the time spent working on application forms and proof of concept documents, ten months where I'd been lying to people slightly, telling them that I was working on one big story when the story hadn't even begun yet, not really. They all asked me what I could tell them: where I was going, when I was going, why didn't the public know about it yet, and I told them that it was being announced that day, that the details were things that even I wasn't sure of yet. That afternoon we sat in the living room and watched the television as they announced it live on the news, a press conference first thing in the morning in New York on Boxing Day, beamed live around the world. They didn't say our names – there would be another press conference in the New Year to discuss the crew, they said, who were about to start a rigorous training process – but they said that the trip was privately funded, a worldwide initiative, the finest minds from every country working on something together, working to further ourselves as a race of people, one solitary race. We were going to travel further into space than man had ever travelled, and that was the point. There's so much that can be seen with telescopes, with probes and satellites, much as sailors used to be able to stand on shorelines and watch horizons disappear, seeing landmasses so far away that they were barely blips, and they would wonder what they were, then travel to them. In the living room, Elena's sister asked me to explain it to her.

'They used to just go, and see what was out there, just because they could. They had a ship, they knew that there was something there, so they went. And it inspired people; it made others do the same, and that led to countries being discovered, populated. After that we went into the seas, sure, and we went to the Arctic Circle and up mountains, but after we made it to the Moon we decided that, what, that was enough? It can't be. This is about man, and what we'll find out there. It might be nothing, but it's worth finding out, surely?' I didn't tell them about the tests we were doing – that we had a scientific reason, because this was never going to be a waste of money, even if anybody objected to private money being spent on something that didn't impact them in any negative way – because that was the part of the trip that even I didn't understand. We were to travel outwards and then plot some map or other, something that Guy was invested in – his life's work, he told us – and then return, and those results would finally enable humanity to map dark matter, to place it in the universe. I left that out, because it was so secondary, such a negligible thing; a discovery that would mean nothing to anybody. Our potential journey was to be an inspiration; that should have been enough.

Elena acted as if she was proud, but she was crushed.

'Do you really want to go?' she asked that evening, as we lay in bed.

'I have to,' I told her. 'Even if I never do anything else, this would be my stamp.' She went to sleep straight away, facing away from me, and I got my laptop out and began to write.

Space is meant to be what we aspire to. We are, by our very nature, a people who explore. It's in our blood. We go back to the times before maps and we just explored whatever we could, in search of something better – better land, better food, better shelter. We follow that line to nomadic peoples, to Vikings, to the Romans, and we explore everything. We discover America, and find that it's already been discovered; we travel the globe and we plot maps that prove there's no edge to fall off, no horizon carved with a blunt knife. We went to the Moon to prove that we could, and we did it as soon as we were able to. We watched ourselves from up there, and we saw that we were exactly who we thought; a people overreaching, stretching ourselves. We explore, and we stretch what we're capable of. It's in our nature. We take steroids to push our bodies; we develop technology to enhance ourselves. With space, we tried before we were ready. The Indian mission went wrong because they weren't prepared. They were barely past the technology of the 1970s, and they decided that it was enough to travel to the Moon faster, to stay there for longer, to orbit it, showing off before they returned. They were wrong, and they paid the price. We watched them – we, the rest of the world – and we knew that they made their mistakes. I remember talking about it in school the next day and everybody being devastated, but then we got over it. And this mission; we're a prelude, a lead-in, a trial run. We're those first people in their boats trying to find something that might not be there; we're guinea pigs being sold as explorers.

Elena stirred and asked what I was writing. I told her that it was an email, that she should go back to sleep. She did, because she had no reason to think that I would lie to her. I had never lied to her before.

5

What passes for a funeral for Wanda is tragic. Emmy says something, because we collectively decide that she knew her best, because she's a woman as well; she's the de facto best friend. With Arlen we were flooded with platitudes and well-wishes and kind memories, because he was the father figure, the bearded joker who we all respected and looked up to. Wanda was something else, something quieter; the girl who sat at the back of class and kept to herself. When Emmy finishes her short speech – which isn't much more than a recanting of things that Wanda had told us herself, about her family, about what she wanted to get out of the trip – she asks if any of the rest of us want to say anything. We had filmed Arlen's eulogy, because we thought it would be nice for his family to watch; with Wanda's we don't bother, because we worry that it'll seem insensitive, or like we somehow care less. Emmy looks at me pleadingly, nods at me that I should say something, but the me that's in the cabin is clueless, doesn't know what Wanda did or why she did it, doesn't know the pain that she was in, how alone she was, how lost. I sympathize, I wish I could have told her: I know your pain, because I'm alone here as well. I'm just as lost, just as trapped, only I don't have the comfort of the others to talk to; I have the lining and the darkness, and the confusion of my situation, the terrifying, bleeding confusion of where I am, how I'm here, and I know what's going to happen as you all die, one by one, and then I'm left alone until this all ends for the second time, and I get to watch it in slow motion, from behind a curtain that nobody even realizes exists. The me doesn't say anything, so Emmy asks again if anybody else wants to. Guy steps forward.

'She died an explorer,' he said, 'an inspiration, right? When they ask us, on the broadcast home, to talk about what happened, we all say that she was a total fucking inspiration.' Only Guy – and now me, as well – is in on the lie he tells; that she was actually just a terrified girl, that she was selfish; that she was burned, just like us all.

When the time comes to speak to Ground Control, for an address that will be beamed across the globe, we discuss the second of our crewmates to die. We sit around the table, strapped in, and we bow our heads, and we explain that she was on a routine walk, one of the many scheduled walks, and something malfunctioned in her suit, could have happened to anybody anywhere anytime. We explain, one by one, that she was a wonderful girl, that everybody who knew her should be proud; that her country should be proud; that her mother, who she is survived by, and will be mourning her today and for the rest of her life, should be immeasurably proud of her daughter.

'We'll all miss her,' the me says.

Emmy cries. In the lining, peering out of a ventilation grate, so do I.

'We mutiny,' Quinn tells Emmy. They don't know that I'm watching them. That I'm popping pills inside the walls of the ship. I'm practically part of the furniture, part of what makes this thing tick. Quinn has cornered Emmy while the me interviews Guy somewhere else, trying to capture footage that I remember being about normality, about purpose, about getting back to what we were meant to be doing. (Guy showed me the instruments that took their measurements of the anomalies, explained what they did, and I pretended to listen. Even now I can't remember them. That was the least interesting thing about this trip, for me.) Quinn pulls Emmy far from the doorway, towards the cockpit section, pushes her up against the table. He doesn't seem to care about her personal space, or his, and she doesn't seem to want him to care. He speaks quietly, so that they can't be heard, bending close to her, leaning in. He doesn't realize that I can do the same. 'We mutiny, overthrow Guy, turn this thing around and go home.'

'We haven't finished the mission,' Emmy says.

'And we won't. We'll get home, and we'll be safe.'

'Ground Control could have us up for insubordination.' She says the word like she doesn't even know if it's applicable, more of a question, really, than a statement.

'They won't dare,' Quinn tells her, 'because we can go to the papers and say that it wasn't safe up here, that we had two deaths and they were fucked up and we wanted to get home.' His accent goes to British for swearing, which I never noticed, and the words cut through the air harder than if they were in his usual sloping speech.

'What about Guy?'

'What about him?' Quinn leaves her at the table, almost gasping, and goes to the console, types something. 'We're on 73% of our fuel, which means we've got another week out here at least, with two dead bodies, Guy, and Cormac.' I don't know what he means by that; why I'm such a problem to be up here with. 'We mutiny, and we go home.'

'I can't,' Emmy says. 'Come on, this will be all right.' She doesn't sound like she believes it.

'They're dead,' Quinn says, not even whispering any more. 'Of course it won't be all right.'

They sleep, all four of them, but I don't. It's what passes for night-time here, and the ship is dark, and two of the beds have been filled even though I did everything I could bar leaping out and grabbing the blade from Wanda's hand, a superhero swooping in to save the day. I take another pain pill, because I haven't felt my leg in hours and hours, not properly, and more antibiotics, dry swallowing them, calling up spit into my mouth to swallow them down, gulping like a turkey because they're formidable tablets.

'I have to sleep,' I say, but all I've done is watch them, and all I can think about is watching them more. I fasten myself to the floor and shut my eyes, and think about nothing but waves, but drifting, trying to lose any sort of focus on anything else. I picture myself on an airbed, on the waves, bobbing on waves, tranquil and calm and the sun is beating down on me, and I'm so far from this place, and I understand everything. I leave the lining and float down the hallway, to the cabin. I take more pills, and then I sit at the computer and punch my password in, and I call up Elena's picture and talk to it, telling her that I miss her, that I'm sorry I ever decided to leave. 'I wish I knew how I got here,' I say. 'Every theory I have, they're all insane.' As she stares at me, I wonder why I'm here: if it's to stop the ship, to stop the deaths; or to help them happen. I'm doing this the second time, and I've already had an effect; there are already things that have happened that I had to be here to enact. Maybe I'm meant to see this through to the end. Maybe I'm part of the problem, and the solution.

The Cormac in the cabin asks everybody for more interviews as they eat breakfast together. Quinn is quiet; Emmy nods, tells him that she'll grab him later; Guy questions it.

'Jesus Christ, that's all you do, eh? Talk to us about ourselves, about who we are?' He prods his breakfast bar at me. 'No. How about that? No more interviews, you can start to make yourself more fucking useful here. We've got so much that needs to be done, okay?'

'He's not trained,' Quinn says.

'Not trained!' Guy laughs. 'I'm not going to be asking him to fucking drive or anything. I have to run maintenance on the panels outside, because Wanda didn't get to do it, so he can help me with that. How many hours did you log in the walking simulators?'

'Seven,' I say. He looks incredulous.

'What the hell were you doing?' He looks at Emmy. 'That's even less than you, right?'

'Shut up, Guy,' she says. She's become so quiet since Wanda died.

'I'm just saying. You must have had your thumb up your ass or something,' he says to me. 'Seven is okay, seven's fine. We can work with seven. At least you know how to cling to the fucking hull, right?'

'I'll do it,' Quinn says, but Guy tuts, shakes his head. 'You have to stay in here, in case.' He sells it like he might need Quinn to run equipment, but I know what he really means: in case something goes wrong. I was always the most expendable in terms of the mission itself, on a practical level. My blog, my video updates, my final story, at the end of it all; they would all work regardless of my presence. If I were to have died instead of Arlen, the final story would have been written by one of my colleagues, and my colleagues would have been quoted, and it would have been tinged with sadness and dedicated to me; but the story would have survived. The Cormac in the cabin barely says a word, doesn't defend himself: he stays quiet. 'This afternoon we full-stop, and we'll go on a walk. You'll be fine, get yourself another hour logged, right?' Guy finishes his breakfast bar. I watch as the me puts his down, half-eaten, and doesn't go back to it. It drifts.

I don't remember being nervous, but the me is vomiting, holding a plastic sack to his face, emptying his guts. He stands in the darkness of the storeroom, only minutes after Guy switches the gravity on and turns the engines off. The engines have smaller engines facing the opposite direction that fire for a single burst to slow the craft down, otherwise the momentum would be tremendous and we'd never get to leave the ship. After they've fired, there's a fifteen-minute wait for the ship's hull to cool, and then we're allowed to go. I remember being sick, but I thought it was because of something that I ate, or because of the change between gravity and not – something that we had been warned could happen, the bracing effect that it could have upon tender stomachs – but now, watching myself from my vantage point I can see the shake in my arms and legs; the breathing that I do when I think that the vomiting has stopped; the quiver that runs through my body when I find more, somehow, and crease myself over. I look so weak, I realize. What was I even doing coming on this trip?

Guy appears in the doorway, tells me to get a move on. 'We have to get changed,' he says, 'we're going to be behind schedule.' I follow myself towards the changing room and watch as I pull my pale body into one of the suits, testing it over and over for tears and rips. There's nothing, so I get a helmet, seal it, check the seal over and over, and then finally join Guy in the airlock. 'Ready?' he asks, but he doesn't care what my answer is, because he hits the button to open the door as I'm still clipping my safety cables on, and then we're floating again, and outside the ship.

This is what it was like. From my vantage I can't see a thing, but I remember how it was cold for a second, then utterly warm, heat still coming from the body of the ship, and then we were floating alongside it, and I was able to recognize what that meant; to be weightless, to be able to see nothing but the expanse of space, the vague murmurs of shapes and colours so far in the distance that we called them stars, whatever they were, planets or anything else; from here, some were so far away that maybe they had never been seen before, that maybe we were seeing their light for the first time, before it even hit Earth's telescopes. We were there at the start. I remember swimming for the first time, moving my arms and legs as if that would work but finding no resistance, then seeing Guy laughing at me. He indicated a button on my arm, the button that controlled the expulsion of CO_2 from the backs of our helmets, a tiny burst of which was enough to push across the expanse. He spoke to me over the headset, telling me to go to him, that he'll show me what we had to do, so I did, I pressed the button and I moved, like a tank with no means of stopping. That first time, I remember, I pressed it too much, for too long, and I overshot, drifting too close to the hull, having to use my hands to stop myself, to keep control. He pulled me backwards, moved me over towards a panel that he then exposed, asked me to hold it open. I did, because it was spring-loaded – for safety, in case somebody forgot to close it, as it was the most important panel, the one that gave access to all the major functions: the engines, the computers, the life support, the communications relay – and he put his hands in, slow-motion tapping at the gigantic buttons, reading numbers off the small LED and nodding in satisfaction as they came up one by one, as he kept saying that everything was okay, everything was fine. I became distracted, because holding a panel open wasn't fun, and looked at everything around me; at the craft we were clinging to, at how its metal body was like a blimp, like one of those old-school zeppelins you see in propaganda films, only new, shiny; yet bruised and dented, a necessary part of the journey. I looked towards where I thought that the Earth was, but couldn't see it – I don't know what I expected, if I wanted to see it, or actually, if I didn't. If it was better being alone, without it. I looked at the Sun, in the distance, the largest thing but even smaller than from Earth, from a garden or from a street. I could stand in my bedroom and watch it rise and it would be closer, warmer, brighter, but so much less impressive, because here I can see it all. It isn't blinding: it's golden. It's the golden disc that people used to write about, before they knew what it was, before they broke it down into science and composite parts, writing it off as a ball of explosive gas. When they thought it was a God, that's how it looks from space, made for worship, for something more special than a casual reliance. Guy told me that he had all the readings he needed from that part; next, we had to check the integrity. He shows me how to grab the ship, shows me the minute handholds all around the hull, indentations and grooves, and then he pulls himself along like a lizard, flying across the metal. He has logged over two hundred hours on the simulations, he told me, and he did walks on low-altitude ships years before. He looks it; everything is easy, fluid. I follow him, stumbling, grasping at holds that aren't there, but eventually finding them and righting myself, and keeping myself pinned down as we revolve around this thing. Then I'm on the other side of the ship and it's an entirely different part of space, and there's Earth: tiny and green. I remember that I barely used to use the Bubble, for some reason. I never went in there to watch, because the overlays were intrusive, as impressive as they were technically; because you were still behind glass. It might as well have been a video. Here, I can see it all. It's too far for me to tell what's what, just a speck, really, green and blue, and it might not even be Earth; it might be me imagining it, seeing ghosts. But it looked like it, even though Guy didn't react. He told me to get up as high as him and unscrewed another panel, this time exposing wires. He told me that they were the core parts for the controls, that they were what kept us on course, and could receive orders from Ground Control to turn us, to change where we were heading, in case of emergency. I asked him if Quinn couldn't just deal with it, and he said that it wasn't that easy. They didn't trust pilots completely; they were only there as watchmen for the project, really. And they didn't trust AIs, because there were so many instances of them going wrong, or being too rigid in their understanding of orders. No, Guy told me, the only true way to ensure that the course is rigid is if Ground Control stays in command, literally and metaphorically. They programmed the course, set the controls, and we just rode with them. Arlen and Quinn were there for landings, there in the case of emergencies, but we were at the mercy of Ground Control. Guy asked me to hold the tool he'd used to unscrew the panel, checked all the wires, all the connections – he pulled on them, to see if they were taut, and then shone his light into the hole to check the ones at the back. When he was done he took the tool back off me, sealed the panel and then seemed to slump.

'Ready?' he asked me, and I asked him what for, and he grabbed me, hurled me backwards. I spun, spiralled away from the ship, slow but fast at the same time. I might have screamed, but I can't remember, as everything turned so quickly, over and over, became like a tunnel of light, of those stars leaving trails in my vision, imprints. Guy's voice rang through the headset then, asking me if I had fun, and then my safety cable went tight and I was being pulled backwards, towards the ship; suddenly stable, righted, in control again. I pressed my button, moved faster backwards. I followed Guy around the ship again towards the airlock, and he disappeared inside, slid over the lip and was gone. I waited a few more seconds, to look at what I was out there with, to take it all in, and then followed, and we drifted in the airlock until Guy hit the button, and we fell to the floor, both of us. The door sealed, oxygen was blasted in, and gravity appeared, and we stood up and took our helmets off. 'Your first time outside the *Ishiguro*,' Guy said. 'How was it?' He didn't wait for me to answer. 'Fucking amazing, right?'

I see my face, gasping for real air again, but not nervous

any more, and I see Guy clap me on the shoulder, then turn and stride down the corridor. He doesn't wait for me or Quinn or Emmy to brace ourselves; he hits the button to make us go again, and we drift upwards. I watch as the me undresses in the changing room, puts his clothes back on, and heads into the main cabin again, where Quinn and Emmy are sitting at the table opposite each other, and stop talking as soon as I enter the room.

I wait for the crew to go to bed, to get tired. I hold the empty pill packet in my hand as I wait, rattling the nothing inside it. Guy is the first to sleep, and then the me, having stayed up with Quinn and Emmy, talking about Wanda, about what we think will happen when we get home. (Emmy is convinced that the governments will give some sort of army-style medal to our dead, a Purple Heart or its equivalent. Quinn tells her that she's insane, that we're private sector. 'Nobody gives a shit about what happens when you're working for money. Nobody,' he says.) When the me goes to bed, Quinn and Emmy stay up. They whisper at the table about what it would take to get Guy to change the computers, to turn the ship around. I want to tell them that they're going to fail; that, whatever they do, the ship will continue unabated. The ship survives to the bitter, bitter end.

'What if we don't get to turn around?' Emmy asks. She seems nervous. I remember the confident Emmy, the Emmy from our training. This one is different. I didn't notice the change; but then, it seems, I didn't notice very much.

'Then we ride this out. There's not long to go.'

'Right, sure. We just stay here, pretend that nothing's happened.'

'It's not like there are lifeboats.' He takes her hand. 'Listen, it'll be fine. Guy's just intense, and Cormac . . .'

'Don't.' She leaves her hand in his as he moves his thumb, stroking her skin softly, slowly, tenderly.

'Fine,' he says. 'Fine. But we'll persuade Guy. He's not as hard as he seems.' He moves his hand from hers, up to her arm, then her shoulder; and then he pulls her closer, not to kiss her, but to put his head against hers, like they're kids, bashing skulls. 'We'll get you home safe and sound,' he says. They stay there like that for minutes, far longer than they should, than makes sense; and when they're done they go to their separate beds, and I sneak out of my hole and drift to the table, the seat, and I sit myself down, strap myself in, and I look at them all asleep, and still needing my pills, feeling that familiar tug of pain all across my body; through my leg, into my head, my brain.

'I wish I could be out there with you,' I say out loud. I think I'm willing them to hear me.

Emmy called me, hotel room to hotel room. It was the night before we were due to leave Florida, return to New York and to – in theory – our families. Emmy didn't have a family, something that never seemed to bother her, but marked her out as different. There wasn't anybody waiting to speak to her on the other side, to tell her that they were glad she was safe. She was bored in downtime. I had been on the phone to Elena, trying to persuade her to come to New York again, but it wasn't going anywhere: she was bored with our conversation, she said, bored of me trying to convince her.

'When you come home, we can talk about this. But I'm not discussing it like this.' She was quiet and patient in her tone, but she looked tired; angry, even. When we said goodbye she didn't keep eye contact. She looked down, at her hands, ready to switch the screen off, and said that she loved me, which I still believed, even without being able to see it in her eyes. I lay on the bed and thought about her, and had the television on – they were showing footage of the London floods from years before, and that made me think about my father, who probably still lived in the city, even though it was barely there any more, and I thought about whether I missed him or not, and how hard it was to decide what was emotion and what was just reaction – and then Emmy called.

'We're drinking,' she said. 'You should *absolutely* join us.' I met them in the bar, where they – six or seven of them, most of whom I knew well enough from the training (with Guy and Quinn among them) – poured drinks straight from bottles that they had taken from the bar, put on their room tabs (paid for by our private investors, no less), and lined up glasses that we downed, one by one. It was eleven by the time that I got down there, and we paid the barman to keep from locking up, to keep the tabs rolling. We didn't have to pay for our room bills, and we never abused it, not until that night. Emmy was the ringleader, we joked, the instigator: she kept asking for different bottles, and kept nudging glasses across the soaking wet bar towards anybody who wasn't drinking. 'What's the point of having a last night if you're not going to make it a last night?' she asked. She was like a teenager, just gone to university, suddenly free of everything and able to do whatever they liked; only she had so many letters after her name already, and must have done that stuff in her past. Quinn was first to bed; he took himself away, quietly, sometime after one.

'I can't fly when I'm hungover,' he said. 'It doesn't work with my insides.' More of the potential crew filtered off until it was just myself and Emmy and Guy left, and I only stayed because I didn't want to go back to my room. Guy outdrank us both, throwing more drinks back into his mouth and swilling them before swallowing. He gasped every time one was emptied, as if he was proud, even when the drink didn't have any burn to it.

'Fuck,' he said. He watched us, Emmy and myself, as he drank, and kept saying that we should go to bed if we couldn't keep up.

'We can keep up,' Emmy said, 'of course we can keep up.' We did. We left Guy asleep at the bar, because the barman had gone as well, locking the metal mesh over the bar as he went, leaving us with a bottle of something viscous and nearly luminous. In the lift to her room Emmy kept putting the bottle to her lips, swigging, letting the thick green liquid coat them where her lipstick had already worn off, and then she looked in the mirror and pouted and laughed, and kissed the mirror to leave a mark, a thick green pitted ring that looked nothing like the imprint of lips. When we got to her floor she asked me to go back to her room with her, and I said yes.

It wasn't like with Elena, which was normal and planned, it seemed; every time nearly the same, no surprises. With Elena I knew what worked, and it became routine; never dull, just a repeated compromise. Emmy was younger than Elena, even if the numbers might have been the same, and she was in charge, which was totally different for me: to be told, to be asked, to be ordered. She carried on drinking, forcing me to, even when I started to feel sick, when the room started moving on its axis. When that happened she focused me, her face on mine, pressing her cheek against me, her tongue – tasting of bitter, sour apple – in my mouth. When we were finished we lay on her sheets, the duvet on the floor, the television on, and she slept, and I watched her – stared at her body, naked on the bed, totally aware but not even caring in a way that Elena had long abandoned. I watched her for hours and didn't sleep, because I knew that this wouldn't happen again. Elena was waiting for me, and I would have to make that decision, because that was how these things worked in the real world, away from space camp.

I watch Guy wake up before everybody else. I watch his routine, as he cleans surfaces, checks dials, reads numbers from the computer screens, makes notes on them. He calls Ground Control, and they answer him. The reception is hazy, filled with static, like an old car radio just heading out of bandwidth.

'Is there an issue?' they ask. It's the night people, the ones we don't usually speak to. We were on a regimented sleep cycle – eight hours for sleep, sixteen hours awake – and they stuck to the same routine at Ground Control. Our mornings were their mornings, so when Guy called them before our morning cycle had begun – when the beds kicked us all out – he probably caught them off guard. 'Everything looks fine from our end.'

'No, no,' he says, 'I'm just checking in. Making sure.'

'Okay,' they say, and that's it, the end of the conversation. Guy is bored. He's lonely. We should talk to him more, I think, and then realize that I have no way of effecting that.

I am so, so tired.

I'm falling asleep, passing out as I try to stay awake: because the crew are awake, because it's daytime, because I should try to keep the same hours as they do. In the cabin, Emmy asks about Quinn's breathing, which seems slightly laboured. It was a common thing, to have trouble breathing. You're not used to being in that sort of atmosphere: your body can't be expected to react the same way every time.

'Were you asthmatic as a child?' she asks Quinn, pulling his shirt to one side, putting her stethoscope to his chest. He tells her that he wasn't. 'Breathe for me.' She puts her hands on Quinn's stomach, asks him to breathe again. The me that's out there watches them, like he knows what's going on. I don't remember knowing anything more than I know now. I don't remember that, but I was definitely there. Guy hands the me a tool, asks me if I'd like to help him work on the engines. The me says yes, but he looks sad, like he would rather be anywhere else than here, there, on the ship, being asked to help. He's not good at seeing things spiral. He's not good at not being in control.

I watch him – me – as he goes about the ship, as he does what he does, his routine. I haven't watched him this intensely before, because it hasn't felt right, or needed. Because, I know what I did, where I was. I wonder, briefly, if one of us isn't real, or if I'm the real one, and he's not, or if maybe he's something that I cannot fathom – more unfathomable than my being here again, for the second time, living in the lining of the ship like a bedbug, scuttling around the walls, foraging for scraps – and if he's replaced me; and then he sighs for Elena, looks at her picture on his screen before he writes his blog update, before he presses the Send button, and I know when I see him do these things – these things that I would do, and have done – that he's me, and I'm him. I have to stop questioning myself. He stares at it: it's one of the few pictures I had of the two of us together, taken when we were on a beach somewhere – Norfolk? I think it was Norfolk, one of the new beaches made after the floods – and wearing scarves, coats, wellington boots. The water was at our feet, but we were totally prepared, and we didn't care. He zooms in on her face, which I remember doing, because if I removed myself from the picture then there was just her, and I was gone; and he presses the screen with his finger next to her cheek, and he presses it so hard his finger goes white and the screen warps briefly, until he lets go.

I crane my face closer, because I want to see her better, just as well as he can. I will him to shift to one side, to give me a better view of her face, but he doesn't. All I can see is the shape of her cheek, her hair, her eye, so dark it's almost black with the glare of the screen against it. You can almost see the wind behind her in the photograph, almost hear her complaining about it, telling me that she's cold, and then we laughed and I tried to pick her up, pretending that I would throw her into the water, even though I had no intention of it. The potential of it all: that was the fun part.

The me closes his folder, takes his fingers from the keyboard, shuts the picture of Elena. He moves to the cabin and puts his hands on the backs of the pilot's chairs, sighs. He leaves and I follow him down to the back of the lounge area, where he climbs into the off-set area with the Bubble, and I watch his body, unable to see his face, as he no doubt stares into space, into the nothingness, and thinks about how large it all is, how insignificant we are, in the face of it all. How we mean so little. I watch as his body shakes slightly, and think, I don't remember crying. I wonder what made me cry.

Quinn and Emmy talk alone. Quinn's breathing is still harder than it should be, so she is monitoring him. ('Ha! Yeah, you monitor him,' Guy said when she told us.) He has taken his top off so that Emmy can listen to his chest and back as he breathes, and he gasps in between sentences, tiny sucks of air to keep him bolstered. Emmy listens to the breaths, and to his words, but I can't tell which are more important to her.

'I'm going to call Ground Control next time Guy's on a walk,' Quinn says. 'When he's checking the hull tomorrow I'll get on the line, tell them that we want to come home.'

'They've already said we have to continue,' Emmy says.

'Sure, but I'll sell it as worse than it is. Say that we're running out of something, I don't know. Say that the computers seem to be malfunctioning.'

'They can check that stuff from the ground,' Emmy says, which is true. Quinn heaves air in as a stutter.

'They'll have no choice. I mean, the repercussions if Cormac writes something that says they put us in – or, *kept* us in – danger?'

'What if they say no?' Emmy's hands sit on Quinn's chest still; her fingernails tangle themselves in his hairs. 'What if they say we have to carry on?'

'You're scared?' he asks, but doesn't wait for an answer. 'We say that there's a problem with the communications. We tell Guy that we have to go home, that it's no longer a choice.'

'He won't listen.'

'Then we make him listen,' Quinn says. He's a different man, all of a sudden. He was so calm, and transatlantic and smooth and cool and easygoing and laid-back. Suddenly he's determined and gritted. They sit in silence for a few more minutes, just listening to him breathe, and then Emmy tells him that she'll give him an injection, because it sounds like asthma. 'I've never had asthma,' he says again. 'Never had any sort of breathing problem. Healthy as an ox.'

'There's a first time for everything,' Emmy says. She injects him, and it's the first time she's had to open the drug-supply box, and I can see it all over her face: there are things missing.

She counts the medicines and supplies: takes everything out, lines them up, reads their names out one by one. She's got a check-sheet on the computer of all the stock we should have, of every single pill packet (and the numbers of pills inside them), every bandage, tubes of antiseptic, antiseptic wipes. She lines up the carriages of medicines, of needles and sealed glass test-tubes – cures for infections, anaesthetics, sedatives, all that ails you. She doesn't tell the rest of the crew why she's doing it, not even Quinn; instead, she tells us that there was a stock-take scheduled.

'It's just something I have to do,' she says. She asks Guy for gravity, says that she needs it because this is something she forgot to do. He obliges, barely.

'You've got half an hour,' he tells her. 'We can't lose time, you know that.' As soon as he presses the button to stop the engines she sits at the table and pulls out the cabinet drawers, laying their contents out, all the colourful little packets and tubes on the strict white surface, and she counts them, sliding them across from one pile to another, marking them off on a checklist. She frowns every time she comes across a discrepancy. The me that's in the cabin mistakes it for her being disgruntled. He jokes.

'Bet you didn't think you were signing up to count bottles of pills all day.'

'I did not,' she replies.

'And we haven't even needed any of it.'

145

'No,' she says, 'because Arlen and Wanda both died before I had the chance to do anything.' She stops, counting the pain pills over and over, opens the caps and spills the pills into a kidney bowl, picks them out one by one. She doesn't say anything else, but when she's finished counting them she pours them out again and starts from the beginning. I watch as she marks them off on her sheets, her face scrunched. 'Shit,' she says. She puts the medicines back in the cabinet and shuts the door. The me at the computer station watches her as she marches down the hallway; I follow her, clambering through the lining as much as I can with my leg in the condition that it is, and from the vents overlooking my original nest I watch her as she rifles through the boxes. Eventually she finds what she's looking for – a padlock, one of the spares for our individual lockers – and she marches back. I listen as it clicks into place on the cabinet door, and as the me asks her why she's locking it, what possible reason there could be.

'It's meant to have been there since the start,' she says, 'I just forgot to put it on. It's the rules.' I look at the bottle of pills I've been keeping in my pocket, and the five tablets that I've got left, and I listen as Emmy hits the button to start the ship. She doesn't bother to tell us: we all just start drifting again.

In the lining, I dry swallow another pill. Four left.

Emmy calls us all to the main cabin, tells us that she's forgotten to give us our psychological evaluations. She's trying to find out which of us is most likely to have taken the pills. Now, this makes sense. Back then, I wrote it off as Emmy being slightly nervous, wanting to find something to do with her day.

'It was part of my role,' she says, 'to make sure we're all doing okay.' She smiles, reassures us. 'Look, *I* know we're all fine, but rules are rules, okay? Especially after everything that's happened.' She's talking to us as she stands in front of the bodies of Wanda and Arlen, forever suspended. At the time, I remember thinking how curious that was. I think I even said that to her when she asked me – or will say it, now. She speaks to me first, leading me down the corridor towards the changing room, where she and I float around as she readies herself. 'I have to record these,' she says, 'because they need them at home. They're private, between you and me and Doctor Golding – you remember Golding, from the inductions? – but they have to be sent.' She presses record on the computer, clears her throat. I lean back against the wall, not having to watch because I remember this perfectly.

'That's fine,' the me says.

'Cormac, are you all right?'

'I'm okay,' I say. 'I miss . . . well, everything. You know.'

'You've been quiet,' she tells the me.

'I've been working.'

'You know,' she says, 'you can talk to me about anything. I'm trained. It's partly why I'm here.'

'Is that an order?' I think I smiled at that point.

'It's a request. I'm here if you need to talk, that's what I'm saying. It must be hard for you: with Arlen, and Wanda. With what's happened to them.' She says it conspiratorially, like she's trying to get something out of the me. As if I'll confess.

'I just can't fucking believe it.' This is like listening to yourself on a radio, or a recording: hearing your voice coming back the same as it is inside your head only different,

somehow more pinched, with none of the power and reson-
ance that you imagine when you speak. 'It seems . . . Cruel.'

'That they died?'

'That they're just there, watching us. I don't mean watching
us, but that they're there. That we have to see them.'

'It's the only way to preserve them. You understand that,
right?' She sounds clinical, because this is how she has to
sound. She's pure business with me. She feels the same, which
I knew then, because I knew her; and I know now that I'm
here again, because I am able to watch her looking at their
bodies and wincing, squeezing her eyes shut and looking
away like she's some over-emphatic actress. 'They deserve a
burial.'

'I know.'

'And everything's all right with the crew? No other
problems?'

'Nothing.'

'You and Guy? You and Quinn?' She doesn't ask about
me and her.

'Everything's fine.' She makes eye contact then, which she's
been avoiding – sometimes glancing towards where I am, in
the grate, like I'm a proxy – and speaks slightly quieter.

'What about your health? Everything okay?'

'I'm fine,' I say. I shake my head, and she picks up on
that.

'What?' she asks.

'Nothing,' I say. 'I just . . . Is everything okay with you?'

'This isn't about me, Cormac,' she says. 'Come and talk
to me if anything happens, or if you need to vent, or if you
just want to talk. About anything. You know where I am,
right?'

'You can't exactly go far,' I say. It's a brief talk, but she seems satisfied, or as satisfied as she can be without running full bill of health tests – blood tests and the like – and we're allowed to refuse those, which she knows. She calls Guy in, and he sighs as he enters the room, drifts around, pushes his hands against the ceiling to steady himself and waits there, almost aggressively. She doesn't like Guy, and never did, and she doesn't mask it. For his part, he revels in it, because it's something I think he's been used to.

'How's it going?' she asks him, trying to be casual, and he laughs.

'Further and further away from Earth, right? I mean, what a fucking question!' He claps his hand against his knee. 'Look, I'm fine. You worry about yourself and the mighty Quinn back there.'

Emmy blushes. 'This isn't about me.'

'No? So tell me, Emmy: who's going to do your psychological evaluation? Who's going to say, Oh, sure, she's fit for duty, because she's fucked two of the crew who are still alive, and the only one she hasn't . . . Well, she isn't his type, or she would have probably fucking tried, I think.' He laughs again. 'I mean, that's not a healthy crew situation, right?' She doesn't reply to him; she doesn't look at him, but she's gone red. We didn't know that she was sleeping with Quinn at that point, or that she had, or whatever; and I didn't know that my thing with Emmy – just that one night, but how ruinous it was, how dreadful – I didn't know that it was common knowledge either. 'Look, I'm fine, I'm functioning perfectly fucking normally, but I've got a job to do, and you're jabbering away, interfering with that. So, let's just say, yeah, I'm fine. Whatever.' He pushes himself to the door, slides it open. 'Quinn?' he shouts. 'Quinn, she's ready for you now.'

She cries, and when Quinn comes in he holds her, and she whispers something to him that I can't hear from where I am, but I think, maybe that's for the best, because it was meant to be private.

Emmy flirted with me all the way to the airport. We were picked up in shuttle-buses and she shuffled behind me in the line, got in mine along with three other people that I've almost completely forgotten about now. (I try to remember them and their faces are blank templates, because all I looked at for the entire journey was Emmy.) She sat opposite me and our knees were touching, and she kept speaking about the night before in vaguely guarded ways, but not subtle, like she didn't care who knew what happened.

'We drank a lot, right?' she asked, even though she knew the answer. 'I woke up feeling ragged this morning.' She smiled constantly at me; the other passengers laughed gently, because they weren't involved in the drinking, weren't even invited. 'I'm shattered.' She kept letting her knee drift and bounce slightly from side to side against mine, brushing against me. 'How are you feeling?' she asked.

'I'm okay,' I told her. 'Headache, but, you know.'

'I know,' she said. I had spent the rest of the night deciding that it was going to be the last time anything happened. Emmy was beautiful and strong and funny, but I loved Elena. I knew that, and I knew it wouldn't change. I decided that I was going to tell Emmy on the plane, where she couldn't make a scene, but I was sure that she wouldn't actually care. It was all so casual, I was sure she wouldn't mind.

We had seats next to each other, because of the order in which we checked in. Guy sat on the other side of me, and I was in the middle, and as soon as we took off Guy went to sleep, his head lolling onto my arm. Emmy found it hilarious and mimicked him, and then her arm slid around mine, her hand on the crook of my elbow, and she shut her eyes. I left her for a few minutes, until the stewardess offered us drinks, and then I shook her gently. She didn't want anything.

'Last night,' I said, 'was really special.' She knew where this was going straight away. Guy stayed asleep – or pretended – and we whispered our conversation to each other. She barely said anything, but left her hand wrapped around my arm for longer than she needed to, until well after it was clear that we weren't going anywhere.

And I kicked myself when she took it away, because of what I did. Because we were close before, and that would ruin it. Because part of me still wanted her – the part that was younger, that had more of his hair, less of a paunch, that still remembered what it was like to stay out until whenever, that wasn't trying for a baby with his wife, that hadn't already lost their first successful attempt, that didn't want to keep her, to struggle with her through whatever it was that was going to come to us.

When we landed at JFK, Elena was waiting on the other side of the gate, suitcase in hand. She had only just arrived, but hadn't told me she was coming. Emmy walked slowly and spoke to Quinn, who darted around saying goodbye to everybody, shaking their hands, and she didn't watch as I kissed Elena hello, and put my arms across her shoulders, folded them around her back, and promised her that we would make everything work.

Three pills left, and I think I can sleep. I hope I can sleep. I shut my eyes but get nowhere, so I sneak out into the expanse of the ship again, pull myself along the corridors to the cabin. I check the cabinet – as if I didn't see Emmy locking it, like, maybe she left the lock open – and I decide that I have to take risks. I open the main food cupboards, take Big Mac bars, dessert bars, Coca-Cola sachets. I sit at the computer and scroll through my photographs up close, and I look at Elena and myself, at my parents. I look at the folders of my writing, the blog entries I've been making ever since I got onto the ship. They detail everything in painstaking fashion, even down to conversations, time stamped, dated.

'I don't need these,' I say, because I've seen it all before, like a director watching the rushes, seeing exactly how it actually looks when taken away from the script. I check the computers and sit in the cockpit seat, the main pilot's seat, and I spin, because that's what I did before, when I was all alone, after all of these people died. I move down through the ship towards the changing room, pull my clothes off, stuff them into the locker with my name on it. I still remember the combination – Elena's birthday, my birthday – and I shower in the pod. The water is amazing, even though it's cold and makes me flinch away from it at first, eventually settling in, and when I'm done I put the vacuum on, put the excess water back into the system. I shave in front of the mirror, and when I'm done – when the vague beard is gone, when my face is clean of all the dirt and grime I've picked up in the lining – I examine myself, pulling my skin, which seems loose. I've lost weight – a couple of stone, maybe two and a half, I'd guess, but maybe more – and the skin seems to have bunched around my eyes. I can pull the skin below them down, see the sting-red of my tired eyeballs. I clean my teeth, swilling water around my mouth, using my finger with toothpaste, feeling the sting where they're sensitive. I'll need fillings, I think. I look at my body in the mirror: my ribs.

I sit in Quinn's seat in the cockpit, flick switches that I know don't do anything, and I call up the computer screen to tell me how to turn the ship. The instructions must be in here, but there are thousands of files, manuals packed into PDFs, all of them interactive and searchable, but the search results turn up nothing. The ship seems to have failsafes, but we weren't meant to know them – or, we weren't meant to read about them on badly formatted online manuals. I think about sending a message back home, to ask them what we can do – to pretend that it's on behalf of the ship itself, say that we have to turn around, that we're all ill or something, that there's an issue with, what, an engine? – but I won't be awake by the time they reply, and it'll be the crew that will get the message, and then they'll know there's an intruder. It might save their lives, but it won't save mine. And which is more important?

I go back to the lining and take another pill, because I can't deal with it. I can't deal with knowing that I'm here with no purpose, and whatever purpose I can give myself – to save this ship, save this crew (or what's left of them), to save myself (other version), to return the crew home . . . I don't know if any of it's right. In TV shows and movies and books, when somebody time travels – those words, like a death knell, a resounding echo in a box I'll never climb out of – they're given a mission, or they work it out, and they know what they have to do. They either have to get back to their time; or they have to change something (put it right or put it wrong, or fix what's been broken by somebody else); or they have to learn to live with what's happened. I have no markers, no clues. All I can do is what feels right: ride out my gut instinct. My instinct has told me not to speak to the rest of the crew, not to let them know that I'm here. My instinct has told me how to save myself, how to ride this out, to do everything I'm meant to have done. Because that's another rule of time travel: it's fixed, and if it's not, it's meant to be. It's like a circuit, a closed circuit: in order to get electricity running, it needs to work at both ends. If it doesn't, it won't even start. It needs to be a closed circuit.

'I think I'm going insane,' I say to the darkness. I told Elena that once, when I had writer's block, when I was struggling to get anything down on paper, to make sense of any of the words I was writing.

'You're just slightly broken,' she had told me, 'you're broken, and you'll have to work out how to fix yourself.' I open my eyes and she's there, for a second, smiling at me. She disappears as I blink away tears, and I remember where I am, where I'm going. Soon Guy will die, and then Quinn, and then Emmy, and then it will be me and him, I and me, and we'll be alone, and I'll have to do something drastic: save the day, become the hero. Bump my name up the credits list.

I spend the next day running through every aspect of my first time: going over every detail. I go through all the details, everything that's happened to me this time, how it jibes with what happened my first time around. I woke up alone in the chamber just after we hit warp and I dragged myself around, and I killed Arlen and then I slept, but I woke up first and I tried to find somewhere to hide, and then I made a tent but it was a stupid idea, totally flawed, and then I found the lining and I slid myself in and I tried to keep it all together, and I took pills for my pain because I'm addicted to them – but how can I be addicted, I've barely taken them for days, only a couple of days before I blew the ship up, but maybe that's enough time, maybe they're just that strong, that potent – and I don't have actual physical pain any more, just the pain left behind when I'm *not* taking one of the pills, and then I watched as Wanda killed herself, and then I started to work out what's going on, because that's the only way this can go, the only way it can, ultimately, end.

The first time we – that is, the trainees, the final few (or as near as for the others to barely matter, because they would soon be sent back to their homes and left unable to speak about what happened thanks to NDAs that could cause them to lose everything they owned if broken) – caught wind that something might have been happening between Emmy and Quinn was during the final stretch of our training. We were spending full days in a to-scale simulation of the ship, putting ourselves to work as we would on the real thing. It was a week, solid and intense, and the DARPA people controlled everything – our light, engine noise, the amount of gravity we had to play with, our level of oxygen (which they fluctuated at whim, to see how we coped with the stress that a lack of the stuff brought on). We obeyed orders, but the whole thing was harmless. One thing that DARPA couldn't stop was us recognizing how fake it all was: because outside the windows it was a grey box, a featureless space of corridors and different-sized basic rooms; and because there was nothing that could really go wrong. When DARPA triggered an alarm, and the sensors threw up that there was a crisis with one of the engines, Guy slowly led Quinn outside the fake ship and they drifted along and fake-fixed the fake problem. Upon their return we tried to clap them, but it seemed stupid to actually do it; like, the idea was nice, but the execution failed. It never felt real enough.

'We get it,' Quinn said, 'I'm going to be the world's biggest hero.'

'Nope,' Emmy said, 'just ours.' And that was it. That was all it took. The comment was totally innocuous, harmless. But she let the words linger in the air longer than they needed to, and Quinn didn't joke after it. He soaked the praise up, even though we knew that it meant nothing at all, but he lingered on it. They didn't hug or holds hands, and there wasn't anything else to give it away, but that set us talking.

'Oh, they're smitten,' Arlen said, 'even if they don't know it yet.' When it had been me, nobody had even suspected. Now, with Quinn, only weeks after Emmy and I spent our night together, Emmy was suddenly gossip. We rode out the rest of the week being ourselves in that fake ship, trying not to laugh when something from the real world intruded – a pipe fell, or a computer booted to Windows, because the real OS we were going to be using wasn't yet ready, so we were on a facsimile, a beaten-up version of Windows, skinned to be what we nearly needed. Quinn joked about eating all the food we had, every part of our supply.

'If I just *gorge* myself, you reckon they'll bring us a proper meal? I'd kill for a steak and fries.'

'Pepper sauce,' Emmy said.

'Oh shit, yes,' Quinn replied. We watched them riff off each other, and we all suspected, but they *knew*.

When the week was over we all went back to the hotel to sleep. We had a few days before the next round, and Elena had flown out again to meet me. She was already in the room when I got there: she had ordered dinner, room service, and a bottle of wine, and we sat at that funny little table that wasn't quite large enough and ate from those plates that didn't seem quite large enough.

'Tell me all about it,' she said, so I did, but I almost singularly left out Quinn and Emmy's names, because I wasn't sure what I would tell her if I even began to think about them too much.

In the ship, the original version of me writes almost constantly, or at least sits at the computer and thinks about writing. He puts his fingers on the home keys and nearly starts so often, over and over again. I remember that it became hard at this point: hard to constantly send something worth reading, hard to maintain that daily rapport with a readership that you didn't know and couldn't predict. Did they want to know more about the ship? About the passengers? About me? I wrote extended eulogies for those who died, and I fed some of Quinn's measurements into the paragraphs of text – here's where we are, here's what we've seen. Sometimes I included pictures of things that we passed, looking totally different on that screen than they did with the naked eye. Photographs of objects so far away that they were barely perceptible are suddenly clear to the readers, close up and distinct. This isn't what we saw, I remember writing one day, because out here it's just black with specks and sparks, like it is from your gardens in the middle of the night. It's no different, really, but here you don't have the mugs of hot chocolate and the blanket wrapped around you and the home-made telescope. Here, you've got the white of the ship and the cold of the outside, and we're not in control of when we stop watching because it's all that there is.

I get to watch the back of the me as he hunches and doesn't type, or occasionally does, and then clicks to send the work, first draft always, no chance to change anything once that button is pushed. I was never a first draft writer, but the occasion, the circumstances dictated that I adapt. The signal is bitten apart and spat out, across hundreds of thousands of miles, further than any information has ever been sent, and I don't know when it will arrive – because of the lag, so it'll get there in two days? Three days? – but that's the nature of technology. I wonder if they're sent before another version of me gets to rewrite them, alter them for my benefit. I hope so, or the stuff that's published back on Earth will be a depressing insight into the mind of a complete madman.

I spend another night roaming the body of the ship. I clean my teeth first, feeling another one wiggle in its socket when I push it with the brush, so I use my tongue to hold it steady as I do them. When I spit out blood into the tube it's not the thin bright red of gum disease; it's thick and dark, and the tooth follows it, clattering into the reedy vacuum before disappearing forever. It was a canine, and the home is wide and sweet to the taste. I shit and I wash, because I feel like that's what I need to do. In the mirror I stare at the scars across my back, like whip-marks, and I find another scar that I've never noticed before at the back of my head, just under my hairline. When I'm finished I dress in a clean uniform, and I shave again, using my own razor, and I cut my fingernails. I rifle through the cupboards for food, taking a Big Mac bar and eating it in the corridor, and I take my last painkiller with it, that single tablet being my starter and dessert rolled into one, changing everything after it hits me. The pain had been back; my leg had been numbing, but now I know that that pain isn't even real. The pain is actually somewhere else entirely. I don't need the pills: my wounds are completely healed. God knows how many I've had since I started this loop – or this pattern, maybe it makes more sense to call it a pattern, because it sounds less insane, more like something mathematical than fantastical – but it's a lot. The scars speak to that. I'm not in pain: I'm addicted. The two feel so similar. I shake and shiver and think about how I'm not taking another pill. I can, I know, survive this.

I sit at the computer and look at how long is left of the trip, how much we've got to go. My estimations tell me that Guy's going to die the day after tomorrow, which means we're heading towards me being all alone, and then the point of no return. It's so dark in the ship, and with the people here – still alive – it feels creepier than it did, as if I'm in a haunted house, waiting for something to jump out at me. From the beds, it feels as if their eyes are watching me, even though they're closed. Back before, when I finished it, I felt totally alone. Now, I feel anything but.

I open files, trying to find any information that might not be in the ship's database. I try to get into Guy's folder, to see if there are any documents in there, but it's got a password for some reason, so I try Quinn's, and I read the titles of hundreds of banal files, bits of nothing. I see a file titled *Emmy*, and I think about opening it, reading, but I don't, because I already know that it'll be a letter or a picture of the two of them together, or something. Something that I'm not meant to see. I respect privacy. I have to.

Then, from behind me, a hiss, the noise of a bed opening

in the darkness, and the thump in my gut that I should move as fast as possible. I hurl myself backwards, scrabbling down the corridor towards the storage rooms just in time to see Guy drift across the doorway.

'Hello?' he whisper-shouts, but I'm inside the storage room already, pulling myself into the lining. The door's shut before he's even halfway down the hallway, and I watch through the vents as he looks in every room. 'Hello?' he whispers again, and he shines a torch, but it only catches the corners of the rooms. There's no trace of me, I realize – except for the files on the computer. I was in Quinn's directory. I rush to the cabin and wait for Guy to return. He counts the bodies in the beds, making sure they're all asleep, and then sits at the desk, straps himself in. He doesn't even notice what files are up on screen: he backs out of the system, to the entrance screen. He's focused, single-minded. He logs in as himself, opens a picture – an old man, an old woman, a very young boy that's unmistakably Guy, only here he's still Gerhardt, dressed in this ridiculous outfit, and I suppose these people must be his grandparents, or maybe his parents, but they're very old – and he says something, very quietly, so quietly I can't hear. I'll never know what he said. He loads something onto one of the handhelds and then closes the screen, drifting from the console and down the corridor. I chase him until he's in the changing room, where he latches himself to the bench and loads an app on the handheld. The program starts establishing contact with home base. Out here, this far, the bandwidth is next-to-nil. The quality is atrocious, the faces of the people in Ground Control little more than grey shapes against a background of static. He pulls an earphone from the device and I can't hear what they're saying, but I can hear his side of the conversation, whispered and calm, but still audible.

'Everything's on schedule. We're only a few days away from entering it. Maybe a week, at most. Everybodys fine here, even Cormac. We'll send a final broadcast tomorrow. Okay. Gerhardt out.'

He closes the application and goes back to the main cabin. He gets back into bed, but I daren't go out there again, because I shut my eyes and nearly sleep and I dream, and in my dream I see myself out there, and he sees me, and he screams and it's all over, which means that, once, I tried to go out there and discovered his open eyes for myself.

6

Guy acts as if everything is normal, not telling any of the crew about his conversation. He doesn't mention anything even related to it until after lunch, when he suggests that we send a broadcast home.

'It's just been a while, and the connection will be getting shakier this far out. Might be our last chance to do video, so let's do it.' It's not a request, but we – the crew, there at the table with him, we merry four – don't care. It's something. Again, though, Guy's lied: first about Wanda, now this message home. I wanted his lies to be to protect us, but there's something else to them, something bitter. He knows exactly how bad the connection will be, and he doesn't tell us: he hides it from us under the veil of his personal speculation. We gather around the table when we've finished, and Guy presses the full-stop button, and we all drift to the ground. Usually I set up the connection but this time Guy takes charge, like a photographer in the olden days, lining up the shot, standing behind the camera to make sure we all look good. 'This will be the last time they see our faces for a good long while,' he says, 'you want to make sure you look your best for it. Smile. Look happy.' We do. 'Hey, remember what's important,' he says. 'We're *intrepid*, right?' He says the word like it doesn't fit into his mouth, into the repertoire of his language.

'Hi, all!' Emmy starts. She sounds happy, still, somehow. I stand next to Quinn, and Emmy is on his other side, and Guy slides into shot in front of us all, kneeling. I remember looking at the top of his head as we spoke, noticing the faint marks on the skin of his neck where there had once been a tattoo, but which was now removed. I remember thinking how little I knew about him; how I would never have guessed that he had once been a rebel. He seemed so straight-laced. 'This is the crew of the *Ishiguro*. We're about to head out of video broadcast range, so we wanted to just send a message with an update, let you know how much we miss you all.' She doesn't say names: she's got nobody there to miss, despite what she says. 'We've been up here for a few weeks, and we're looking forward to the next part of the trip. In two days?' She looks at Quinn for confirmation, and he nods. 'In two days we're going to have travelled further than anybody else has ever travelled, which is an amazing feeling.' She's like a TV presenter. 'All that we've ever had out this far before is probes and satellites. We're doing what man has never done before.' We all thought she'd have a career as a personality when we got home. It was her destiny.

'We're all excited about it,' Quinn says. 'We'll try and broadcast again when it happens, so you can celebrate with us.' He puts his hand on Emmy's back, squeezes the folds of her suit, pulls it tighter so that she knows he's there, that he's with her.

'And then, not long after that we'll be coming home,' Emmy says. The me doesn't say anything. Guy doesn't say anything either, but when Quinn says that we should sign off he waves, shouts goodbye with the rest of us.

'That was good,' he says when we've severed the connection. That was, I remember, the last time we spoke to home.

Elena used to worry about how we would survive the gap between us, the ever-increasing distance.

'You won't be able to speak to me directly,' she said, 'I don't know how I'll survive.' We had just been told that personal contact was a no-no; every single broadcast we did home cost millions, each blog post I made thousands. At least I would still have contact with her through those, I said.

'You know that I'll be thinking of you with each message I write,' I told her. 'Every one is a letter to you, think of them that way.'

'It's not the same, Cormac.' I had been finding her hairs on the pillows of the hotel-room beds, thick and black and coiled like snakes, and now she bit her fingernails down past the line of flesh, towards what my mother used to call the quick. Her hands used to be pretty; I don't tell her that. 'It's not the same. Because I'll miss you so much, and this all seems so unfair.'

'But think about how important it is,' I said. We had been on the cover of *Time* that week, in an article pre-empting the one that I would be writing, a lead-in that featured sound bites by almost anybody who mattered in pop culture and politics. They opened it with this quote, from Captain Cook – about how exploration was seeing how far it was possible to go, not about what you find when you get there, but the journey itself, the *find* – and they equated us to the greats. There wasn't much about us as a crew, just a few details here and there, and a few details about the ship, the course we would be taking, the things that we might see. Mostly, the article – and the people interviewed – cared about what it meant. Elena didn't understand that.

'You shouldn't go,' she said.

'I have to,' I told her. 'It's so important.' We had that same conversation over and over, like a loop, a single moment that she never let drop.

'More important than me?' she would ask, and I would tell her that I loved her, but that I had a chance to do something great. How many times did I say that phrase? How many times? 'What am I to you?' Elena asked.

'You're my wife.'

'And does that even mean anything? How can you prove that I'm so important? That I'm most important?' Every time she asked that I nearly told her about Emmy, but then didn't. At that point, I wonder if she would have even cared. Space was the only other woman, not the pretty Australian girl.

Guy lives the penultimate day of his life as a man unaware of his ticking clock. He sends facts about the ship back to Ground Control and eats with the rest of us, and stays quiet when we talk about things that he doesn't care about. We used to be close, I think.

He isn't the fascination to me. I am, the me out there. I am so quiet, almost sullen. I remember myself as being full of life. Instead I watch everything as the outsider. What am I thinking of? Is it Elena? Is it Emmy? I don't remember this: what thoughts went through my head as I geared myself up to write. I sit at the computer and type another entry, and I remember telling Elena that they were all for her. This one isn't. I'm asking Guy for facts and figures about the trip to pepper the update with, and he reels them off, things that sound unimportant but probably mean the world to our continued movement, our survival.

'Oh,' he says, 'I'll need your help tomorrow outside the ship. Another routine check, okay?'

'Fine,' the me says, but I remember that I didn't go on that walk. I remember that I slept in, for some reason; missed my chance. When he got back we argued, and then . . .

'We have to go early, so we'll set the alarms, get up and do it. Okay?'

'Okay,' I hear myself say. I didn't get up. I didn't go on that walk. Guy was a stickler for routine – if he said something he did it – which means that I'm being called up: the me, here and now, in the lining. We're on my page of the script, and my stage directions are written in bold italics.

An hour after they all go to sleep I prowl again. Emmy's medicine cabinet is locked; I itch, the ache in my leg having spread to my belly. Everything aches, but that's understandable. I want to smash it open, gobble at the drugs. I don't. I can't give myself away. I read up on walking again, reminding myself of how to do it, but even reading it seems second nature. When I'm done with that I take up the portable device that Guy used to contact home, turn it on, try to re-establish the last connection. It's to base camp, and they fuzz through, their faces indistinct through the static.

'Gerhardt?' they ask. 'Why are you making contact? Is there a compromise?' I switch it off, quickly, as quickly as I put it on, before they can see who's called them, and I close the apparatus down, make sure the application isn't running. It feels wrong: again, in my gut. My gut says, don't speak to them. Instead, I silently drift towards the bed of the other me, tap on his alarm settings to turn them off, make sure we're not interrupted; then I tap on Guy's bed to wake him slightly earlier, to give us as much time as possible. I watch him through the glass: he's sleeping soundly. He seems totally unconcerned.

There's another motive in time travel stories, of course: just to find out what's going on. I go to the shaver and the shower, do what I can to make myself mimic the appearance of the original me – I will keep my mouth shut as much as possible, puff my cheeks to not look as gaunt as I do, keep the lights low to mask my thinness with shadows – and then I wait in the darkness of the lounge until Guy's alarm trill and his bed hisses, and then I greet him, tell him that I couldn't sleep.

'Lights,' he says, but I quickly snap that they should stay off, before he can turn around and see that I'm actually still asleep in my bed.

'Let them sleep,' I whisper, 'they've had a rough few days.'

'Right,' he says, nodding. 'Sure, whatever. Let's get changed and get the fuck out there.' In the changing room I face away from him and pray that he won't notice the scars or how thin I am, but he doesn't look at me, not even once. He focuses on the floor, and on his suit, and then on the security line, checking over and over that it's tight enough, that nothing can possibly go wrong.

It's like riding a bike, or one of those other things that people say you never forget how to do. Breathing, that's another one. It's swimming, gentle and loose and graceful, even for me, in my state: so, so tired, tearing myself apart, almost collapsing. Out here, in the dark, it's like night swimming, that sense of not knowing what's below you because everything's so dark, so filled with absolutely nothing. I glide around the ship in Guy's wake. He tells me that we're going to check the ship's guidance systems again, then the communications system, then the life support.

'You can just hold everything for me again, okay?'

'Fine,' I say.

'It's all so fucking delicate, this stuff.'

'You must miss Wanda,' I say. He doesn't reply. We pull ourselves over to the first panel and he lifts it off, delicate work, concentrating as he does it. 'Why did you want me to help you?' I ask him. 'Wouldn't it have been easier to have Quinn?'

'Less fun, though,' he replies. He turns, looks at me, smiles. 'Besides, good to get you out, right? Get you out of that ship.' He turns back to the panel; I can see his face reflected, his tongue sticking through his teeth, his eyes squinting to see what he's doing. 'Must be hard, seeing Emmy and Quinn like that, right?'

'Why?' I ask, but I know what he's talking about. I want him to say it.

'Oh, fuck off, you know why. You know why, don't be so fucking coy.'

'I'm not.'

'So nothing ever happened? Oh, okay, fine. Let's pretend that you and she were like fucking strangers, right? That you never did her.' He laughs.

'You're forgetting about Elena,' I say. 'Don't talk about something you don't know about.' We didn't tell a soul, Emmy and I. We didn't tell a soul. All Guy can know, unless Emmy told him anything, is that we flirted, danced around each other; or maybe he was awake on that plane flight, maybe he was listening in.

'I'm not forgetting,' he says. 'Maybe you are, though? Maybe?' He seals up the first panel. 'Fuck's sake, there's a

168

problem. We'll be out here a little longer. Okay?' It's not a question. We move to the propulsion panel and he unscrews it, hands me the tool.

'I heard you messaging Ground Control yesterday,' I say. He stops moving, puts his hands on either side of the panel.

'Okay,' he says.

'Why didn't you tell us all?' He doesn't speak. His whole physical presence changes. I had worried, as the words came out of my mouth, that he'd be angry or bitter or violent, but he seems disappointed. He deflates. 'What was such a secret that you couldn't tell us?' No, not disappointment. Relief. 'Why was it such a secret?'

'We're not going home,' he says. 'They want us to stay out here.' He doesn't give me a chance to process it, to question him. He already knows what I'll be asking, what I'll want to know. 'They want this mission to be a glorious failure; they want the world united in their search for us, in their desire to see what we've seen, to discover what happened to us. Where we ended up.' He doesn't move from the panel; doesn't face me, doesn't even think about turning around. I think he's scared to see my face. 'We'll be heroes for eternity – the crew of the *Ishiguro*, lost in space! Adrift among the stars! – and they'll rush-build another ship to search for us, this time with a bigger budget, co-funded by the governments, because how can they not? We're everywhere. We're on the cover of *Time Magazine* twice. We're on the boxes of Happy Meals, on the sides of cans of Coke. DARPA won't be on its own, and the ship they can send will be twice as big, twice as powerful. It will be able to see things we only dream of. And we've got a beacon in the ship, so when they find us we'll be taken home, buried in the most glorious way, and the world will remember us. Don't you get that?'

'They'd remember us if we got home.' I'm shaking. Inside my suit, I'm actually physically shaking.

'For a while, sure. But what would we have actually done?'

'We'd have gone further into space than anybody before us.' I must sound desperate, pleading: it's the anger.

Guy laughs. 'And you actually think that people care about that? Who do they remember? The guy who went *quite far* into the Antarctic? No, of course they don't. They remember two people: Scott, who beat that fucking place, and Oates. *I'm just going outside and may be some time*, right? That's what he said, and we remember that shit, because he tried, and he failed. Think about Amelia Earhart, right? She went missing, and she was fucking *trying*, Cormac. She was trying, just like we are. We can't be Scott, Cormac. There's nowhere to go from here. We're done. So we're Oates, right? We tried and we failed. But better than that, because maybe we didn't! Maybe we didn't! Nobody's going to have a fucking clue, because when we drop off the grid they'll just never hear from us again, and they'll speculate for years about what happened to us: why we didn't come home. Why we stayed out here. For all they'll know, maybe we chose to.'

'But how does this help?' I gulp back tears inside the helmet. The reveal of motive should bring relief. It doesn't. It terrifies me.

'This way, maybe, the governments might get involved. Space travel's bigger than it's ever been, there's more to discover, more to see. The technology is astounding. And we're going to be sending back results from the deepest part of space, deeper than anybody else has ever travelled.'

'We've already done that.'

'*Even deeper*. Think about it: we're not even halfway through our fuel. We're going to keep going, and I'll get to research things that we don't even fucking know what they are! Anomalies we only dreamed of seeing! There are things out there, Cormac: things that are bigger than us, bigger than all of this. You know the anomaly we're going to see? It's like nothing else. We've never seen anything like it. Can you believe it? Something truly new. We can see it first hand, we can report on it. We can uncover the secrets of space. And you: you can write stories about us that will live forever.' He's begging, almost. 'The governments will see what we've achieved, and they'll put money back into this. It won't be to rescue us: it'll be to look at what we've found.' His voice cracks under the stress, and he starts crying I think, but I don't know if it's fear, or pity, or pride. 'We're meant to explore, Cormac. We lost the urge, but this will give it back to us. Think about when children get kidnapped, or when there are hostages, or rescue attempts to people lost at sea. It starts a new wave of human interest. Think about what this will do for humanity,' he says. I look into his eyes: he really believes in this.

'Who knows?' I ask him.

'Only me, now. Wanda knew. She hated it, but accepted it. She wanted to be remembered, just like everybody. She wanted to leave her mark.' My hands shake inside the suit, and I have to keep reminding myself to cling on or God knows what will happen. 'Shit,' he says. 'You should never have found out, right? It would have been so much easier. You would have written your own obituary, the dying throes, your last hurrah, right? It would have been so important. Studied in schools around the globe forever: the document of our glorious failure.' He slides towards me slightly. 'You still can.'

'Why us? Why this crew? Why bother training us, going through the fucking rigmarole of all that shit, those months of shit we went through. What was the fucking point?' Even when you shout in these suits, your voice sounds like a whisper through the headsets.

'It needed a crew, Cormac. This only works if it's people that the world cares about.'

'But why us? What made us so fucking special? What made them think we could be fucking sacrifices?'

'Oh, that's easy,' Guy says. 'We're all alone. Every one of us: no parents, no kids, no loved ones. Until you and Elena broke up, I don't even think you were going to end up being picked for the mission. And then – '

'Elena,' I say, and then everything goes black, and I've let go and I'm drifting, spiralling away from the ship slowly, facing the stars, thinking about my wife, relying on Guy to save me.

'Don't go,' Elena asked me, over and over, until it nearly became all that she said. She would wake in the night and throw herself over to me, shake me. 'I've had a dream,' she would say, 'a horrific vision, and I saw you dying, not even making it past launch.' She would cry and lay her head on my chest. 'Oh Jesus Christ, Cormac, please don't go. Please.'

'What's wrong with you?' I asked her one day, not meaning it to sound the way that it did; or, actually, meaning it to sound that way, but not expecting it to.

'We've been through so much, and I can't stand to be alone,' she said. She told me anything she could to get me to stay, because she was fragile – snapped – and I didn't care. She told me that she was pregnant, and I knew that she was lying but played along until I could prove it, until we sat in the doctor's surgery that I forced her to go to and he told us, in blunt terms, that she wasn't. She told me that she was ill, which she wasn't – not in the way that she meant.

'I can't stand to see you like this,' I told her.

'Why am I not enough for you?'

'Maybe you should go and stay with your mother for a few days.'

'In Greece? You want me in a different country?'

'No. I don't mean that.' The launch was happening a month after we had that conversation: and she bought a ticket for her flight, and left without telling me, and then called me from Athens, shouting at me down the line.

'This is what you wanted,' she said, and I sat against the wall in the kitchen and wept, because how could I fix her? Had I done this in the first place? 'Why are you even with me any more?' she asked. 'If you love your fucking job so much, you should just have that. Forget about me. Forget about what we were. Why are we even together?'

'I don't know,' I said. She hung up, and when I called back the phone just rang and rang, and I could picture her screaming at her mother to let it ring, because she knew who it was and she didn't want to talk to me any more.

Guy grabs the end of the tether rope and pulls me back towards the ship. He looks genuinely concerned; I don't know if it's for me, or because now I might expose what's been going on to the rest of the crew. He pulls me up to him, holding me by the lapels of the suit, staring into my eyes.

'You with me?' he asks. I'm not sure how he means it. 'We have to finish this.' I have the tool in my hand, still; something not unlike a power drill, only with encased parts, a sharp end, like a thick metal knitting needle. I could do this, I realize. I could take him out, throw the tool into his face, rush inside and tell the crew what he tried to do. I think back to my first time here, as Quinn tried to turn the ship around, alter the course but couldn't, and I realize what Guy's doing out here:

he's breaking it. He's breaking the ship, and I can't do anything about it, because this is what's meant to happen.

This is the way that fate occurs: I am out there with Guy, and I hold panels of the ship's hull for him as he cuts wires and reroutes things, removes plugs, all easily labelled for him so that he, a man with a PhD in both Astrophysics and Engineering can't fuck it up, that's how little they trust him; and I pass him the tool when he needs it, letting him seal the sections with their special screws, like you'd find on the back of household technology, underneath the Warranty Void If Broken sticker; and I watch as he declares that he's finished, and he hangs there, fixed to the hull, and he seems to be thinking about something.

'Do you understand?' he asks me.

'No,' I say.

'You're going to tell Quinn and Emmy, right? It's okay, I understand. They should know. Maybe I'll tell them.'

'No,' I say again. He doesn't ask why, but I tell him. 'They shouldn't know that they're going to die. Nobody should know that.' He nods. He has under an hour to live, and it's so tempting to break my word and tell him, to see how he reacts, but I don't. *It's in my gut.*

I don't know how I'm meant to do the next part. I assume that it will all make sense. We pull ourselves along the ship to the airlock and slip inside, and Guy instigates the procedures. When he takes his helmet off he doesn't look at me. We take the through-door to the changing room and he strips, steps into the shower, facing away from me. He keeps his head down. I hang my suit up and dash back down the corridor, back to the lining, hide myself away. I watch as Guy dries himself, dresses, then heads to the living quarters. The me is at the computer, as always, like a fucking corpse

174

already, hunched over that table, barely typing. Emmy and Quinn are eating breakfast.

'Morning,' Quinn says as Guy walks in.

'Morning,' Guy mumbles. I watch as he fetches himself a breakfast bar, sits at the bench alongside them and eats, silently. He keeps coughing, as if he's about to speak, and he cradles his side. Soon, he'll plummet down that canyon of a hallway. The me ignores him. Emmy ignores him. Quinn starts to make conversation, just as Guy finishes eating, moves to stand up. I watch the players move to their marks: Guy, holding the table, but floating in the centre of the room; Quinn, opposite him, but further back, towards the cockpit; Emmy, seated at the table still; and me, at the computer, craning my head to look at them; and me, here, in the lining. I shuffle around to get a better look, pulling myself as close to the grate as I can, my eye pressed against the bars. 'We can start up again,' Guy says, and Quinn presses the button. The engines roll into action, and the crew latch themselves onto the furniture, so that they don't drift away.

'You've been out walking?' Quinn asks. (We always called it that, though you didn't do anything even close. It was so far from walking that it sounded odd, like the word suddenly had a different meaning.)

'There's a problem with the comms,' Guy mumbles. He's not convincing anybody, but none of us are really listening to what he's saying. We're waiting for Quinn to call him on the next part, the part that we discussed when Guy was outside: how he was breaking rules when he walked outside the ship alone, and how we have no confidence in him, so we're voting to turn the ship around and go home, orders or no.

'You went out alone,' Quinn says. 'You know that's against protocol.'

'I wasn't alone,' Guy replies, 'Cormac was with me.' Emmy and Quinn look at the other me for confirmation. He shrugs.

'I was in the shower,' he says, then rubs his wet hair as evidence.

'What the fuck?' Guy asks. 'You were with me. Tell them!' He looks at the me in the chair, in front of the computer, begging for confirmation of his story; he doesn't offer it. He's clueless, because he genuinely doesn't know what Guy's talking about.

'I was getting ready to go with you, like you said. I figured you just decided to go without me,' Cormac says. Guy's face goes white; his jaw hangs. He's second-guessing himself; he's wondering if his memory of what happened was a complete fantasy or not.

'We've all been talking, and we're turning around,' Quinn says. 'We don't care what you say, Gerhardt, because we're sick of this, and we're going to turn around. Something's not right.' He's suddenly the leading man again, all power and charisma and charm. If I hadn't been out there with Guy, he might have even persuaded him. 'Help me or don't, but we're going home.'

'We can't,' Guy whispers. 'Something's stopped working, in the uh, the uh, the navigations, in the engine.' He looks at the me for help, but my face is blank, because the me doesn't know what he's talking about. 'Come on,' he begs, and he rolls his eyes and searches for something he can use, anything at all, scanning every corner of the room for proof that he isn't insane: and then he sees me, in the lining, pressed up against the grate, a fairy-tale child peering through the frosted glass of his favourite toy shop. He sees me, and our eyes meet, and I wonder how he is the only person to have ever seen me, the only one to have ever looked up at that exact angle, to have perfectly lined up his vision with the slats of the grate, and I realize that it makes sense: it's fated to happen, destiny. He was meant to see me, so he does. I am going to cause whatever will happen. He locks onto me, and he instantly recognizes me. You can see it in somebody's eyes, that recognition, and I see it in Guy's. He sees me, and he *knows*. Guy gasps, and clutches at himself, and he has the heart attack I knew he would have, that I had to be here in order to instigate, because this is all about me, all hinges on my being here. He paws at his chest and then lets go of the table and lurches, and that's when he plunges down the hall. Quinn races for him, Emmy unbuckles herself to do the same. Both versions of me watch as he dies, as they open his suit and try to kick his heart back into play; as he throws his arms around when he gives up, when he knows that he's fighting a losing battle, and they try to restrain him, but they fail, and he stops moving as they finally manage to, in synchronicity. They aren't sure if they've won or lost. I watch as Emmy cries: not because she liked Guy, but because this is all too much. It's all too much, all the death and the tragedy and the lack of this being what she expected. She gasps back the tears.

'We'll turn around and go home,' Quinn says, making the decision that it will be so. I wish that I could warn him that he can only be disappointed, now. I wish I could, but I don't, and I can't.

7

Emmy keeps telling Quinn and the me that it'll be fine.

'We'll get home,' she says, though she doesn't sound like she believes it. The trip has sliced the crew in half, reduced our number by 50%. We're being culled, and she knows it. 'It would have happened anyway,' she says as we put Guy's body into his bed. 'This trip puts so much stress on the human body, so much stress. It would have happened anyway.' She says it as if she's consoling us both, but it's all aimed at Quinn. He was the one in the argument; he's the one who'll feel guilt, for shouting at Guy and causing his heart to collapse, to rupture, to fail. I didn't feel any guilt at the time, because there was none to feel. I had backed them up, but it wasn't my fight. Now, however, the guilt swarms me. Emmy is trying to be the strong one, but she's fighting a losing battle. 'We'll turn around, and we'll get home, and we'll bury them all.'

She doesn't even sound like she's *trying* to believe it, not really.

* * *

They were down to nine people in the running for the final crew places. Myself, Emmy, Quinn, Guy, Wanda, Arlen; and then another assistant engineer (far more qualified than Wanda, but with so much more arrogance, the sort of dickhead who speaks about themselves in the third person on occasion); another pilot (who could have replaced either Quinn or Arlen, as there was no hierarchy to their roles at that point, but they were slightly more jittery, slightly less at ease with the idea – the possibility – of dying, or of the higher risks involved in something going wrong); and the only other remaining journalist. Her name was Terri, and she was Asian-American. She pointed it out every time somebody referred to her as just one of those ethnicities, correcting whoever said it with her disappointed little squeak of a voice. She was driven, totally and utterly. I managed to never spend any time with her during either the interview or training processes, because we were up for the same job. There was no point in us sharing any experiences together, because that would never happen in real life. Emmy and Guy, they were constants. They were part of every variation at that point. They knew that they had the job, if they wanted it; and they both wanted it. Terri hated Emmy, and Emmy hated her. That made Guy laugh when he spoke about it, when neither of them were around.

'It's like warring fucking rabbits,' he said. 'You ever see rabbits fighting? It's hilarious, because they don't even fucking try. It's lazy viciousness, like they can't really be bothered but they still want to win. Emmy doesn't give her the time of day, but when she *has* to, she does it so fucking snarkily. Like, Fuck you, bitch, but without saying those words.' That made him laugh. He even sent me a link to a video of rabbits fighting when we were waiting for the final line-up to be announced. Terri had nobody. She was focused on her job, her career. Everything else was just flotsam.

'She'll be picked,' I said as we reached the last few days. We knew that the final crew was to be announced a week later, so they only had a few days to decide. 'She'll be picked.' I was so sure. Myself, Emmy, Quinn and Arlen were drinking, even though we had been told to stay off the stuff. We knew that we four – we wanted us on the trip. We would be a good crew, a wholesome, relatable, well-adjusted crew. We would overcome all obstacles, and we would serve as role models. Emmy wouldn't sit next to me, though. Apart from in the group, we weren't talking.

'She won't be picked,' Quinn said. 'Have you read her stuff? It's all gimmick. She won't be picked.'

Quinn presses the button and the engines stop, and the gravity comes back. I watch as the me and him pick up Guy and move him to his bed – which we should have done before this, because his body is heavy, mostly muscle, even what we assumed to be a slightly paunchy belly – and we strap him in, fasten him to the bed.

'He didn't deserve that,' Quinn says. *He did*, I think. *If you knew what I know.* But he doesn't, and he won't. He closes the bed, gives it minimal oxygen, lowers the temperature – which actually means not heating the pod, relying on the outside vacuum to keep it cold, keep the body frozen – and seals it. 'We're going back,' he says. It's not a question, or a debate. 'We should tell Ground Control, but the mission's over.' He asks the me to shut down what I'm working on – one of my blog posts, one of the last few that will get through because of where we are. I do. I watch as I save it, close the program, log out. Quinn opens the comms link, but there's nothing there, just static. He closes it, opens it again, and still there's nothing. He asks me to help him, then calls for Emmy – who is in the changing room, crying, trying to hide it from us, but we *knew* – and we all watch as he shuts it down again, opens it, shouts at the screen, hits the computer with his palm. 'We're going home,' he says. 'I'm turning us around.' He spends the next twenty minutes staring at the screen as he types code, as he tries to activate things, but nothing happens. 'Fuck,' he says. 'I can't get into the fucking systems.'

'What does that mean?' Emmy asks.

'It means we can't change course.' He's shaking, having trouble breathing fully again. (It's a red herring, his breathing: it'll never have any effect. He'll die when his head smacks against a wall. Even now I wonder if I'll have anything to do with that.)

'Can't you just turn us around?'

'No,' he says. 'It doesn't work like that. It needs preset coordinates, and the ship only moves in that direction. Manual control doesn't kick in until we start to enter descent, when the landing gear's deployed. This is all automated. It was meant to just work, and if it didn't, we could hack the system and enter coordinates and . . .' He looks white, sick. He asks the me to go with him on a walk. 'We have to check the comms relay,' he says. I wonder if I shouldn't just tell them, save them the trouble, but even as I gently contemplate it, I know that it won't be happening. This is inexorably set. My gut aches as I even think about the alternatives to the predestined.

I watch them suit up, and then I watch Emmy, alone, brutally affected. She is a shell. She sits and bites at the flesh around her fingernails, because her fingernails are perfect and manicured, cultivated over months; but that flesh will heal quickly. She doesn't make it bleed. She only nibbles at the hard part, pressed up against the nail itself. She keeps looking at Guy, before eventually sitting in the seat in the cockpit, too far away for me to see her. I'm shaking, and I'm sweating, wet running up my back, making my top stick to me. This is the start of my cold turkey. Quinn and the me are outside, only they don't know what they're looking for. Neither of them saw what Guy destroyed. I did. If I'm meant to fix it, only I can, now.

Every part of me aches. Before this, I wouldn't moan. It wasn't in my DNA. Elena would take the piss out of me: she would say that I was willing to worry about everything else, but sickness . . . Sickness was something I liked to pretend I was impervious to.

'It's like you can't even begin to admit defeat,' she said. 'You can't accept that it's okay to just let go.' She would tease me, because I would plug on and make myself worse. I would have the flu and it would last weeks because I refused to take a sick day, to plant myself under the covers and eat soup and watch TV and stop. For me, the work was the important thing. Having a runny nose wouldn't stop me writing. If it's what you want, you persevere. 'If you had even one day off you'd get better straight away,' she would tell me, waving vitamins under my nose as she threw them into her mouth every morning. 'A little vitamin C, you might stop getting these colds, and then you wouldn't have to pretend that you felt okay all the time.'

'I feel fine,' I would say, when I didn't. Now, though, I might be admitting defeat. It's the shivers: they run through me completely, pushing me to the point where I can hear my own teeth rattling against each other at the back of my mouth, making my jaw grind in my ears; I can feel my elbows and knees on the metallic grating thing that I'm lying on; my clothes are drenched, like when I woke from the sleep pods for the first time, sodden, dripping, gasping for dry air; my head aches from the sheer pain of the vibrations coursing through me. It's all too much. I shut my eyes and try to sleep, but even now I can barely get there. The rattle of my bones gets too loud inside my ears, and I pray that they'll put the engines back on soon, just to drown it out, to maybe let me sleep again, or pretend to. They have to. And they'll run out of air if they're not careful. That's the beauty of the ship: if it doesn't move, the crew die. If it moves, the crew die. It's a perfect, closed system, just like time itself.

Quinn marches back into the ship, throws his tool – the manual version of the tool that Guy hurled into the darkness, which is now probably a satellite, far out and orbiting something somewhere – and he shouts at nobody in particular. I remember being out there with him, struggling to open the holes, looking at the damage, not having a clue what to do. Or, rather, he knew what it should have looked like, but it didn't, because Guy had made it so. In the ship, I watch as Quinn opens the comms app again.

'We can try emergency frequencies,' he says, 'they should be monitoring them, so they'll pick those up.'

'We stay here?' Emmy asks him from her vantage point in the cockpit.

'We don't move a fucking muscle.' I can't see the screen that says how much oxygen we've got left, but I remember that we were moving when Quinn died, so I know it can't be long, because he's on his penultimate day. As Guy died, so too comes the tragedy of Quinn's impending death, because this is a constant and I can't change it.

Quinn spends the rest of the day trying the emergency band, but there's no answer there either. We don't even have static on this system: if you don't make contact it's just silent, totally black. There are no frequencies to shift between, no manual toggle, no choice. There's Ground Control and then there's emergency, and there's a button toggle for each. I can't tell Quinn that it's all in vain, whichever one he chooses, but as I watch him press alternating buttons and repeat the same message over and over – 'Come in, Ground Control, anybody, this is the *Ishiguro*' – I think he already knows. My telling him wouldn't actually change a thing: he would still be there, hammering at the screen, trying to get it to suddenly understand what he wants it to do. Eventually Emmy and I go to other rooms – her to the changing room, the me to the corridors, where I walk up and down – just to get away from the noise of Quinn's tapping. From the lining I watch him as he sits in front of the screen, sitting too close, focused, intent, driven, working.

They sleep with the gravity on, no longer drifting. I wonder how long it takes for the momentum to die out here; if we're endlessly moving, no matter what we try to do. The speed we have behind us when the engines are on, I wouldn't be surprised, even with the slight reverse thrust given when we go to full-stop. I wonder how long it takes us to reach terminal velocity; and when you reach it, if nothing presses against you to stop it, do you ever stop? What is the resistance of space?

I have to creep, because suddenly I have footfalls. I leave my boots in the lining and tiptoe through the house, wary

of waking anybody. Every single noise in the ship makes me
think that somebody's watching me: that the ghosts of those
who have died are here. Guy, Wanda, Arlen: they're peering
at me as I sneak. I feel another tooth move, and I scratch at
my stubble, and I ache in every single one of my ribs. The
tool that Quinn threw is on the floor; I take it, latch it onto
my belt. Inside the changing room, I pull on a suit, and then
I head to the airlock. I shut the outer door totally silently,
or as silently as I can, and I free myself from the airlock
with a press of the button. I've tied the safety line myself:
I'm in control. I drift out onto the ship and cling on, clambering around the hull. My gut burns, telling me I shouldn't
do this. I do anyway. I haven't changed anything yet. I move
to both panels that Guy opened, open them again, and I look
at what he did. I can't see anything. There are wires inside
the panels, and some of them are attached, some of them
cut, some of them loose. I can't tell what he did. I push the
wires to one side, try to see if there's a picture on the under-
side – like underneath the hood of a car, where the oil and
water are marked with graphic representations – but there's
nothing. The wires are loose, and then I push them back,
and they look different. One of them is looser, as well; a
pink one, thick and taut like strawberry liquorice. It hangs
loose, drifting, but looks like it's meant to be a part of something, like it has a purpose. I think about plugging it in but
my gut tells me not to. It's the strongest feeling yet, from my
head, my belly, telling me to leave it as it is. I don't know
what happens if I do plug it in. I don't think I want to know.
I don't even know which plug it was attached to, so I can't
put it back, I tell myself. Anything would be futile. I shut
the panel and move to the next. Again, I don't know what
I'm looking for. I was hoping for sparks, or for scratches, or

badly cut wiring. There's nothing. Whatever Guy did, it was meant to be done, or could be easily hidden. I can't fix anything. I head back to the airlock, and the wheezing in my belly subsides, putting me back on track.

As I stand in the changing room and put the suit back where I found it, I wonder if I've missed my birthday; what happens to dates, things like that, when you're time travelling.

Quinn is first up. He hammers on the frontage of the me's bed, calls for me to get up. No answer. He shouts at me to get up.

'What about Emmy?' the me asks.

'Let her sleep,' he says. We sit in the living room together and he asks the me if I've got any ideas what Guy did. 'Anything at all?'

'Nothing,' the me says. 'Sorry.' He's going on a walk, he says, and I remind him that he shouldn't go by himself, but he ignores me.

'That's what I'll have to do,' he says. 'I need you to tell me if the computer changes. All you need to do is hit return every time I tell you? Okay?' He patches his helmet microphone into the computer headset loop, which the me puts on, and he enters the airlock. We can't hear anything inside here. Every so often the me reacts to him, presses the single key on the computer but nothing happens. Occasionally Quinn shouts into the microphone, swears, hammers on the hull. Sometimes I think we can nearly hear it. When he comes back in he's frowning, and he heads to the engines. He shuts the doors after him; the me sits and types at his computer, and stares idly at space, at everything around us. He doesn't have a clue. Half an hour later, Emmy wakes up. 'Where's Quinn?' she asks the me, and he tells her. She sits down near him, asks what he's doing.

'He wanted to find a way to turn us around. Maybe he thinks there's something in the engines that he can do.'

'Oh,' she says. I watch us not talk, and I wonder what happened between us, because I don't remember how it got like this. I just don't remember it being this bad between us. 'Are you okay?' she asks the me, and he/I turns and smiles at her.

'Fine,' he says. He shrugs, and she looks away.

'I should find Quinn,' she says, and then he reappears and waves to us, down the corridor. From here, I can see that he's acting suspiciously.

Elena never stopped asking me to pull out of the programme, even when the names of the final choices leaked to the press – nothing to do with me, or any of us, and we speculated that it was in fact a strategic thing, a calculated leak – and the press seemed firmly behind me over Terri, the other journalist. We were the last two to be picked between. Emmy, Arlen, Guy and Quinn's places were secured, and Wanda's, and it was just myself and Terri vying for that final place. They interviewed everybody else, asking them who they would rather have on the trip.

'Camaraderie is of utmost importance,' they told the crew, and asked them to answer honestly. They all told me that they picked me, even Emmy, even though we had barely spoken since our night together. She pulled me aside and said that she hoped we could move past it.

'Look,' she said, 'we got on really well, and this is just stupid. We should get over it, right? It happens all the time and other people deal with it, and I would far rather spend

months in a tin can with you than her. So, what do you say?'
She held out her hand for me to shake, but I hugged her
instead.

'I missed you,' I told her, and I meant it. She folded herself
into me and put her head on my chest. It was still too familiar,
but I didn't say anything.

That evening I told Elena that I was down to the last two.
'There's only me and this woman, and she's not much
cop.' She acted as if she wasn't listening, pushed her food
around her plate, into her mouth as I waited for her to reply.
'The rest of the crew all want me to go, and they told the
bosses that. Hopefully I'll get to go,' I said. 'Can you imagine?'
I never said it, but I hoped she'd suddenly come around, tell
me that she was proud of me, that she wanted me to go. She
would tell me that she understood, but that it hurt, that she
would miss me, that we would pick up where we left off
when I returned because I mattered to her.

'Don't go,' she said, which was all she managed before
she collapsed. I took her away from the table, put her on
her back, checked she was okay – breathing, which she was
– and then carried her to the bedroom. When she woke up
she told me that I was the worst person in the world, that
if I loved her I would never go. The argument began, and
grew. She threw something at me – a book? – and it hit my
head, next to my ear. I didn't throw anything back. She
carried on, circling the bed like I was going to pounce for
her, when all I wanted was for her to calm down.

'Don't do this,' I said to her.

'This is your fault,' she said. 'This is the worst thing that
you could ever do. You would leave me when we're so happy?
Why would you do this to us?'

Then, because I wanted to hurt her, but I had no other

weapons, nothing I could use, I told her about Emmy, and about our night in the hotel.

'This is so fucking stupid,' Quinn says. We're eating lunch – which makes me, now, in the lining, hungry, because I've been so intent on watching, so intent on seeing this through, not missing a single second (in case it's important, something that I need to pass on to a future version of me to help him complete this), and I haven't eaten a thing in a while – and trying to work out what's wrong with the ship. I could be the curtain drawing back, the reveal, dropping down from the vent and shouting about Guy's misdeeds, about the rogues and vagabonds at DARPA who decided that we were arbitrary sacrifices in the name of human endeavour; but I don't. I don't need dreams (echoes?) to tell me that that won't work, that I'll be reset before I can finish my story, wildly spouting conspiracy theories to people too terrified to listen properly. Emmy asks if Guy might not have done something, and Quinn defends him, slightly.

'He said there was a problem and he was trying to fix it,' he says, but from here I can hear the doubt in his voice.

'That's what he said,' Emmy replies. 'Doesn't mean it was true.'

'What are we going to do?' the me asks.

'There's other stuff we can work on,' Quinn says, 'but I'll need to be writing code.' He thinks for a second. 'You could go out, do the stuff outside. You've seen the panels, right? Inside them?'

'Yes,' the me says, 'once.'

'Okay. I can tell you what to do, and you can do it, right?' He's all affirmation, enforcing my self-belief. My skills are up to this, he tells me with his words. You, Cormac, are capable. He stands up, heads to the computer, pulls up schematics, shows me the wires, how they should look. 'Some of the connections seem to be severed,' he says, 'so they need to be reconnected, rejoined, but I don't know which exact ones. So you go out there, try changing them around – you know how to strip a wire? Use the solder clips to attach it to another one? – and I can try running code here while you do it. You tell me every time you've done a different wire, I work on that code.' He sees something in my face. 'Don't be nervous,' he says. 'You'll be on the safety cable, I'll get out there if you have any problems, and you won't be out there long. Hour at most.' He tells me to go and suit up, and I do, walking down the corridor slowly.

'Will he be okay?' Emmy asks, and Quinn nods. He's gone quiet. Something's wrong. I didn't see this in him before; either because I missed it, or because I wasn't here. It feels private, secretive, but I watch anyway. He follows the me, watches me dress, talks me through more of the details, and then tells me that he'll fasten the safety cable for me. He does, and it's secure; and then he says that he'll work the airlock. I remember standing there, terrified at being on my own, and Quinn telling me that I would be fine, reassuring me, totally confident; then pressing the button, and then I was gone for that second. I listen now to the sealing of the airlock door, but can't see myself sucked out, suddenly free again. I don't need to, because I remember it like it was yesterday.

I remember feeling totally alone for those first few minutes, so alone, more alone than ever before, because there was just me and the metal and the stars. I remember thinking about what happened if I cut the cord; if I let myself off, to drift, to plough onwards on my own, a one-man satellite, a moon, a comet. There's that story about the astronaut who wasn't Armstrong or Aldrin; how he spent half an hour on the dark side of the Moon, away from any communications, cut off from everybody. He said he felt alone, but that it was great. You're at one with the universe. That was what the trip was all about in the first place: achieving greatness. I could drift off and try to find God until my oxygen ran out, and then I would die, but I would be content, maybe. I remember pulling myself along the cord to the ship, moving to the navigation panels and starting the long process of unscrewing them.

In the ship, I watch as Quinn goes back to Emmy in the cabin.

'It was Cormac,' he says, 'not Guy. Guy said he was out there with him, right? And Cormac denied it, said he was in the shower, but I checked the tapes, and he was outside, just like Guy said.' We recorded everything that happened to the hull. I forgot. There was a camera on the outside of the ship, pointed behind us, recording everything, because if something physically broke, it was the easiest way of the engineers back home seeing exactly what went wrong. 'I watched the tape, and he was there. He was out there with Guy, helping Guy, just like he said. And get this: he walked again last night, while we were asleep, and he opened panels – and why the fuck would he be opening panels? What was he doing to them? I think he's . . . I think he's sabotaged us. I can't say for sure, but he's got something to do with this, with our situation.'

'Cormac wouldn't do that,' Emmy says. She has faith in me. It's warranted, I suppose. 'He wouldn't lie like that.'

'Don't defend him. He's been lying about his wife,' Quinn says, 'and that's pretty big, right? He lied about that, he might be lying about everything. What's he got to live for, now, anyway? He's unhinged.'

'He's not unhinged.'

'Oh, come on, Emmy. You know. You know him better than any of us, from the psych stuff, from being with him before.' It stings her, you can see. I didn't know that Quinn knew. Emmy must have told him. 'He's not right in the head. Why bother to lie to us? What's the point in it?'

'Don't.'

'He's sabotaged this, him and Guy. They must have done it together. He wants . . . I don't know what he wants. He wants us dead.' His chin shakes, and he balls his hands, and Emmy keeps gasping, as if the shock hits her every few seconds, as if she can't comprehend it all. Here, in the lining, I know how she feels. I didn't know that any of this happened. I didn't have a clue.

'What do we do?' she asks, seemingly having decided that he's right, swayed suddenly, persuaded.

'I don't know,' Quinn says, and then the me that's on the hull, the guilty before being proven innocent, asks Quinn over the speakers what he should do.

'The panel is open,' he says, 'and I can see the wires. Which one shall I join first?'

'Start from the left,' Quinn says. 'Let me know when it's done.' He doesn't stand by the computer; there are no tests to be run, no equations or codes to be rewritten or altered. He thinks I've already been out there once, that I already know what I'm doing. He's just buying himself time to think, time to work out how to deal with me. I already know that he won't get the chance.

I watch as they pace, as they discuss it. Emmy favours tying me up, leaving me in the storeroom – 'Nobody goes in there,' she says, and I stifle a laugh at that – but Quinn keeps his cards to his chest. I know what he's thinking before he says it, and when it's out there, he can't take it back.

'We could just shut the airlock,' he says.

'What do you mean?' Emmy asks, but she knows exactly what he means. If she pretends that she doesn't, if she plays dumb, then she can act as if the thought has never crossed her mind. *The idea was all Quinn's*, she can say, to herself, or to whatever tribunal she might still hope they get to face when they're rescued.

'We shut the outer door. It'll sever the safety cord.' He doesn't look at her as he says it. She doesn't look at him as she processes it.

'He'll die,' she says.

'Yes.'

'You think we should kill him? You think he deserves that? He's not a murderer.'

'Yes, he is. He's tried to stop us getting home, Emmy. We'll die if we don't get home. We'll drift and drift, and we'll die, because we'll run out of food or oxygen, and that'll be it. Besides,' he says, 'maybe he was the one who tampered with Wanda's suit.' It's founded on nothing, because that was an accident, but it's enough. A line can be drawn between all my actions, my guilt proven. Outside the ship, the me has completed his second-to-last connection. He tells Quinn, and Quinn tells him that it hasn't worked. 'Keep trying,' he says.

'Okay,' my voice says. 'Last one now. I'll tell you when it's done.'

'We've only got a couple of minutes,' Quinn says. 'I'm going to do it.' He stands up, walks down the corridor towards the airlock. Emmy runs after him, begging him to stop, even though I can't tell if she means it in her voice, not really.

'Yes,' I say, 'stop.' I shake. I shake, and I ache, and my gut is tired and hungry and hurting, and my head hurts, but this didn't happen. I didn't die out there. I came back in and Quinn was dead. Emmy's going to kill him. She's going to kill him, for me. To save me. I follow them down the corridor towards the airlock, not worrying how much noise I make, because they're lost already, stuck in their own world of murder and tears and the speculative insanity of Cormac Easton.

'Done,' the me outside says over the speakers.

'Doesn't work,' Quinn says. He's standing by the console outside the airlock.

'I'll come back in, then,' I say. 'You should try, maybe. I don't really know what I'm doing.' I sound disappointed. I really wanted to help save the day. Quinn doesn't say anything. He starts to key in his security code, and I watch for Emmy to make her move but she doesn't. She stays totally still, shaking, crying. He looks at her.

'This is the right thing to do,' he says, not a question, an affirmation, but she nods anyway, giving him permission. It's not her: it's me. I'm all that's left. And if I'm not, this will reset, and the next me will know, somehow. I kick open the wall and run, and in a second I'm in the hallway, charging into Quinn, my hundred-something pounds of frail, worn body thudding into his muscles, his brawn, and he would have been able to overpower me if I didn't push his head with my hand, take him so completely by surprise, slam his skull against the wall so hard that it sounds like the slamming of a door.

That's all it takes; his skull cracks, and he slides down, collapses under my pathetic weight. Against the white panelling, he leaves a red trail, a streak down to the ground. The blood starts to puddle as Emmy screams. I look at her and she takes me in, and her face looks like she's seen death, but she can't comprehend it, not properly, and then I hear the me that was outside clambering into the airlock, hear the doors start to shut, their mechanics making the whole ship rumble. I have to go, I realize, so I do, back into the walls, but Emmy doesn't see that because she's too busy staring at the now-corpse of Quinn on the floor, too busy screaming. I listen as the me takes his helmet off, asks her what's wrong before he's seen it, then sees the body and tells her that he's sorry, asks her what happened, but he's talking too fast and it almost all sounds like gibberish, like blabbering, so he does what he thinks he should, what he thinks is appropriate, and he puts his arms around her to console her but that only makes her scream louder, so he thinks she's reacting to the death and he restrains her with his arms, holds her as she beats at him, tries to fight him off, her hands leaving blood prints on his suit from where she had grabbed at Quinn to check his pulse, to see if she could save him.

'Shh,' the me says to her. 'It'll be all right. Honestly, it'll be all right.'

He takes her to the main cabin, tries to get her to sit down but she won't. She screams at him.

'How did you do that?' she asks. 'You killed him! How did you do that?'

'I didn't,' the me says. He is honest, genuine in his confusion. She takes it as a lie.

'Get away from me,' she says, 'you're a fucking murderer.' She spits it, and I'm the villain. My face is hurt and shock. I remember thinking, *She's lost it. Quinn's death was the end.* I remember thinking, *I wonder if she killed him*, because that was a natural reaction, just a quick thought, and I dismissed it, because I knew she would never be capable of it.

'We've only got an hour of life support left,' I say, because we used so much of the battery operating the airlocks, changing the suits. 'We have to start the engines.' I go and clean up the blood first, from the puddles around Quinn's head, sucking it up into a smaller liquid-hoover. *I can't imagine anything worse than blood in zero gravity*, I remember thinking. *Poor Quinn*. I press the button for the first time that trip (and she doesn't try to stop me, though from the lining I can see her flinch, as if she's considering it). It's the first time I note how much fuel is left.

'57%,' I say to her. 'We'll be turning around soon enough.' She ignores me, her eyes dismayed and reddened. 'We'll be okay,' I tell her.

'How could you do this?' she asks, but it's a rhetorical question, because – then, at that point – I don't know what it is that I've supposedly done. I remember even wondering if it wasn't her that did it, that killed Quinn, or pushed him by accident, or something. Now, remembering that, I can only feel guilty for ever having doubted her.

The me pulls Quinn's body down the corridor, clumsily (because Emmy won't help), his limbs hitting the walls, his leg dragging on the floor as if it's somehow heavier than the rest of him: which it isn't, it's just luck that it looks that way; or a better word, chance. He puts him into his bed and does the straps up.

'We should say something,' he says, which nobody did for Guy, but he's trying to be nice, trying to be considerate of Emmy's feelings. She obviously cared about him. 'Do you want to say anything?' She doesn't reply. He turns on the computer screen, the camera. 'We'll tape this, so we've got something to show when we get home.' The blunt insistence that we'll be saved, that the technology will work. Everything should have told him that this was a folly. He endeavours. 'We should say stuff about him, like we did for the others. I'll start, if it's too hard.'

'Go to hell,' Emmy tells him. He looks hurt.

'Fine,' he says. 'I'll write something.' He leaves her at the table, strapped in – where he did the straps himself, to keep her in one place, to let her calm down – and sits at the computer, starts to type. He opens a new file, and I remember this: he writes an update, talking sadly about the accidental death of Quinn. He leaves out any suspicion that Emmy might have been involved, because he can't bear to imagine that she would have anything to do with it. He thinks too highly of her.

This was my last day with any of the rest of the crew, because tomorrow he'll sedate Emmy permanently, sealing her bed, putting her in the equivalent of a coma until they get home, because she can't be trusted, because she's too far gone. I'll bet that if I read it, that last piece of writing still has something resembling hope in it. Tomorrow, that will be all but gone.

He asks Emmy if she wants to eat, but she doesn't, and when he lifts his own bar to his mouth she swipes at it, scratching his face. It's not hard enough to break the skin, but it's an attempt. She unbuckles herself, pushes off the wall towards the computer, then down the hallway. The me follows her, stuffing his meal bar into his pocket, and I mirror him as he drifts down the corridor.

'Emmy,' he says, 'why are you doing this?' She gets to one

197

of the engine room and shuts the door behind her. He doesn't try to force it open. 'What's wrong?' he asks again, as if her answer might suddenly change. She doesn't say a word, so he gives up, floats outside the door and then returns to the cabin and stares at the faces of his dead crewmates.

I always wondered if the DARPA people listened into our conversations. When we got into the training facilities, there were always faceless, personality-free rooms that we were given to stand around in, to make cups of coffee and talk about ourselves. The morning that I found out I had made the cut – over Terri, noxious Terri and her over-eager ways – was the morning that I told my future crewmates that Elena and I had argued, and that she had left me. She had taken a bag, packed it with her best clothes – the stuff she wore when she had important meetings, when she wanted to impress somebody – and left. She smashed my mobile phone, throwing it into the bath (which was empty, but a hard porcelain, and the phone screen smashed all over the plughole); she tore at my shirts when she filtered through for hers, pulling them off hangers, tearing the occasional seam; she took the car, and didn't tell me where she was going. I got a phone call – to the house phone, which barely ever rang – telling me that she was leaving me and never coming back.

'Every single thing you have done the past year tells me exactly what I need to know about you,' she stammered, 'what sort of man you are.' She sounded as if she had written this down and was reading it out. I could almost hear her mother standing behind her, egging her on. We had never seen eye to eye. 'You have proven that you're unwilling to make this work, and have betrayed my trust in the gravest way. What's done can't be undone.' I could see her mother bent over, scribbling the words onto the page. 'When you leave our home, please don't expect to come back. Don't call me.' I could see her mother calling the lawyers, telling them what an awful person I was.

When I got into the waiting room – that's what we called it – I told the rest of them about what happened.

'She'll come around,' Arlen said.

'She won't,' Guy said. 'Lovers never come back when they've gone insane. I've seen it happen.' I didn't tell them about Emmy, about that being the reason. I just said Elena couldn't deal with the trip. It was always about the trip.

'Maybe you won't get onto the final list; then you can go back to her,' Terri said. Two hours later they called us both into an office and delivered the news: that I had been chosen, and Terri was thanked for her time, reminded that she had signed non-disclosure agreements, and then told that she would receive her final pay cheque at the end of the month.

'Congratulations, Mr Easton,' they said to me, and then sent me back to the waiting room, where they then appeared with bottles of champagne. We cheered and clapped and were happy. That afternoon they did the announcement, a television press conference for the world. They introduced us one by one, said what we were going to be doing, and then we answered questions. Somebody from a tabloid asked us how our families felt about it, about us going. None of us really had very much to say. When the press conference was over I tried to call Elena, first on her mobile, then calling her mother's house. There was no answer either time. I don't know if she was watching.

I wait until night-time, when the me goes to sleep in his bed, next to all the other bodies. Emmy is still in the engine room – I listen against the door and she's snoring gently, asleep, passed out, probably. I sneak out, again, to the computer, grabbing food on the way, wolfing it down, stuffing it into my mouth, three or four of the bars, enough to make me feel sick even as I'm eating them. I look at that thing that the earlier version of me wrote, and it's cloying and tacky. I delete it, and write something else, something new; part eulogy, part tribute, part statement. It's nice. It feels like something I would do, something I would have written, at my best. It's truthful. When I'm done I press the button to send it, and I sit back and watch as it struggles to make contact. It times out, saying that it's been sent, but I can't be sure. The message could end up anywhere. It could be our last words, or it could be nowhere, floating in the ether. Or it could have stayed on the hard-drive, and it'll never be read.

I try to sleep, but I can't. An hour, maybe two, broken up over the night. I keep leaving the lining and looking at the reflection of myself, trying to see the real differences. I can feel another tooth loose, so I work it out, giving me mirrored gaps: both canines gone, the inverted vampire. I clean the ones I've got left – I forgot what it was like to have them clean – and I shower myself. The water pressure is almost so strong it hurts, burning the skin that barely coats my ribs. It washes away the sweat, though, and I realize that I barely thought about the shakes, about the tablets over the last day; watching Quinn die took all my attention.

I can't warn myself how I'll be woken up, so I'm forced to watch as Emmy gets up first, unrestrained, untied, unsedated, because the me trusts her, foolishly; trusts that she'll see sense and realize that he's not the devil she thinks he is. She rushes to the medicine cabinet and fiddles with the lock, entering the code, then pulls the door open. (My heart skips as I watch it open, a box of treasures shining yellow light on the face of the opener.) She's after a syringe, one of those mechanical injectors, and she finds one, her hands still fumbling, and slides the needle into a bottle of something viscous and transparent, like egg white in a bottle, and then turns to face me. She leaves the medicine drawer open and the contents start to drift upwards, but she doesn't care, because she's headed for my bed where the me sleeps still. She opens the door and holds onto the lip, and then waits, about to inject me, but she can't do it. Her hand is poised, ready to strike, wavering slightly even here, even this close, but she can't do anything with it. He wakes up and shouts something, sees her there, grabs her hand, and *then* she decides that she wants to do it, tenses her arm muscles and tries to jab the needle forward, aimed right at my neck. The me swings her around.

'Stop it,' he says, trying to stay calm – he's a good man, I realize, he's trying to do this right, and if I ever had any doubts about him I don't right now – but Emmy is insistent. 'I'll sedate you,' he says, and she hears it as a threat. He can't win, whatever happens, even if he doesn't quite know it yet, so he squeezes her wrist and takes the syringe as she drops it and it drifts, and he puts it into her arm because he's already got a hold of it, and he presses the booster, to inject the contents and she slumps almost immediately; either it's taken hold, or she's given up.

He straps her back into her bed, fastens the straps harder than before to make sure she stays where she is, and then starts collecting the loose medicines. When they go back into the drawers he doesn't lock it, and I decide that I'm already off the wagon, that I'm already contemplating when I can get to the pills. I would stay strong, but I know that I don't, because when I wake up next time around I'm already addicted, and my leg – I had forgotten all about my leg, which is healed, totally, has been for God knows how long – I'll think that my leg is in pain but it'll actually be the addiction. It's so easy to mistake the two.

He talks to Emmy as he straps her in.

'I'm sorry,' he says, 'for everything.' He feels guilt that he shouldn't – as if, by even coming on this trip he's somehow cursed them all, opened a well to God-knows-what, but he hasn't. He apologizes, nonetheless. 'For what happened between us, as well,' he says, 'and because you lost Quinn. He was a good guy.' He means it. This Cormac bears no ill will. He sits at the computer and writes, to keep this all in check, to make sure that, when they get home, it all makes sense to Ground Control. From here, he knows, he'll just sit tight, twiddle his thumbs. He's got an excess of food, he's got reading materials on the computers, he's got company – because Emmy will calm down, she has to, and they always got on so well – and he'll just sit it out until they start their descent, and then he'll worry about the landing when it becomes an issue. He's sure that, as soon as they're back within contact radius of home they'll be able to talk him through it. He sits in the cockpit, in the pilot's chair – Arlen's chair – and he looks at the buttons and wonders, for the first time, what it would be like to be a pilot, a childhood dream suddenly realized, one he didn't even know that he had.

When he's done fantasizing he goes to the computer and calls up his pictures, and from here I can see him, so attached to Elena still, even after this gulf of time and space, even after everything that happened.

The last time I spoke to Elena was the day before we left. From announcement to launch was only a period of days, a frantic week where we were paraded, hailed, the press barely given time to breathe. The world got to know us in one quick, brutal burst, on the covers of their magazines and the front pages of their newspapers. We were everywhere for that week, because DARPA said these things worked best if it was like reality TV.

'People get bored,' they said, 'so we put you everywhere and they'll really care. They'll care enough to follow every tiny part of your journey. They'll really want you to succeed.' We did everything we needed to – all the final health checks, all the final training – but so much of it had been covered in the preceding year, in our groups. 'We've made everything so simple that you'll barely need to think,' DARPA said. 'Press the button, get there, come back. Simple as that.' Guy was the wild card, because he had been working on the project with them for years – his entire adult life, as it turned out – and because (though we didn't know it until that last day, when something was in one of the papers about it) there was never a chance that he wasn't coming on the trip with whichever other crewmates made the cut. That final week was insane, and we barely breathed. I kept trying to call Elena every day, when I woke up, but she never answered. Then, one morning, the hotel woke me with a call in the middle of the night.

'Hello?'

'Cormac,' she said, 'it's me.' She told me that she was in Greece with her mother and her uncle, and that they weren't sure when they were coming back.

'Can you get work there?' I asked.

'I'm not sure if I want to,' she said.

'So you're never coming back?'

'Are you?' she asked, and I said that I was, of course I was. It was one trip – the trip of a lifetime, the best opportunity I'd ever have – and then I would be home, in London, and I'd work there for the rest of my life.

'I miss you,' I said.

'I miss you too,' she said.

'I'm sorry,' I said.

'No,' she replied. 'No, you're not.' She hung up the phone, and I realized that I was apologizing for Emmy, for having slept with her, breaking Elena's trust; and she thought I was apologizing for the job, for being a part of the space trip. I tried to find out the number she was calling from, call her back, but it was blocked, so I sat by the phone for the rest of the night and didn't sleep.

In the morning, Guy joked that I looked so tired I must have been up all night.

'Nervous?' he asked, and I said that I wasn't, and he laughed, and called me a liar.

It has been hours, and he does nothing, and Emmy stays asleep. I don't know how long it is because I can't see a clock, but it's hours and hours, and he's already starting to look bored. *You've got weeks to go*, I think. *We've got weeks to go.*

Emmy wakes with a cough, and I wake as well, hearing the sound of her lungs kicking in, a human alarm. The Cormac in the cabin is already there with her, holding a flask of water for her, pointing the straw towards her face. She leans forward and sips, like a reflex, then adjusts her head.

'I didn't want to have to do that,' the me says, 'but you were getting pretty crazy there.' She doesn't say anything. 'Are you feeling better?' She shakes her head.

'No,' she says, 'I'll never be better. Why did you do it? Why did you do this?'

'I didn't do anything,' he says. 'Please, I really didn't.'

'You're so different to when we met, you know? What the fuck did I ever see in you?' She's so angry, like I've never seen her. Bitter. 'Let me out of here.'

'I'm sorry I hurt you,' the me says, because he thinks this is all about him and his mistakes, and that makes her laugh so much.

'You're an arsehole,' she says. 'You're a fucking joke. I feel sick with myself for ever thinking you were a good guy.' He stands there, ashamed by what she's saying, put up, downtrodden. This is the lowest point. And then, the knife: 'No wonder your wife killed herself.' It hits him like a brick, because he had kept it all inside, buried down; not denying it, but not talking about it, not telling them that it happened. I remember the feeling, of being betrayed but not knowing by whom; and of picturing my wife hanging from the low beams of her mother's house in Greece, her feet – her toes – scraping the floor as she swung, as they tried to get her down, but the knot in the bed sheets was so tight they had to cut it, and they couldn't find the scissors when they really needed them, but it was immaterial, because she had been dead for hours. In that bedroom, the wood was old, and I imagined the beams buckled under her weight, slightly bent, to stay like that forever, her final signature, her lasting, indelible mark.

We were waiting to get onto the ship, because the press were lining themselves up and there was an order of importance, and they were all arguing about it. We were in another of the white rooms with nothing in them, and I ducked out to use the toilet, down the corridor. I borrowed a mobile phone from one of the rogue journalists wandering the halls – we had met a few times at random parties, and I remembered his first name but nothing else, not even who he wrote for – and I called the house, and her mother's house, and then remembered that I should try her brother – that he might have the number. He lived in Islington, and it wasn't hard to get his details, so I called him. He answered and assumed that I knew.

'Jesus, Cormac, I'm so sorry,' he said, crying himself, which I had never seen or even heard – his voice was so deep and coarse, and it sounded wrong coated in thick wet sobs – and it took me asking what he was sorry for for him to realize that I hadn't heard yet. He told me, laid it out in the order that they think it happened – she went to bed; she called me; she said goodbye; she told her mother she was going to sleep; she tied the bed sheets together, then to the ceiling beam; she climbed up and put her head through what shouldn't have worked as a noose, but the knot was so tight it actually didn't snap, and held; and she stepped off the edge of the bed. He told me that some of her toes looked like they were broken from where she kicked the footboard, trying to get back onto the bed, to save herself. She regretted it, but couldn't change it. What's done can't be undone.

I got off the telephone as somebody was looking for me, trying to find out where I was. We were meant to be lining up for the photo call, because it was time. We were boarding. I can't remember how long I contemplated not going for, and going instead to bury my wife, but it wasn't long. I told the reporter what had happened, told him that she would need to be honoured or something, but I don't know what he made of it. He told me that he would, and I went back to the waiting room, and from there to the gangway leading towards the lift that would take us up the length of the shuttle, and to our new home. We posed and smiled and waved, and they called us explorers and heroes, and we applauded them just as much as they applauded us.

'See you when we get home!' we said, in a joint statement where I didn't have to actually say anything, thank God.

The Cormac in the cabin is shaken, because he had blocked it out, almost, and he thought he was alone in the knowledge of what had happened. He clutches the corner of the table.

'Who told you?' he asks. 'Who knew?'

'Ground Control,' she says. 'And we all knew. We had to know. We were your crew, Cormac. Your friends.'

'How long have you known?'

'Before we even took off. You think they'd let somebody doing your psych evaluations not have that sort of information?' She looks sad for him. 'You didn't talk about it, and we weren't going to force you, but now I see that maybe we should have.' She starts crying. 'Maybe this wouldn't have happened if we did.'

'I didn't need to talk about it,' he says. 'It's okay. We had broken up.'

'Not really. You hadn't.' She softens. 'You hadn't. You wanted her back, you told me that much, and so I *know* how hurt you must have been.'

'Of course I was hurt,' he says. 'I apologized, but she wouldn't accept it.'

'So you know why she did it?'

'Because I came up here,' I say. She shakes her head.

'You're a man,' she says, 'who thinks that the world revolves around him. That what happened is because of your choices, not hers; that you can feel guilt because, how could she live without you?' She shakes her head, disappointed in me. It's a look I've never seen on her before, and it feels wrong, like it's Elena's, a gesture that I saw in my now-dead wife's face, put onto Emmy, there to punish me.

'You're wrong,' he says. 'She loved me, and I loved her.'

'She was sad before you came along, and you were a trigger,' Emmy says. 'When somebody does something like that, all they've ever needed was the trigger.' She softens again, and Cormac – the Cormac out there – changes. 'Can I come out?' she asks. 'We can talk about this more.'

'No,' Cormac says. He closes her bed and seals it, because he knows that she's lying; that she'll attack him in the night, try to get the upper hand, because she hates him and thinks he's done all these awful things.

I watch him inject her to make her sleep, then make her comfortable, unstrapping her, fastening her headrest in a secure position, then seal her bed, and then he stands back and watches as she drifts off. He brings the picture of Elena up on the screen again and stares at it, and then he tries to make contact with Ground Control, a feeble, pathetic attempt, and then he floats there, in the middle of the room, thinking that he's alone.

We climbed onto the ship and were told how the bed process would work; that Arlen would be put under first, using something hardcore to send him to sleep. Emmy would help the doctors administer it, because sometimes the body flinched at the drugs.

'It's like a coma,' the doctors said, 'but totally safe. A timed coma. We've got it so that the nanites in the drug can tell to the minute when we want you to wake up – unless they're interrupted or their schedule is changed, that is.' Arlen lay back in the bed and grinned.

'Always wondered what it'd be like to sleep with a robot,' he said, and we all laughed. The camera crew filming us laughed as well – it was all loose, documentary, fun – and only Guy suggested he say something else.

'You're sure you want that to be the last thing you say before you go under?'

'Okay. Sure. Let me try again.' Arlen hammed it up for the cameras, knowing that they would show the whole scene. It was camaraderie. 'We're going deeper into space than anybody has ever gone, and I'm going to sleep the whole way there. See you when I'm famous.' He was smiling, and his charm meant he could get away with it. 'Better?' he asked Guy.

'No,' Guy said. We all watched as Arlen went under – no countdown, just Emmy holding his shoulders, the doctors injecting him – it looked like mercury, the liquid in the hypo – and then his body bucking once before he slept. We were to be sleeping for weeks; that didn't come without a price. They did Wanda next – she flinched.

'Can't stand needles,' she said.

'Then don't look,' the doctors told her. She looked over at me instead and winced, and bit her teeth together in an almost-snarl.

'Shit,' she said as the needle slid into her neck, and I saw one of the camera crew note something down – a reminder that they would have to bleep her. Guy was next, and he didn't say anything until after the injection.

'See you on the other side,' he said. Then it was my turn. Emmy leant over close to me as she held me down.

'Are you okay?' she asked. Back then I wondered why she was so concerned about me. Could she tell that I had been crying?

'Yes,' I told her. 'I'm just thinking about Elena.'

'I know,' Emmy said.

The sleep felt like a crash: like that feeling where you can't stop it, where you're helpless for a few seconds. You can see the car coming, you can brake hard, but it's never enough, because velocity is what it is, and because physics are what they are. I remember blinking to see through the fug, because that's what it was.

I leave the lining and watch him sleep, lying in his bed, next to her. She looks dead, I think: dead and tired. Her eyelids twitch. She opens one eye. He didn't do it right: she's awake, and she looks angry, as if she's worked out what's going on. I rush for the medical kit again, to put her under before she has a chance to wake up properly, but she's already opened the door to her bed, already pushed off. She flies towards me, and I'm still fumbling with the sedation when she hits me. The syringe flies loose, tumbling away from me, and she's there first. Her hand closes on it, and I don't know what to do, because there's one weapon in this room, and she's got it. She swings it at me, totally silently – almost as if she knows how much I'm praying this doesn't wake up other Cormac – and then I lash out and grab her ankle, and manage to pull her towards me and turn her as I'm doing it. I grab her, thinking I can wrestle it out of her hands, but she pushes me backwards again. I hit the edge of the table at the worst angle: it scrapes down my back, and I can feel the skin tear, the blood start flowing. My back bends at an awful angle, and I realize that I've felt this pain before, in the twinges as I've knelt or crawled or drifted through the lining, the exact worst spot it could have hit me.

'Cormac,' she gasps, 'what happened to you?' and then we're fighting again, struggling with each other, even through my pain. She jabs me with the needle, straight into my arm, but doesn't manage to push the injector; I grab her wrist and then pull the needle out, and swing her arm around, and watch as the needle – three inches, thin, made of some new metal that can't break or split or bend, even – slides into her chest, finding a perfect space between her ribs. I press the injector, and she collapses, falls limp. She's immediately adrift. I don't know if she's asleep or dead; if I hit her heart or her lungs, maybe she's already gone. Maybe, all those times I looked at her and thought that she looked as if she was already dead . . . Maybe she was.

I shunt her body back into her bed, strap her down – in case – and then seal it. I set the timer myself, making sure, this time. I set it for years in the future. My blood, from my back, has painted the table and the wall near the computer; I wipe it up, hit the vacuums to take any excess out of the air, and then I pull myself along the floor to the changing area. I take off my top, sodden with damp red, and I throw it into the refuse, taking a fresh one from my locker. In the mirror, I try to examine the damage, the space on my lower back where it hurts, nearly at my coccyx. I have to crane my neck to see, using one hand to steady myself in case I start to drift: it's a mess of blood, the cut long and thin. I take a towel and mop away what I can, using antiseptic wipes to clean it, and then I bend again to take another look. I can see it, clear as day: a slash, a neat line. And, next to it, there are more scratches, or the scars of them; pink dashes lined up, occasionally intersecting, tens of reedy pink lines alongside my fresh new wound. It's the same injury done over and over, the same result, the same scar. I've been here before.

Everything falls into place: my gut instincts, stopping me doing things that I felt I shouldn't, like reverse déjà vu; how far I've degraded, as if I've been here for months – years, even – without medical help, living off ship's rations; and where I'm going, aimlessly here, not knowing what I'm meant to be doing. The lines on my back are notches, one for every time I've done this trip. I try to count them, but lose track at fourteen, because they're layered, or can't be seen thanks to my new fresh tear.

I've been here before, over and over and over again.

PART THREE

We shall not cease from exploration
And the end of all our exploring
Will be to arrive where we started
And know the place for the first time.
                              – T. S. Eliot, *Little Gidding*

1

We work in shifts. When he's awake, I'm asleep, or watching him sleep, or trying to sleep. The abundance of tablets helps matters, and I tell myself that I shouldn't feel guilt for taking them, because I'm helping maintain a constant timeline. My addiction is part of the cycle, because – I work out – the first time I did this I still had a broken leg, still had all that pain to deal with, and I took the pills for as long as I could. I don't know if the timeline changed when I changed it – if I did things differently, told my crewmates I was here, for example, if that broke everything, somehow. I don't suppose it matters. All that matters is that I've been here before, and that I'm back here again, living this over and over. Each time I started the cycle again I kept on taking the pills, and every time I woke up back at the start I carried my now-addiction with me. At nights, when the first version of me – the original, the best, untainted by whatever the fuck has happened to me – when he sleeps I sit at the computer and try to work out how many it's been. I want to know how long I've been doing this for. I think it's been years. I think I'm significantly older. If I were a tree, I would have rings to count. Here, I can only rely on the rate of my body's degradation, on the grey hairs I've got. How long does it take for a broken leg to heal? For those sorts of cuts I have on my body – and those clustered on my back, echoes of Emmy's last gasp – to scar the way that they have, and to heal into fresh pink puckered skin? How long for addiction to set in, real genuine addiction, thick and cloying in your blood so that you shake and shiver and sweat when deprived of your craving? How long for teeth to loosen under decay, to not be cleaned and to start freeing themselves, their bone-loss aided in part by the lack of gravity, the lack of anything to test them on, the lack of vitamins, the sporadic food, the constant periods of wake, the gritting of said teeth? How long to lose those teeth? How long to see a hairline that recedes by a full centimetre at the peaks, to reach behind and feel what might be the start of a friar's patch? To see your skin yellow under the weight-loss, to see your ribs jut forth? It's probably close to a hundred times I've done this, gone back to the start and seen how far I can get; but then, sometimes I think I've gone insane: that a number like that is a vast understatement, or maybe an overstatement. I can't tell. There are no videos, no logs. All I have is fourteen scars, and all that tells me is that I reached the point of fighting with Emmy before I put her to sleep at least thirteen times before this.

The other Cormac still sits at his computer and writes his diaries every day, because there's nothing else for him to do. I have a recollection of the boredom, but it's been replaced, sort of, turned into a feeling of calm. This is less stressful than it was when I was perpetually hiding. Now, I know where Cormac will go and what he will do, because I was there for everything that first time. It's hazy, but I've watched the start of this over and over again, and somehow . . . It's like muscle memory. You repeat something enough, it becomes an ingrained habit. You don't even think about it. I know that when he sleeps, he will sleep right through, and I can be there instead of him. I know that he doesn't keep a day/night cycle with anything resembling structure or order, which means I have to abandon mine, if I ever even came close to having one in the first place. He writes his blog entries and presses send on them all because, at this point, he still thinks he'll get home. When they reach the 51% mark, he thinks that the ship will do as it's meant to and turn around, and he'll reach Earth again as that intrepid hero-explorer, him and Emmy; and the people will congratulate him, because he survived. He's the one who saw space as it was meant to be seen: dangerous, unbridled, as wild as the mountains and seas used to be in the days when they were uncharted, when they were unmapped.

'I wonder if they'll call me an explorer,' he asks aloud. I wonder the exact same thing.

I spend the first couple of days doing nothing, because that's what the other Cormac does. He seems wilfully ignorant of the subterfuge, steadfast in his belief that he'll get home. All of this is reasonable to him. It's all acceptable, at the very least. Sometimes he looks at Emmy and thinks about opening her bed and seeing if she's better yet, if she's willing to sit down and talk, but he decides against it. Instead, he sits in the cockpit and watches out there, at the dark, or he goes to the Bubble and looks out of that, or he slides around the living area and touches everything. He's bored, and he watches the percentages every time they click down. This was when

217

the clock-watching began. 52%. It'll be tomorrow that he's crushed, that he works out he might not make it home.

Cormac watches as the numbers change, bracing himself for what he assumed was going to happen. I can't see him because he's in the cockpit, but I can remember how it felt: the disappointment. After a while he hits the button and the engines stop, and we're drifting. I'm on the floor, and I can't see through the vent I was looking through, so I move, adjust my position. He breathes, pauses, speaks to himself.

'Okay. Maybe it needs a reset,' he says, and then he hits the big button. 'Go,' he says. It does, and he watches out of the cockpit at fixed points in space – stars in the distance, the vaguest suggestion that the rest of the solar system still exists out there – but they don't move. We're still moving forward; we don't rotate. Our axis is immobile. He looks around the room, sighs. 'Come on,' he shouts. 'It's on 51%, we're going home now.' He wills it to do something it hasn't even got the slightest intention of doing. This – anything he'll attempt now – is pointless. 'Come the fuck on,' he shouts again. From behind my bars, this reminds me of nothing but a zoo: of seeing an animal, caged and boxed and limited in his scope, and desperate to try to break free but totally unable. That's the point of a cage. If you could escape, it wouldn't be a cage in the first place.

50%. Cormac has decided to press the button again. He does it almost nonchalantly, throwing his whole weight into his arm in exasperation. The ship whirs as the reverse boosters kick in, and then we drift to the ground, and the engines fall silent. He stomps around the cabin and hits the computer screen, and shouts for Ground Control to answer. He either doesn't know or doesn't care that it won't work; I can't remember which. I watch him call up Elena's picture, standing on my tiptoes to see through the right grate at an angle that'll let me see her as well.

We took that picture in Cromer, on the seafront. It was blustery, and that's why she liked it; the wind behind her, her hair loose, her skirt puffed up, and she's laughing.

After a few minutes Cormac darkens the screen and paces around the room. He eats a meal bar, even though he only had one a few hours ago. He breathes deeply. He stares at the dead faces of his crewmates, and he listens to the creaks of the ship as it gives him air, as it slows down, as I shift inside the lining trying to make myself comfortable. We've got a few days of this coming, because he – I – thought that somehow, through miracle or coincidence or something, somehow I might be rescued.

I won't be, obviously. I just want to tell him to get on with it.

He stares at the computer because he doesn't understand it. I understand it slightly more now, I think – all this time watching Quinn and Guy from the outside, being able to actually see what buttons they press, as opposed to the frantic guessing that Cormac is doing, pressing them to see what they do. He shouts at the screen as it dribbles to 49%, screams that it has to go back now or he won't make it all the way.

'This isn't fair,' he says. He sounds brattish, petulant. I pop another tablet into my mouth and wait, because soon he'll get tired – by my estimates he's on a 36-hour stretch of fake daytime, and night'll happen fairly soon. I need more of the pills (for the addiction, and the shiny new ache running through the small of my back), and more food, and a replenishment of my water. I can remember when I wrecked my leg in that first run – when Cormac will hurt his, soon, all too soon – and I can remember looking through the medicine cabinet, thinking how empty it was. There were painkillers left, but not many, so I know I can't take them all. Just some. That's okay: some is all I need.

He gets tired, starts pressing the buttons with less gusto. I'm tired too – you give me gravity and there's only so long I can stand here for. Every part of me shakes as I think about food and the pills and clean water and sleep, so I lie down, listen as he presses the buttons and mutters to himself. Eventually there's the hiss of his bed – the air being let out, the oxygen flow starting, the second hiss as it seals after he gets in. I look for him but can't see him, so I run to the hatch and open it, watching until the lights click off, one by one. It's night: I'm allowed out.

I take food bars – we're out of the popular brands now, because we ate them first, there being something comforting about them – and we're down to the curry bars, the pie bars, the goulash bars that Guy insisted we bring, all labelled by supermarkets or bad television chefs. I carry handfuls of them from the storeroom to the lining, dropping them to the floor, and I take water, extra flasks – the ones that would have belonged to Arlen and Quinn, I think – and fill them with clean water, along with filling my own. I don't know when I'll next get out.

Cormac starts the engines again, because he knows that it's pointless to not: his life support relies on them. (This is before he will do the maths that will change this, that will tell him he can stay still for longer: right now he's running on Guy's rules, where he had two days at most before charging the batteries; and it's before he finds the button on the computer to display the amount of battery charge remaining.) He wonders if, actually, the ship isn't going the right way: maybe he's got everything wrong. We drift up and float again as he scours through the maps on the systems, calling screens up in the Bubble, getting courses plotted and matched. It takes him most of the day to work out how to use the systems, because they weren't a part of his training, but when he does he's quite nimble with them. He rotates the map to see if the overlays fit – it's not an exact science, because stars go dark, he knows, and because nothing is as pixel-perfect as the computer suggests – but if he can find Orion he can find almost everything else. He sighs as he does everything, because this feels futile, even at this point. All of his friends are dead. There's nobody waiting for him back home. He's Ground Control's perfect candidate: he's alone, and he no longer cares if he lives or dies, not really.

He hasn't told himself that, yet. He's got a while to go before he reaches that decision. Tonight, as he sleeps – forcing himself to, knowing that he has to or he'll lose it totally, and that it relies on him to get himself home, and Emmy, don't forget her, she's still alive – tonight, I decide that I'm going to watch the launch. We watched it when we first got up into space, after dealing with Arlen's body, but I didn't really see it. I told myself I would get to it another time. For some reason I never did. My plan was to address it when I got home, maybe edit it into something, splice some interviews and soundbytes into it . . . That will never happen. I find the file on the hard drive and boot it up, and I make the screen as big as I can. I want sound, I decide, so I need to keep the earlier version of me asleep.

I open his bed as quietly as I can and then take the same
sedation kit that I watched him use on Emmy, and I draw
a shot into a fresh needle and slide it into his arm. He
shoots awake as I press the button, and his eyes are only
open for a second, not even long enough that he'll remember
this, the dose strong enough to keep him down for hours
and hours. I make the screen large and turn the volume
up, and I watch the video. There's no commentary; it's the
footage taken from the cameras fixed to the side of the
ship, rigidly pressed against the body of the craft. The
countdown is on there: it was played loudly to the crowd
below over huge speakers, like New Year's Eve celebrations,
and it counts from twenty, waiting for the ball to drop. As
it hits one the noise of the crowd cheering swells, and is
replaced by a rumble of the engines. They're unnatural, the
most unnatural noise ever made, the loudest grind and
churn of technology, designed to do things that have never
been possible before. The flame spits from them, and then
the smoke. It looks for a second like it's billowing underneath the craft, like the craft isn't going anywhere, and
then it does. It pushes away from the ground, and everything
– the launch-pad, the crowds and crowds of people, thousands of them, like at a festival or something – everything
disappears as quickly as it can, spiralling into miniature.
The smoke continues until I can see the coastline as a crack,
and then the coast itself. The launch was designed to be
faster than man had ever travelled, to get past the gravi-
tational pull of the Earth with the minimum of fuss. It
manages it. The East Coast of the US is a smirk for a
second, then a grin, then every detail is there, and it's like
those pictures they showed us in school, or on those old
BBC identification cards, the Earth as a perfect sphere of

green and sand-colour and blue and then clouds, and then space behind like a black halo. I watch as it pushes further and further away, until it's a marble, and then it's only the size of the Moon from my back garden, and then it's almost nothing. I watch this all, and I write down exactly what I can see, and then when it stops – as we're in the darkness of space, filming nothing but the hull, the occasional sputter of the engines – I start again from the beginning.

When I've finished writing, I press Send on the entry. The earlier version of me will never know.

It's the most intense déjà vu, watching yourself doing what you've already done; less like seeing a recording, and more like catching a glimpse of yourself in a mirror that you didn't know was there, seeing that flash of your limbs, instantly recognizable, but you still wonder if it's a ghost, an intruder, somebody spying on you. With all the other versions of me, it's worse still: like a mirror in front of a mirror, hundreds of your hands flashing around, even though you can only see the ones in the here and now with any clarity, only your body itself and the initial reflection. Everything else is background, mountains beyond mountains stretching into the distance. Watching Cormac doing what he's doing puts everything that I am into context. He calls up that damn picture of Elena so often, stares at it, weeps – those early days, when he was weeping for himself, not actually for her, but because he felt so guilty, and I just want to say, You should see how I feel, because I was here when it all went, I made this what it is. You want to talk about guilt? Try aiding in the deaths of at least a few of your crew.

When I try to work out why I had to do that my head hurts. When Cormac sleeps I read entries on the ship's computers, in the encyclopedias and textbooks, looking up entries on time travel, reading about it in fiction – books, movies – and trying to equate the examples to my own situation. Everything points to this being a paradox: I was on the ship when these things all happened, and they happened because I was here, which means I was always here twice. When I break the paradox, it resets: like, when you have a cut and you pull the scab off, you reset the wound, put it back to zero, because you need that scab to stop from being infected. Every other version of me is the scab being knocked off by something or other, and the body resets itself. You need to heal, it says, so it makes a new scab. I'm older, I know that: if I was a betting man I might say years. Two years. Maybe three. So, for three years, this body – which is time, in this example – has been trying to heal itself, and I've been the shitty, flawed little scab that keeps catching on kitchen surfaces and shirt sleeves. Time fixes itself, but my body is staying the same. You stick your hand into a fire once, you learn not to do it again. My body – or my mind, or whatever bridges the two – has been learning, I think. Every time I do something over and over I learn not to do it again. I can't remember it, but that doesn't matter. Maybe part of the key to time fixing itself is that the me that's here can't remember being here. Maybe my journey – ha! – is part of what has to happen.

I still don't know how I get out of the other side. I know that I can't go on like this. I'd go mad, if I could remember the other times. Or maybe I already am?

I lose another tooth as I'm eating: I pull the bar away, the taste of coronation chicken in my mouth still, mixed with blood, and the tooth is embedded in the soft paste. I swear quietly, pull the tooth out. It's black and sore, like bruised fruit around the root, and I feel the hole it's left – front and centre, top row right – running my tongue into it, poking around. I put the tooth in my pocket and strap myself to the floor, to try and sleep, because I'm so tired constantly now, trying to match Cormac's hours. He's been doing this for far, far less time than I have, and his stamina is enviable. As I drift off I think about how much the body can fall apart before it dies. I worry every single tooth in my mouth, and most of them seem to shift as I poke them. How long can you go without cleaning your teeth, without seeing a dentist? How did they used to survive in the days before toothpaste and dentists? I wake up and feel another tooth loose in my mouth, swirling in blood and saliva, and keep my mouth shut. I pull it out gently, slide it into my pocket and close it, trapping it with its friend.

I spend the rest of the night reading about famous explorers: every single explorer who did anything worth their salt, who found something or went somewhere just for the sake of it. I read about their exploits and their adventures – even those who we know next to nothing about – and they're still remembered, still written about. What they did is sometimes lost – they tried to reach somewhere; they disappeared, searching the seas and were never found; they went into jungles looking for lost cities of gold and never came back – but they're remembered. They fought trials and tribulations, fought nature and chaos, and diseases – scurvy, insanity, malaria, frostbite. They fought all of those things, and they persevered.

Guy always said that we only did this because we wanted to see something that nobody else had ever seen, and because we wanted our names to go down in history. We'll get that, even if it's as the long-disappeared crew of the *Ishiguro*: the *Marie Celeste* of the mid-21st century.

He can't surprise me: not with the things he does, because I remember them. Every moment is a recollection, a brief, tiny memory slipping in. The way he does things, though. They're nothing like I remember. He seems angry, hitting the buttons on the computer, thudding away as if it's the thing that has wronged him. He swears under his breath, and he keeps talking about everything that's happened. They say that, in quiet solitude, people are inclined to talk to themselves, to work things out that way. I have been alone – surrounded by others, but still – for so long now, and I haven't lost it. If you count all the times that I've done this, my loneliness can be measured in years. Compared to Cormac, my loneliness is extravagant.

I don't even feel like we're the same person. We have the same face, sure: his is somehow more defined, having more clarity to it, his stubble manicured, his hair kempt. From here, he almost looks like *he* could have been the leading man, not Quinn; compared to me, he's an Adonis. We have the same face, but his is all gritted teeth, hard and firm and determined. Mine has become loose and tired. Where it used to have definition, mine has dropped at the jowls even through the weight that I've lost. His teeth are perfect, or as perfect as a childhood without orthodontics can give him; neat slides of blunt white knives. Mine . . . I look punched. I look wrecked. He is tense and angry, and when he talks to Elena – which he does, calling her picture up, chatting to her, telling her how sorry he is – he sounds weak. He queues up the videos that we sent home, copies them to a playlist and sets it going, and watches as we get onto the craft in the first video, and then get knocked off, one by one. Each subsequent loss makes him wrench at his hair – which is fuller than mine, closer to the front, his widow's peak less strict – and he runs his hand through it, pulling it into shapes. His has grown since he stepped onto the ship, but mine is somehow static, or shorter, or delayed. We're brothers, not twins, a year or two between us; the same parents, but different genes.

And he's dull. Watching him do the same things over and over is mind-numbing. I have spent so long watching other people, struggling to get past the fact that I can't speak to them – that I can't go and hold them or shout at them or argue with them – that now, as he does nothing, and I have no desire to interact with him at all, it's more frustrating. It's brutal.

I send another message home as Cormac sleeps. I spill it all. I tell them what's happened, in case they ever come to get us, open the door and find us stuck here in some crazy perpetual loop, enacting the same thing over and over. I tell them what happened to me, and I write to them about Cormac.

He's so boring. Maybe worse? Maybe even worse than nothing? He's moping and tired, and the way that he looks at those pictures, over and over? I remember watching videos of the crew from the first time around: I can't wait until he gets onto that. He will do it out of boredom, and I want to grab him and tell him that the boredom he feels is nothing. Try watching it, I want to say. Try watching boredom.

I feel angry at him, at the pictures he stares at, the constant mourning he's undertaking. I think I'm not mourning Elena any more. Like, maybe mourning is a chemical reaction, and I'm past it, time having done its job. I think about her and she's like a ghost, you know? Like a reflection. She can be erased, because she seems like somebody who's barely real. When I picture her in my mind, she seems different to how she looks in his picture. In that picture she looks happy.

I don't know what happens at the end of this. I don't know if this resets, or it ends and then it's actually over, or what. I don't know. I can't possibly know. I've been here before, and I keep thinking of this as being like a circuit. Like, maybe I haven't been able to close the circuit? You think about a current: it needs to reach point b from point a. What if all the other times I've been here, I've failed? Maybe this time I have to complete the circuit. That makes sense, right? You land on the snake and get sent back, and you desperately try to roll a six to get to a ladder and claw your way out? Maybe this is the time I roll double sixes, snake eyes.

I send the file, and then regret it. Because, if they are still receiving these, they'll think that I've got Space Madness, and that'll be my legacy. The thought of that alone makes me laugh, and I have to bite my lip to stop from waking the sleeping Cormac.

He bangs the dials at the front of the ship and swears at them again, and then he sees it, on that screen: I had almost forgotten. 250480, it reads, that chain of numbers and nothing more, and the beep from the systems, and the little red light.

'What?' he asks the air, and doesn't get an answer. He sits in the chair and finger-taps the screen, using his nail to make a thin sound that I can't hear from here, but I remember. He reads the number aloud and then presses buttons to try and make sense of it. Within minutes, the screens are covered in PDFs of the manual, everything you could possibly want to know about the operating functions of the ship laid out for you, exposed. He searches the indices but nothing, then does a full text search, but nothing; so he looks for warning messages, and spends the next few hours of his life comparing the few hundred plausible warning messages that the system can throw up with the one on the screen. They're nothing alike. A real warning message will have a key, and will darken the screen, and will beep, this constant tinny recurrence that sticks until the problem is fixed. This time, when the beeping starts – an hour after the message appears – it's a drone, a thin whine like a dog feeling sorry for itself. 'What the hell?' Cormac asks, hitting the speakers to see if the noise will stop. He sits back and looks at the screen, at his depleting fuel gauge, and he knows that they can't be entirely coincidental. Coincidence doesn't exist. When your body is ill – symptoms – they're related, because everything in a body is related. Everything in this ship is related, tied together with wires instead of muscles, but still. You pull a wire, something else is going to stop working. We didn't turn around, even though that's what we were programmed to do, and then this message and this noise . . . Well, they *must* be related. It's a fault.

Only I know that it isn't a fault, that we were never meant to turn around. I know everything, because here, in the lining, I am almost omnipotent. I have seen things I shouldn't have seen, and I *know*. The ship wasn't meant to turn around: we were meant to carry on into nothingness, drifting into space, going – yes – further than any man had ever gone before, but with no chance of return or reprieve. You follow coincidence to its natural conclusion, that message isn't a fault, or a chance warning. We were meant to see it. It was meant for us. I look at the string of numbers, straining to see them with my eyesight how it is, but able to read them because I

229

can remember them so clearly, so indelibly printed onto the back of my eyelids, or somewhere deep inside my brain as they are. I can remember them, and I laugh at their purpose, and I slip off and fantasize – not dream – because this is the lining, and I am still alone, and nothing can change that.

When he's asleep I go and look at what he has looked at; and I look further. I look past the computers and the screens at out there, at space. The stars are gone. It's pitch black out there, total darkness. Nothingness.

Whatever the number is, it is this. This is it. It is nothing.

2

Here is what might have been.

The first bed to hiss open stays shut until it's meant to open, because there is no hand of a stray Cormac to open it, to yank it wide in a desperate act of self-preservation. Arlen steps out, dripping wet, groggy, sweat all over him, running down his beard. He dries himself and turns the ship on, lighting the rooms, and then starts running diagnostic programs. He sings to himself, because that's the sort of person that Arlen was: he sang a lot. He makes sure that the ship is safe for the rest of us, and then greets us as our beds open and we all drift out. He steadies us until we get to the shower, and then he leaves us as we say hello to each other, laugh at the fact we're all in our underwear, all soaking wet. I stand next to Emmy and we don't really look at each other, because there's bad blood there, still – and because she knows about Elena. She knows how much I loved her, how much I wanted to make it work with her. She'll say something at some point, but now is not the time.

When we're showered and dressed – in our identical

jumpsuits, slightly different colours on the badges like some prototypical sci-fi TV show – we each start our jobs, checking we've got everything we need. Guy runs more diagnostics; Quinn sits in the cockpit, reads all the readouts and checks they're fine; Wanda resets the beds, setting the water to drain, starting their cleaning cycle; Emmy feels our pulses, one by one, and takes our blood pressures; and I sit at the computer and boot it up, and start writing something, my first entry. *We've just woken up*, I type, *and it feels amazing.* I decide to leave Elena out of this, because I've got a job to do, and it's important that I do it. Elena will always be a part of me, but she's gone, and this is now. It's important – and that's not to demean her, God no, but this is important for humanity. I have to carry on. I have to be strong.

We gather for the broadcast and greet home, and tell them what it's like. It's televised, beamed to hundreds of countries. Arlen does most of the talking, because he's the elder statesman, with his beard and his vitality and his healthy heart. He jokes about the rest of us, says that we're still finding our feet, and then he drifts upwards, out of shot. It's a gag, but we all think it works, that it'll play well back home. Who are the audience? It's the kids. It's the children, cross-legged on the floor in front of their TV sets, smiling at us, putting our faces on their walls. When the broadcast is done we all gather and chat, and eat our first meal on the ship, processed bars still, Big Macs and Quarter Pounders and McRibs, but we revel in how they taste, because they're an experience that we're having independent of everybody else in the world. I say that, and Quinn asks if we can even say that up here. Can we even say in the whole world when we're no longer there? he asks, and we ponder it, because he has a point. In the universe? I ask, tentatively, as we agree that it's better, for the best. We're part of something bigger.

We do our jobs. Wanda goes on a walk with some of the friends she's made amongst her crewmates, and she never feels guilt. She's constantly happy, so awed at being in space when she's still so young. Who gets this opportunity? she asks, and we say, Well, you do. You deserve it. She blushes. She walks outside the ship and finds the rush of it incredible, and we all want our turn. Next time we stop, Guy says, the rest of you can try. Guy is hard and quiet, but we trust him, because he knows more about how this all works than the rest of us. We listen to him when he tells us what to do, and we do our jobs. We write and speak to home, and they send messages back, and everything is amazing. One day, Emmy sits me down. We should talk, she says, and she asks me about Elena, lets me know that she's aware what happened. You can talk to me, she says; just because of what happened between us doesn't mean we're not friends. So I tell her everything: about how it happened, why it happened. I tell her about my guilt and she listens to me, and I weep into her shoulder and watch as my tears, which are droplets on my cheek, thick and salty, drift away from my face and into the air to be sucked up by the vacuum pumps in the air filtration system.

We gather around to watch the fuel tick from 52% to 51%, and when it does the ship hums and grinds, and we watch as we turn and start heading back home. We cheer when it does it, because we've reached the peak, the furthest point ever. We've seen space. We shoot a pod from the ship, a collection of flags of all the countries united in this project, and it unfurls, and there's the money shot: one giant, unified flag, not fluttering apart from in our wake, square and blunt against the nothingness of space, and it flits off as we move, there for eternity, to drift.

We land in the sea, the Atlantic, the coast of Ireland. It wasn't expected, but was nearly impossible to predict. We knew it would be a water landing; that was part of Arlen's training. We would be coming in so hot we had no other choice. The camera crews sprint to catch us as we disembark, the craft steaming in the water as the door hisses open and we wave, one by one. They cheer our names. Quinn and Emmy are together, and we all know about it, but we're happy for them. Quinn asks if I care; he didn't want it to upset me, because of Elena. I have been open with them all. I'm fine, I told him. They do articles and interviews in glossy magazines, holding hands, talking about the future, about kids, a wedding. I do interviews that are more serious. I write my final article, then get a book deal, high six figures, and it's an easy write. There's a chapter on Elena, on the circumstances heading into the trip, because I argued blind that she was key to my mindset, that she was totally important. Without her in there, there was no book. The publisher liked it. Human tragedy sells. It gave the book a personal touch. I don't win the Pulitzer, but who cares, right? Instead I keep writing, and I write a novel, a pulpy, sci-fi thing about a man who is trapped in a perpetual loop, a time loop, like so many other sci-fi stories wrenched from the back of magazines – there are no original ideas, not any more – but this one is more human, or trying to be. I write that and it sells pretty well, and they turn it into a movie and they cast it, and the Cormac isn't the star and it makes a bit of money and I'm set, because I invest, and I meet a woman, but she looks just like Elena sometimes, and in the light she looks like Emmy, and I sometimes confuse her with them, because her name is Emily, and it's so easy to get these things confused.

When I die, my obituary calls me a writer and an explorer. That's all I ever wanted, I think.

My fantasies always involve other women; never Elena. I can't picture her there when I really think about getting home, because she's gone, and I killed her – or, near as – and nothing I can dream of can change that, not really.

3

The beeping stops in the cabin, and that's enough to wake me, just the cessation of that noise. He's asleep, so I sneak out. How quickly you collapse: he's stopped shaving, stopped caring. I don't remember showering this little. When there were people on the ship, I had one a day. He hasn't, not since Emmy was put away. I'll bet he stinks. I know I do.

I shower myself, and shit, and shave. I decide that, even though I'm falling apart, I can do it with dignity. He doesn't know how good he's got it. I eat, and take the pills, which I barely notice now, and I sit at the computer and know what's going to be there, because I'm already thinking it. He's still writing the blog entries, Cormac; he's charting what he's done that day, his thoughts. They're not worth reading, because he's so naive, so clueless.

Instead, I try to work out how this ends. I shut my eyes and try to picture that final scene of my life, as I drifted into space. I remember feeling like somebody was holding me: maybe that was me? Maybe the me now saves the me then? Maybe I tried but failed? I should be more diligent. Maybe

I'm meant to save him, and maybe there'll be a DARPA-funded craft only a few hundred klicks back, and maybe they'll grab him and take him home and patch him up and maybe give him his life back.

I know that they won't. Which means, the best I can hope for is to stop me coming back here again. Because this – reliving these memories, this pain, this confusion – it's not something that I would wish on my worst enemy.

I watch Cormac open a bottle of champagne, and I watch as the froth dances around the cabin, and he floats with a straw and hoovers it up, giggling, the bubbles and alcohol going to his head. He's drunk within seconds. I remember this. He goes to the computer and starts hammering the buttons, and he messages home, even though all he gets is static.

'I miss her,' he says into the microphone, 'and I want to come home, because I'm so alone and this is so unfair, and this is no way to die. It's going to take so long, still. I can't take this long.' I remember this. He tells the computer that he's going to end it, and he takes a thin shard of plastic from the medicine box and holds it against his wrists. He's still broadcasting to the static. 'You can all see it,' he says. 'You can all see how much pain I'm in, right? Because they're all dead, every single one of them. Elena!' It's a cry. From here, if it didn't sting, I'd almost think it was pathetic. He can't go through with it, because he's too weak. There's nothing there: the ability to kill himself is wholly absent from him. He cries instead, and drops everything, and cleans up after himself, and then he drunkenly tries to sort out the ship's course, hammering the keys, opening software he doesn't understand. I remember all of this. When he finally gives up it's to go to bed: he slides into the open-front coffin and shuts his eyes, and I watch until he stops murmuring, then sneak out of the lining. At the computer I can see that his hammering has been useless, ineffectual. He doesn't know that. Tomorrow, he'll see that the fuel is rapidly burning itself out, and he'll think it's because of something that he did.

I inject him with the final dose of sedative and watch him slump when I put gravity back on. I suit up, tie myself a security line, take the spare tool with me. I cling to the outside of the ship, and I open the panel that controls the engines and stare at the wires. I don't know what I'm doing, but I grab a thin blue wire and pull at it. It feels like enough. I know that when I go inside and start the engines again, the fuel will be burning faster; that the blue wire somehow controls the accelerant, or the speed with which the fuel is fed into the engines, and that the ship will gradually get faster and burn more and more of it as it goes.

I stay outside and watch space until the air in the capsule starts to run out. It's still calm.

He notices that it's going down faster than it ought to, that the fuel supply is ticking quickly. He watches out of the Bubble at the nothing, and he tries to discover what's making it happen.

'Are we going faster?' he asks aloud, which we are, of course, because that's how the fuel is going so quickly. 'Holy shit.' He keeps reading the manuals over and over, and searching the database, trying to find anything that can point the way for him. I feel sorry for him, because I remember how this felt, and now know why it's happened. He sits and watches the numbers as they tick over, and he panics when the numbers and the beeping starts. It doesn't herald the change in fuel content, but it seems related. Coincidence, he will start to fathom. He writes something, and leaves it on the screen, unfinished, it seems. It's the first piece he hasn't bothered to send.

That night, as he sleeps, I leave the lining to read it. It's normal: an outpouring of emotions, self-pitying and terrifying to read. It's my voice, but nothing like I remember it.

I'm trying to keep myself stable, and constant, and normal, but I've been here so long I can't even remember what that feels like. In the daytime, I treat everything like I should: I keep my spirits up, and I look out of the Bubble, and I wonder where the stars have gone; and I try to fix this, to turn the ship around, but I know it's all useless. I'm so far out there will be no getting home: maybe I could make it to the Moon before I choked and died from lack of oxygen, from the power giving way, from the fuel running out, but then, what's the point? They'll see something in their telescopes and find me months after I've died, drifting and rotting and boneless. What will a lack of oxygen do to the body? Will it preserve it? Will it make everything worse?

Maybe I'm better to be out here, alone, and drifting. Maybe I'm better off dying when my time comes. They'll remember me at home, just like Guy said that they would. They'll remember us all. I try to stay chipper in the days, because otherwise I should just end it all, here and now. But at night, before I sleep, it sounds like the ship is creaking, and it feels like I'm being watched, and the watching eyes are just thinking, End it, Cormac. End it.

He's all talk.

I'd forgotten about being actually alone. For the last – how long has it been? – I've had the rest of the crew, and Cormac, all doing things I didn't necessarily see the first time around, managing to surprise me, to confuse me. I've been alone but never lonely, not really. Now I am. Cormac isn't real company. I know what he's doing, just as the left arm knows where the right is. He doesn't do what I want when I want. He sits at the computer and mopes, and watches the videos over and over. He focuses on that video of Emmy, talking to him, addressing him like they were strangers.

'I did my training in Brisbane and Sydney,' she says, to the camera, cool and delivered like we were taught during our training, preparing us for the media interviews we did before we left. They told us that they would book us more for when we returned, fill our calendars, put that training to good use. She reels it off to camera like she would for anybody, but Cormac reads it as something for him, personal insight. She's repeated her story thousands of times before, in every interview – press or job – that she's ever done. Cormac is blind to it; blind to her.

He switches all the lights off, all over the ship. Everything, room by room, goes dark, apart from the main cabin, lit by the neon coming from the computer screens and HUDs. He sits in Quinn's chair and pretends to be pilot, but I have to strain to see him, even more now it's so dark; and he talks himself through rescue attempts, speaking them aloud, reciting them. This much trauma – to have your wife die, then to see your friends die, one by one, not knowing that (you) Guy was to blame for it all, or near as damn it – this much trauma can only fuck with you. I thought I was totally holding it together. I thought – hindsight being a wonderful thing – that I was an exemplary example of a stranded

240

astronaut. If they managed to retrieve the black box, it would stand testament to my skills and mental fortitude.

We both watch the numbers on the screen, although I can barely see them from here – a fuzz of red faux-LED, where the distinct shapes – 1s, 4s – make sense, but the rest require fathoming. We're on 39% fuel, 94% piezoelectric. Nobody can ever claim to having felt déjà vu until they watched the same thing, the exact same thing, for the second time in their life, waiting for the exact same moment where the numbers tick down, 39 to 38. Cormac watches and waits, and it finally happens. He doesn't look satisfied, or dismayed; he just looks blank. He opens a file on an adjacent screen, types something, brings up a stopwatch and sets it off; and he watches the numbers fly on that screen as well. He just sits and counts. I decide to sleep, so I strap myself down further towards the back of the ship – in case he hears me, if I snore, or cough, or anything. I dream about myself in space, the way it ended, spinning, alone, everything exploding, both the ship and myself, because that's what happened in the pressure of that vacuum; and I dream of the thick blackness that engulfed me. In the dream, it swallows me over and over.

I wake shaking, sweating. I take another painkiller, dry swallowing it, gulping it down with saliva from my mouth, and I lie back and put my hand on my heart, because it's racing, thudding like it wants to come out of my chest. Through my paltry flesh, it feels like it's going to split my ribs.

'Please,' I say, because I don't want to die, not now. 'Please.' Cormac is asleep, finally; draped over the captain's chair, head lolled to the side. I leave the lining, still holding my chest, wrapping my right arm across to my left as if it will hold my body together. I don't know what's happening, but

I pull myself to the medicine cabinet, open it as quietly as I can, and it isn't until I'm standing over it, using my other arm to stop the contents drifting everywhere, that I realize the pain has gone, that I was just dreaming. I'm alive, still, and my heart is racing, but I'm fine.

Who am I kidding? I'm not fine.

In the bathroom, as Cormac's head lolls backwards in the cockpit, I examine myself again. Another tooth, but that's to be expected. I crick both my knees, having the room to extend, and listen as the bone in them grinds against itself. They told us that the cartilage would be the first thing to go. It's a wonder I'm not in more pain. (Then I remember the painkillers, strong enough to dope a horse, and I'm no horse.) I look at the scar on my leg, the others on my back, and I wonder how long the bone in my leg took to heal here, where bones don't work the way they should, where the body isn't right? If I had to put pressure on it for any real amount of time, sans self-medication, would it hurt? Would it even work properly? I try to feel the bone through my skin, and it seems fine: but I can't believe that it is.

I'm a fucking disaster. I don't have any chance of getting home, no chance of putting right any of the shit that went wrong, no chance of doing anything to save myself. I'm expendable. Cormac out there, he's the important thing. If I can get the circuit complete, maybe he'll wake up and won't have to do this again. Or, maybe he won't wake up at all.

That's the first time I realize what I think I have to do: to save Cormac, I have to kill myself – this later version of me.

Cormac is angry, furious, even. He screams at the computers, which will never answer back.

'Why is the fuel going down quickly? This is going faster than it should.' He finds our speed and writes it down, and then searches, and he can't be sure, but he thinks it's faster than it should be. It is. I know about Guy's tampering, now; about trying to make it easier on us. In some ways, maybe we should have been grateful – or maybe I should have been, because I was all that was left. *Am* all that is left.

I'm having trouble with my tenses, sometimes. Is this now or then? It's so easy to get them confused at times like this.

In the movie of this, assuming that anybody's still watching, that anybody has stayed in their seats and dug in for more popcorn, this is the scene where I pace up and down a room, working through ideas, dismissing them or scrawling them on a giant blackboard. In reality, I lie down in the lining with my pen and paper and make tiny, almost illegible notes about nothing. I can't change anything, because every time I do – or have, previous versions of me – everything resets, back to the point where, what, we entered hypersleep? We hit warp? To that point I can't change it. I wonder if the loop ends when Cormac's life does. Will I just wake up back at the start – or, another version of me – and have to do this over and over again, forever, until my body is so crippled that I can't even open that door and kill Arlen at the beginning, so the loop resets as soon as it starts, and that's it, hell, for me, forever? Maybe that's the answer: this is hell. When I die, I start again, looping, somehow back alive, my body broken but going again. Maybe I'll do this until I get into that loop, stuck in agony and going round and round, dying over and over and over again, the pain and the torment and the loop, and nothing else until the end of time.

Fuck.

Cormac has managed to work out how long it is between percentage points, which means he's made a spreadsheet of sorts, telling him how long he's got left. It won't stay like that: something happens, and the fuel goes down faster. For now, at least, he's got it down pat. He sits and counts down from ten using the stopwatch app until the numbers roll over.

'Three . . . Two . . . One . . .' He's perfectly on. The fuel counter drips down to 33%. It'll be about a week until it accelerates. What are we going to do with all that time?

The only thing stopping me from killing myself is the knowledge that I'll probably wake up with my throat slit on the floor of the ship, and I'll keep dying until I manage to, somehow, heal, and then I'll keep reliving that pain, that agony, for the foreseeable. It's got to be better to see this through. It has to be.

4

He sleeps so much. He sleeps, and then he wakes up and writes his fucking blog entries, and he reads the manuals for the ship cover to cover, the stuff that only Guy read. He searches on the computer for the meanings to some of the phrases, the equations, and he nods as if he understands them. He doesn't. He's fucking clueless, spiralling along like a patsy. He goes to the Bubble and he calls up overlays, and he makes notes, and in his blog entries he writes about the things that he's seen, because if they do recover the broadcasts – they should reach Earth eventually, he knows, though they might be scrambled, and they might be late (and I know now, given DARPA's intentions for us on this flight, they might be conveniently ignored, or buried, because who wants those ramblings becoming public? They aren't heroic, aren't intrepid, aren't anything but one man and his head) – because if they do recover them, they'll be the last things he'll have ever written. In his delusions, he writes that he thinks they might be his own eulogy.

Who knows? I wanted to go for the Pulitzer, for a work of journalism that broke boundaries, that told humanity something new. Maybe, through these dying thoughts, I'll have achieved that.

He speaks about things he knows nothing about, inserting the names of galaxies and nebulae and words of description that mean nothing to him, flowery language to somehow offer the punctuation of meaning, to imply knowledge that he doesn't have. If Emmy were awake she would tell me that I was being narcissistic. She would point out that he's me, and that I did all of this, and that I'm only seeing it this way now because I'm on the outside, because I can appreciate it for what it actually is. I would argue with her, and tell her that even first time round I knew this was fucking pathetic. Everybody needs an antagonist, I would say, and he is mine.

'See? Classic narcissist,' she would reply.

After days and days of sleep, I wake up when he presses the button and we stop. I almost shout, because I fall a foot or so, the straps slackening, and my back hits the floor, the exact same spot where it was cut, where it's scabbed over. I already ache constantly: this is just another complaint. I try to not make noise, but I barely care. I don't think he would notice if I did. He puts on that video of Emmy again, and he watches it on one screen. On the other he's got his pictures of Elena, and he picks the one of her taken in Cromer, and zooms in, and he weeps. He watches them both and he sits there feeling guilty and he cries for himself. If you could only see yourself, I think, and that makes me laugh, because it was entirely accidental. Jesus Christ, Cormac. Pull yourself together.

With the lights off, it's harder to keep track of him. I can see his shape in the cockpit and the lounge, but when he's in the hallways he's a ghost. He can see better than I can, I guess; and he's got a little torch on his suit, the kind they have on

246

life jackets, so I can see that when he shines it. He finds the food he wants: when I leave the lining, I'm left grabbing whatever bars I can find first, fumbling in the dark and trying to stay silent. Somehow, despite his self-pity and mourning, he's the alpha male, and I'm left scrabbling for his scraps.

We spend two days there. Two full days, doing nothing, watching as the numbers on the piezoelectric counter tumble, as the air starts to thin. His shitty calculations are based on him being the only person who needs to breathe, and here in the lining, at the back of the vacuum pumps and air-dispensers, I'm suffering. I feel light-headed, and spend much of those days lying down. First time around, it felt – I remember it feeling – almost like an adventure. I remember trying to keep my spirits up, or, at least, that's how I wrote the blogs. I read them now and they're awful, mournful, dark as anything. He's suffering and I hate him for it. He should have just killed himself. He should have had the nerve to end it like a man, in the bathroom, in the shower, a knife into his neck or his wrist, or put the gravity on and use the safety cord, tied off around something. I see him contemplate it, when he looks at the pictures of Elena: he looks at them and at something that he's written, a file on the computers about her that I can only read a sentence of before I have to stop, because it's still so fresh. Did I think I wasn't still in mourning? I'll *always* be in mourning.

If you could, you might say it wasn't my fault, but it was, and it is, and it always will be; and I will never see you again.

Instead he watches all the videos, but he's barely watching them: they're just there as company for him, voices in the quiet of the ship, something else to bounce off the walls. I go out and watch him as he sleeps, and picture myself putting my hand over his mouth and nose, bracing my weight against him as he wriggled away from it, stopping him: but that's not how it happened. If I kill him, I'll only end up here again. I might as well see it through to the end for once, if I can.

(That makes me laugh, again, another thing that I find funny in this fucked-up situation: that Guy would be proud of me. I'll be the first Cormac to complete a loop of this particular section of his own life, and the only man in history to see the furthest point in space *twice*. I should get a medal.)

He moves on to videos of Quinn when he's exhausted the trove of Emmy interviews he's taken. There's no malice in them: he watches them for company, occasionally chipping in as the videotaped version of him asks a question. He mirrors the question, vocalizing it aloud, and sometimes, once or twice, I catch myself doing the same: three of us, different times, all saying the same thing. We're so predictable. Can a man change? Only with hindsight, and even then I'd be suspicious.

Eventually he starts the engines again, and he shouts, into the deep of the ship.

'I'm going to bed,' he says, not aiming it at anybody, but it's my klaxon. I drag myself to my feet and count down to a hundred. He always found it easy to sleep. Tonight won't be any different.

It's as I'm staring at his face, thinking about how much of a stranger he is. I write something else to send home.

I can try to reconcile this, to make sense of it – to say, I wasn't here the first time, and so I'm just trying to make it all work, but I was here the first time, because those things happened, and they can't have been a coincidence. Which means I've always been here. Time is a straight line, and my life on it is a line, until I reach that explosion, until the first me, the original – or am I still the original? I don't know – until the first me goes back to the explosion, and then he does it again, over and over, scratching over the timeline like a scribble. I don't think that time is looping: it's just me. Back home, they don't have a clue. They're just carrying on as before.

Don't even get me started on why this is happening. I think about that for too long, I'm liable to go insane (if I'm not already there). If this is how it's meant to happen, all I can do is see it through to the end. If I complete the loop and I come back next time, then, well, another plan. Something else. We'll cross that bridge when we come to it.

And if we don't come to it, nobody will ever have read this, and none of it will matter.

When he wakes up, he'll see that we've carried on losing fuel, because that's what happened before, and he'll panic, and none of that can change. All I can do is stay out of his way, now, and watch as he pushes us towards . . . whatever.

He wakes up and panics, as I knew that he would, and he grabs his suit.

'If I go out there, I can maybe fix it,' he says, but he can't, and we both know it. Still, at least he's trying. It's the most admirable thing he's done so far, the most proactive. I watch him change into the suit, step into the airlock and seal the door behind him, and then I watch as he disappears from my field of vision. I've got a few minutes so I sneak out, and it's the first time I've been on the ship by myself. Sure, before – when I was still the first Cormac – I thought that I was, but I wasn't. Now, here: this is me truly alone. The devilish part of me thinks that I should start the engines, fry him, drive off, the most expensive joyride in history. I don't, of course. Instead I take more painkillers, drink clean water, and I look at the picture of Elena that he's left on the screen, that he's been staring at and reminiscing.

I can berate him for doing it as much as I like, but, truth be told, given the opportunity, it's what I would be doing as well.

Outside, he can't see anything wrong with the ship, because there isn't. No pipes need fixing; no holes have appeared; nothing is leaking. This is how it's meant to be, Cormac. This is just how it all happens.

Cormac turns the lights on and it blinds me, for a minute. He's listless and lost and he flits from terminal to terminal, from action to action. He's still watching the videos, accompanied by the faces of the dead as they tell us about themselves when they were alive – not who they really were, but who the public perception of them was. Quinn talks about his life as a pilot, but he was more than that. Emmy speaks about doctoring, about healing, but she never mentioned that in person. In person, she drank and she laughed and she joked and she flirted, and she never once mentioned that she was a doctor. It's a different voice in the tapes, almost, a professional sheen that she never carried away from the training rooms. He's given up. It's so hard to watch him like this.

He finds the rest of the champagne. He gorges himself on food, eating dessert bars instead of a meal, and he laughs and laughs, and he tapes himself doing it, and then broadcasts it. He drinks the champagne and he sobs and sobs into the small flasks of it, as he drinks it through the straws. When he's not quite finished he drifts around the cabin in a ball, and he convulses. He drinks more when he thinks that he's ready, and then he's sick, remembering to do it into a bag, and then he cries more, great heaving wheezes of tears, and he says Elena's name over and over, over and over as he cries. When he passes out – floating in the air like some possessed child in a movie, his back arched, his arms and legs dangling, his head lolling back, tongue out, eyes twittering – I leave the lining and help him into his bed. He could catch me – and this could all be over – but he won't. I put him into the bed and strap him down, and he doesn't stir.

I take a champagne back to the lining with me, and a burger bar, and a cherry pie bar, and I sit and eat them and think about how little time is left.

I always said that the thing I was saddest about, when they had pretty much stopped printing paper books, was that I couldn't tell how long was left until the end. I could find out, but that feel, that sensation of always knowing was gone. I used to love the way that the cluster of pages grew thinner in my hand, how I could squeeze it and guess the time it would take until it ended. I loved endings, when they were done well: I loved knowing that it was finished, because that was how it was meant to be. An ending is a completion: it's a satisfaction all in itself.

From here, I can squeeze the pages, and I know there's not long to go. I've been here before, but I don't know the actual ending yet.

He recovers by vomiting, by holding his gut with both arms, holding as tight as he can. It's worse in zero gravity, I remember that much: it feels like you can't even get close to making your stomach settle. That sense of your insides swirling you get after being sick? That doesn't leave. He heaves into bags and then puts them in the chute, and he clutches his gut and whimpers. He's still drunk, so he swigs water until that makes him feel ill again. He sleeps and he cries as he sleeps, and he's like a child. Staying away is hard, but it's how it has to be. I remember everything, almost, even though I was in that state. I remember that I was on my own. When he wakes up, he sits at the computer and he cries and cries: because he feels awful, sick and ruined; and because he misses Elena, and because of how she died, and how much guilt he's storing, that he didn't even go to her funeral; and because he's alone. He knows he's going to die, as well. He might not have admitted it, at the time, but he knows it. Watching this – watching the movie – everybody knows it. The only reason I'm sure of it is because I've seen this already.

Hangovers in space don't work like on Earth: there's nothing to ground you. When the room feels like it's spinning, it's because it is. Your blood pressure is already fucked up, so that sensation – the feeling of being drunk rather than the alcohol actually being in your bloodstream – that lasts far longer. We were warned by DARPA not to over-drink before we left.

'The champagne is for celebration, for you all to share. Don't drink it all at once: it'll make you sick as dogs.' I remember that, and Cormac remembers it now. I'm not sure that we did before we drank it. Or, maybe that was the point. He cowers and stares at the numbers – at his life-clock, ticking down – and then puts on Arlen's videos, and watches the big, bearded, larger-than-life man laughing and joking his way through the very first video any of them recorded, before they even took off. He yammers as he waits for the camera crew to leave, to stop their panning shots, epic, widescreen, 3D shots; and for the injections to start before lift-off. He talks about the crew.

'They're good people,' he says, 'really good people. It helps;

you have a good crew, this whole thing will go a lot quicker.'
Cormac cries, his standard reaction to almost everything, it
seems. I'm well past it, by now.

Guy's videos. Fuck. I don't think that I can watch them.
Cormac laps them up, because he thinks that they will contain
the secrets of the universe. He trusted Guy implicitly, and
these videos – these brief, utterly vacuous interviews – are
probably nothing but lies. Guy smiles, and jokes, and tells
Cormac not to touch anything. He's lying about everything,
and Cormac doesn't have a clue. He tells the me in the video
about what it means to be an explorer, proselytizing about
how good the feeling will be to have done what we will do.
When he's done, Cormac writes a new blog post, about how
Guy would have known what to do.

He could have fixed it all, he writes. *He wouldn't have
been in this mess, and he would have made it home, and it
– this – would all have been worth it, for him.*

When Cormac has finally gone to sleep I rush out and
alter his post.

Guy was a real fucking traitor, I write, *and if you're reading
this, Ground Control, the rest of you are too. I hope you
hate yourselves for what you did. I hope you feel guilty.*

It feels good to write it, to put it down, to actually speak
it. I send it.

When he wakes up, Cormac puts the Guy videos on again,
as background noise. Guy talks about famous explorers.

'They'll remember you forever!' he says.

'Fuck you,' I say out loud. Cormac doesn't hear me.

The next day he reads the numbers, over and over, and he sees
the numbers and he tries to work out what it means again, as

if the systems encyclopedias might somehow have updated, and might magically give him the answers he desires. He types it into the computer and I watch him as he spends the day reading stuff he's already read. He gets into a thread about aliens – we're back here again, that thinking that something internal might be something, that something – a flight of fancy – can spiral into thoughts of invaders, of extraterrestrial life, of so much more than being stuck in a tin can until you die. He knows they don't exist. He knows that, here, so close to the Earth, really, not even a tenth as far as some of our deep-space satellites and probes have travelled, there's no chance of finding anything. He knows, but he hopes. I don't. Not that I've given up: I just don't know where we go from here.

'Save me,' he whimpers.

'I would if I could,' I say. I wait all day for him to sleep, but he doesn't, and we've totally lost track of time again, because it's like the Arctic here, no lack of daylight from the strip lighting. I take the painkillers in the lining and sleep, so lightly, barely even sleeping. I can't remember when I last had a full night; what it's like to put my head to a pillow, to feel that stillness of a bed, of drifting into proper sleep. I can't remember what it's like to actually dream: the things that I had before, the echoes of previous versions of me, they weren't anything to do with me letting go. If anything, they were me clinging on. I wait for Cormac to sleep so that I can go out there, but he doesn't, so I watch him.

I realize that I won't get to sleep again before I die: at least, not in a bed, with a duvet, pillows, a mattress, the warmth of another person next to me, sharing my space.

'I just want to get to say goodbye to Elena,' he says. He's looking at her photograph as the ship is full of the noise of the crew cheering, that first video home, where we lied and didn't say anything about Arlen. The cheers seem to cling to everything Cormac says, rising and falling with a strange serendipity. 'I miss her so, so much.' He strokes her photograph on the screen, and then clutches himself, pulls himself tight, winces at whatever it is that he's thinking. 'This is so unfair.'

He reaches over and puts on the videos of Emmy again, to punish himself: because she's as close to an admission of guilt as he can offer. He watches her talk about her training, smiling in her casual, semi-professional way, and he hammers the keyboard, writing letters to Elena, to his parents. He knows that they'll never read them – that there's no possible way that they ever could – but that doesn't stop him. He cries as he writes them, finding it cathartic and powerful at first, because there's real meaning there: and then he realizes that he's done, that the people he's writing to are even more dead than he is, and that there's no going back from here. All he's got left is to join them, and he's always been an atheist, never believed in a higher power, especially not out here, where it's so cold and dark and so absolutely full of nothingness.

Tomorrow he'll break his leg. We're nearly there, Cormac. We've nearly made it.

5

As the other Cormac gives us gravity, I brace myself against the lining, pushing back to stop from falling, and I don't get to see him fall because of that: but I hear the crack of his leg as he lands oddly, such a small fall, but so vital. It makes me wince, and I take a painkiller like a gut reaction, a reflex. He howls, and by the time I'm on tiptoes back at the vent all I can see is the blood, soaking through his white uniform, the bend in the trouser leg like a right-angled pipe, where the bone is jutting through. My own leg starts hurting just to look at it, and I rub at the scar, ill-formed and only barely healed. In the cabin, he pulls out Emmy's medicine cabinet, yanks the drawers to the floor, growling like a chained dog as he does it. He's remarkably resilient, holding himself together through the pain far better than I thought he would: there aren't tears, just howls of agony. He paws at the anaesthetic needles, jabs them into his own neck and presses the button, and I watch as he gets that glossy look in his eyes and the drugs run through him, taking the edge off. It's not enough: he immediately sticks himself with another, and he tries to ignore the angle that his jutting bone is making, and the blood. If he concentrates on the blood, he's likely to lose it. Antiseptic injections, to prevent infection, are next: he sticks himself like an old pro, desperate to save himself on some battlefield, and then he laughs, as he remembers that he's going to die, that antiseptic won't help that, that none of this – the pain, the bone, the risk of infection – will make the slightest bit of difference when he's dead. He decides to bind and tie off his leg, because he needs his mobility. He isn't just going to lie on the floor of the craft and wait to die.

I can't remember exactly, but I think that that was the moment that I decided to end it for myself, rather than ride it out. I watch as he passes out, just as I did, as he keeps coming to, his mind rolling around from consciousness to not. He splints his leg, because he thinks that he should. He keeps sleeping, and if I didn't know better I would be worrying that he was dead, but he isn't. I do know better. I'm tempted to head out there, see what I can do, but there's nothing. This is sewn-in, hewed. I could change something, but then only a few seconds – half a minute? A minute? – later I would be right back at the start. I've made it this far: let's see what it's like to die.

He puts gravity back on when he wakes up again, starts the engines, watches as the 9% on the screen shouts at him, as the beeping of the 250480 tells him something he cannot understand. After a while he sleeps, in his bed, strapped in but with the door open so that his leg can drift. He leaves that part free and it swings around as he twitches in his sleep, like a cat's tail. I manage to leave the lining for a few minutes, and I write a blog entry myself.

Acceptance: the final stage of grief, right? Is this all I've been working towards?

He coughs in his sleep, and I put myself back into the space between the walls. He doesn't wake up, but I decide not to risk it. My daredevil days are over.

My first interview, after I got past the paper stage, the form sent in and stamped and approved, my name written down somewhere by somebody as a potential candidate. We were sent to a building in New York, unlabelled from the outside, like a secret. We waited in a nondescript waiting room, the magazines on the table reflecting nothing but the secretary's tastes, and we leafed through them and tried to not make eye contact with each other. We didn't know why the others were there – we didn't know what field they were from, or even if they were here for the same thing. The building had so many offices, and any one of them might have been for a different DARPA project, and it wasn't right to probe, so I didn't. Nobody else did either. There was a part of me that wondered if it was a silent first test: can you make it through the first stage without getting excited, without spilling the beans? I passed, with flying colours.

When they finally called me through to the room, I sat in a comfortable chair, one of those expensive ones they fill fancy office spaces with, and faced a panel of three, two women and a man, all older. They told me their names and shook my hand, and asked me why I had applied.

'Because I want to explore something,' I said. 'It's all that I've ever wanted to do.' They wrote that down. 'May I ask why you want to know?' It was cocky, bolshy, but that was who I was, who I used to be, as a journalist. Before Elena died, and my world fell apart.

'It's crucial,' they said, 'because some people do this for the glory, for the rewards, and that's not something that we necessarily want to encourage.'

258

'So my answer was the right one?' I asked, and they smiled, but didn't reply. They asked me other questions – about my health, about Elena, my parents – and then told me that they would be in touch. They stood and shook my hand, and they each shook it harder than the last, and I thanked them for the opportunity and left. When I got out, the same people were in the waiting room, and they were all biting their nails or checking their emails, and I wondered about every single one of them: about whether they wanted onto the trip because they were excited about the opportunity, or because it was something to put on their CV. I looked at every single one of them and hoped that it was the latter, that they didn't get the job and I did, because, I thought, my intentions were pure. I deserved it.

Wanda's videos fill the screens. She feigns excitement, and then leans in and whispers to me that the controls are fake, and then makes out that she's joking. She's not. She knows what's going to happen. She knows everything, and she can't deal with it, and she knows we're all going to die. It's just a matter of when.

The me sits at the computers and reads everything again, and then stumbles upon the bit about the Crash Assist, where the craft jettisons the cargo to lose weight, then fires the stasis pods towards Earth with their own parachutes, and the rest of the hull collapses and falls apart, to harmlessly tumble towards the ground, the people, the sea, whatever. It's a eureka moment. He's in agony, still, dumb and blinkered by the drugs he's taken – aren't we all? I think – and he reads how to do it, over and over, and then starts typing into the computer, commands that he doesn't understand but that he's been instructed to use. Only now do I wonder why it was there, that fail-safe we would never use, and I realize that it was only ever intended to be used if something happened during take-off, the cargo being jettisoned from the rear to allow it to safely hit the sea we launched over, allowing for recovery of the ship's guts, and maybe us, if there were even parachutes in the first place. He presses the Enter key, and the main hull door seals, and I realize that I'm locked out – my entrance to him is through that door, back past the lining, past the cargo rooms.

He presses the button again, and the noise is awful, grinding and churning of doors that have never been opened before, and then the cold rushes to me – not actual cold, just the pull of the outside. There's barely anything between me and space, nothing sealed, nothing airtight. I've got seconds, I reckon, until all the doors are open. I plough myself to the vent overlooking the changing room, kick at the vent as hard as I can, shoulder it, and it starts to give way, and then it does, and I'm into the room, pulling on a helmet as fast as I can manage, yanking my head into it as the air rushes out, slamming the visor down, breathing, fiddling with the dials to give myself some time, to get me breathing, and then the door to the changing room flies away from me, and I've got no time. I fix the bungee, because I'm suddenly afraid to die. This isn't what I want.

The ship is suddenly still, all the air gone. Everything from the cargo rooms, the changing room, all the loose bits and bobs are suddenly floating. They drift, and I go with them, knowing that Cormac is about to initiate the countdown, and I float to the doorway between us, stare through the transparent window set into it. I have to stop him doing this. If I have a reason for being here, it has to be that, surely?

It has to be to save him. I hammer on it, but I know he won't hear me, so I hammer harder, because there's nothing else to do. He presses the button, and the lights dim, and the numbers on the computer screens wipe away, replaced by that countdown.

30. He just sits in Arlen's chair and watches it, 29, 28, 27. I in turn watch him, and then I can see it, out of the front window: that blackness, totally stark against the rest of the stars, like a puddle of oil; but slick, floating in front of us. I didn't see it first time around: my eyes were too full of tears. 26. I get to the Bubble, 23, and look at it, and it gives me a reading straight away: ANOMALY, it says, ANOMALY 250480. I didn't do this last time – the first time – because I didn't see it, not until it was too late. What could a computer tell me about what was happening to me, or what was going to happen to me? Now it tells me everything: there's something out here with us. With me.

This something was our secondary objective; or, maybe, our primary objective, and we just didn't know it; the thing that Guy yammed on about and we ignored, because he was a scientist doing science. It was the thing that he was going to measure, that he acted off-hand about, off-the-cuff, almost. He was lying. He knew about this – about how vast it is, how massive, how it must mean something. Where it was: that it was further than we could reach. He knew how we *could* reach it, though. This was his life's work, and he knew that it would kill him. That's why it was throwing up the message on screen so much: it was a warning. We were meant to fly into the storm, but we were never going to tell home how strong it was, or tell them how to combat it, or what it was going to do. We were just meant to tell them where it was. Anyway, maybe it would turn out to be harmless, just a smudge on a window. Or, maybe it's something more important, deadly to the human race, sliding across space to swallow us whole. I suppose I've been inside it for awhile: I suppose it's why this is so dark. Why I'm doing this over and over. I'll never really know, not now. Now, it doesn't actually matter.

14 seconds left, and I read something on the screen about how much it's grown, and then, based on that, projected growth, and I don't know how big it's going to get, or what that means, but I like to think that it means Guy was actually trying to save us all – like, maybe it's going to get big enough to envelope the Earth, and maybe he was there all along, not the bad guy he ended his life as, but the one I made friends with, who seemed reasonable, who seemed penitent for what he had done. There's a greater good.

3, 2, 1, and the ship cracks up, and the pods jettison, because I hear them roar past, and then everything is silent. This is how it should be. The front wall of the Bubble splinters and I'm suddenly floating, attached to a large lump of hull that looks like an airlock, still, a metal box, dragging backwards. Cormac is in front of me, twisting forwards, still strapped to his chair, heading towards the blackness of the anomaly. He's going to hit it, and that's what sends him back to the start, makes him do this again: I have to stop it, save him.

I push off the Bubble as fast as I can, blast CO_2 for a boost, knowing that he's only got seconds before this is pointless, before he's done, and then I'm at his chair and pull him out of it, and the bungee goes taut but he's still ahead of me. It's attached to the helmet, so I yank it off, because I have to do something. The pressure makes me blind, and we were told to shut our eyes but I don't, because this only ends one way. I have seconds, seconds, and then it hits me: this is what happened. I was here the very first time, because I have to have been for this all to happen, and I felt hands on me, because I was heading towards what is almost a wall of blackness, cloying and tangible, like thick ink, and I felt somebody – myself, this future version of me, the me from now – save me, pull me away from the blackness, and towards the nothingness behind us. It's a paradox, a closed loop: I was here so this could all happen as it did. You can't change time, because my gut tells me I can't. I parse it: I can do exactly what happened the first time, grab him, push him into the blackness, because that's what I'm meant to do. Every thought I have that doesn't involve it makes me hurt. But, then, here and now, that pain means very little to me. Cormac is the definitive version; I'm just a later version of him, a version that never has to exist. I have seconds to change everything, seconds when this might become something different, and I have to let us both go. The blackness – whatever it is – will cause him (or me) to go back to the start, prolong our lives for however long, cursing us. Now, I have to have the courage to do what he couldn't. I make the decision, and my gut screams at me, aches, burns, and it feels wrong, but I have to do it, because this might be the only chance I get. What if every other time I've been here I've thought I'm meant to make it happen as it did? What if I thought I was meant to make the circuit closed, make it perfect, complete? Save Cormac by pushing him into the anomaly, because that way leads to life?

Maybe this time I should try something different.

Before, I spun around and I was saved. Now: I open my fingers and he opens his eyes, and he sees me, and I tell him that it will be all right, but this time I'm lying. I clutch onto him and fire the CO_2 again. I look back and see it push apart the blackness, like throwing a stone onto the surface of a lake, once so still, now broken and disturbed, and I clutch Cormac as we push away from the anomaly, going away from the still-exploding ship, away from the blackness, away from everything. All we've got is each other, he and I, I and he, and I did what I had to do. He coughs and chokes in my arms, and I don't look as all those things they warned us about start happening to him. I can feel him going in my arms, and then I can feel it happening to me, because now my eyes have been open, and you can never survive this, no matter what you do, who you are. I opened my eyes to look at the blackness as it swallows the wreckage of the ship, the hungriest thing I've ever seen: the darkest part of space, swallowing everything in its path. I let go of Cormac, because he's done, and so am I.

I wait and feel my lungs stop, and I open my eyes wide and stare forward at the nothingness, going onwards forever, it seems, on and on, with or without me there to see it, and my head feels like it's about to burst. I'm not back on the ship. I don't have my scars. I've not opened the door and killed Arlen, and I haven't started this all again, confused and lost and alone but not alone. I haven't done that. I wait to see if it'll happen before I die, and if it does, if I'll even remember this moment in the first place.

From here, space looks like it does from any garden, anywhere. It's so still.

Acknowledgments

Thanks go first and foremost to Robert Simpson, astrophysicist. When I started writing *The Explorer* I threw ideas at him, over and over. A lot of the science (anything that's right and logical) is down to him. The other stuff? Blame me for that. You could do worse than googling him and finding out about his mind-boggling array of wonderful space-projects.

Sam Copeland is my agent, and I couldn't be more grateful for all of his hard work. He saw this novel in its earliest form and knew what it ultimately could be. Thank/blame him appropriately. Thanks too to everybody else at Rogers, Coleridge & White. Thanks to my early readers, as well: Holly Howitt, John Smythe, Kim Curran.

Thanks to my wonderful editor Amy McCulloch, whose insight and thoughts were utterly invaluable. Thanks also to my wonderful copyeditor, Joy Chamberlain, and to all at Voyager Books /HarperCollins UK for everything that they do so very well.